PENGUIN BOOKS

PINEAPPLE STREET

Jenny Jackson is a vice president and executive editor at Alfred A. Knopf. A graduate of Williams College and the Columbia Publishing Course, she lives in Brooklyn Heights with her family. Her first novel, *Pineapple Street*, was a *New York Times* bestseller, a Good Morning America Book Club pick, and has sold around the world in sixteen territories.

Praise for *Pineapple Street*

CHOSEN AS A BEST BOOK OF THE YEAR BY

The New York Times • *Time* • NPR • *USA Today* • *Elle* • *Harper's Bazaar* • *Town & Country* • *Vogue* • BBC • *POPSUGAR* • *Goodreads* • *theSkimm*

bighearted, and full of emotional truths. It's the kind of novel you hope will never end."

—Adrienne Brodeur, *New York Times* bestselling author of
Wild Game and *Little Monsters*

"I was entranced by *Pineapple Street*. Smart and complex, rich and gorgeous, this novel drew me in from page one."

—Amanda Eyre Ward, *New York Times*
bestselling author of *The Lifeguards*

"A charming, funny, and keenly observed story about New York City's one percent—and what it means to find yourself among them, whether by birth or marriage."

—*Town & Country*

"A delight to read from start to finish, Jenny Jackson's *Pineapple Street* is a cancel-all-plans kind of book. . . . If I could have put this novel on a drip straight into my veins, I would have!"

—Ashley Audrain, *New York Times* bestselling author of *The Push*

"A blissfully enjoyable novel."

—*The Sunday Times*

"*Pineapple Street* encapsulates the oftentimes ridiculous nature of the ultrawealthy. The author seamlessly immerses readers in the lives of the Stocktons . . . [who] must ask themselves the uncomfortable question: Is it possible to be 'good' with this much money?"

—Shondaland

"Full of witty and caustic observations about a privileged class of New Yorkers, *Pineapple Street* is a sharp and juicy satire."

—Nita Prose, #1 *New York Times* bestselling author of *The Maid*

"There is a particular pleasure to reading about the languid rich. . . . In her debut novel Jenny Jackson delivers a very funny domestic drama of a family drowning in their own excess and overeducation. You will heartily enjoy judging them."

—*Glamour*

"I devoured *Pineapple Street*. . . . [A] messy, hilarious, and ultimately relatable family story."

—Cristina Alger, *New York Times* bestselling author of *Girls Like Us*

"*Pineapple Street* is that rarest of gifts—a novel you don't want to put down for anything. Transporting and laugh-out-loud funny, this intergenerational story is a perfect tale for our times."

—J. Courtney Sullivan, *New York Times* bestselling
author of *Friends and Strangers*

"A family drama dripping in gossip, sabotage, and old-school New York luxury."   —*POPSUGAR*

"*Pineapple Street* might be the Edith Wharton novel for our times.... Wise, funny, tender, and utterly relatable."
                         —Susie Yang, *New York Times* bestselling author of *White Ivy*

"Jenny Jackson's deft debut takes on the topic of generational wealth with a keen Austenian eye.... An engaging and absorbing read, with a supremely satisfying conclusion, perfect for book groups or to pass along to a good friend."   —*Bookreporter*

"I sucked it down like a milkshake.... My favorite part of the novel was the heart. All the characters mess up but make amends. They TRY. And they keep trying."
                         —Helen Ellis, author of *Bring Your Baggage and Don't Pack Light*

"I'm not sure which is bigger: *Pineapple Street*'s heart or its humor. It's smart and surprising and, yes, scrumptious. I devoured it. I can't recall the last time I read a novel that was both this heartwarming and this hilarious. One word of advice: clear your calendar before you start reading. You won't stop until you've finished. It is, pure and simple, a treasure."
                         —Chris Bohjalian, #1 *New York Times* bestselling
                                 author of *The Flight Attendant* and *The Lioness*

"Jackson has a deft hand.... Rich-people jokes, cultural acuity, and entertaining banter keep this novel moving at a sprightly pace.... A remarkably enjoyable visit with the annoying one percent, as close to crazy rich WASPs as WASPs can get."   —*Kirkus Reviews*

"Brooklyn socialites, trust funds, and family secrets are at the center of this unputdownable comedy.... [*Pineapple Street*] grabs your attention and keeps it."   —*theSkimm*

"[A] brilliant debut ... It's both sharply drawn and compassionate." —BBC

Penguin Reading Group Discussion Guide available

online at penguinrandomhouse.com

Pineapple Street

A Novel

JENNY JACKSON

PENGUIN BOOKS

PENGUIN BOOKS
An imprint of Penguin Random House LLC
penguinrandomhouse.com

First published in the United States of America by Viking,
an imprint of Penguin Random House LLC, 2023
Published in Penguin Books 2024

A Pamela Dorman/Penguin Book

ISBN 9780593490716 (paperback)

THE LIBRARY OF CONGRESS HAS CATALOGED THE HARDCOVER EDITION AS FOLLOWS:
Names: Jackson, Jenny (Editor), author.
Title: Pineapple Street : a novel / Jenny Jackson.
Description: New York City: Pamela Dorman Books; Viking, [2023]
Identifiers: LCCN 2022018944 (print) | LCCN 2022018945 (ebook) |
ISBN 9780593490693 (hardcover) | ISBN 9780593654705 (international edition) |
ISBN 9780593490709 (ebook)
Subjects: LCSH: Rich people—New York (State)—New York—Fiction. |
LCGFT: Domestic fiction. | Novels.
Classification: LCC PS3610.A3519 P56 2023 (print) |
LCC PS3610.A3519 (ebook) | DDC 813/.6—dc23/eng/20220429
LC record available at https://lccn.loc.gov/2022018944
LC ebook record available at https://lccn.loc.gov/2022018945

Printed in the United States of America
1st Printing

DESIGNED BY AMANDA DEWEY

For Torrey

Millennials will be the recipients of the largest generational shift of assets in American history—the Great Wealth Transfer, as finance types call it. Tens of trillions of dollars are expected to pass between generations in just the next decade.

—Zoë Beery, *The New York Times*

I live in Brooklyn.
By choice.

—Truman Capote

Pineapple
Street

Prelude

Curtis McCoy was early for his ten o'clock meeting so he carried his coffee to a table by the window, where he could feel the watery April sun. It was a Saturday, Joe Coffee was crowded, and Brooklyn Heights was alive, women in running tights pushing strollers along Hicks Street, dog walkers congregating at the benches on Pineapple Street, families dashing to soccer games, swimming lessons, birthday parties down at Jane's Carousel.

At the next table, a mother sat with her two adult daughters, drinking from blue-and-white paper cups, peering at the same phone.

"Oh, here's one! This guy's profile says he likes running, making his own kimchi, and 'dismantling capitalism.'"

Curtis tried not to listen but couldn't help himself.

"Darley, he's twice my age. No. Do you even understand how the app works?"

The name Darley rang a bell, but Curtis couldn't quite place her. Brooklyn Heights was a small neighborhood, she was probably just someone he'd seen in line ordering sandwiches at Lassen, or someone he'd crossed paths with at the gym on Clark Street.

"Fine, fine. Okay, this guy says, 'Cis male vegan seeks fellow steward of the Earth. Never eat anything with a face. Except the rich.'"

"You can't date a vegan. The footwear is ghastly!" the mother interrupted. "Give me that phone! Hmm. The whiffy here is terrible."

"Mom, it's pronounced 'wai-fai.'"

Curtis risked a quick peek at the table. The three women were dressed in tennis whites, the mother a blonde with gold earrings and a notable array of rings on her fingers, the daughters both brunette, one lanky with straight hair cut to her shoulders, the other softer, with long wavy hair loosely tied in a knot. Curtis ducked his head back down and broke off a crumbly bite of poppyseed scone.

"'Bi and nonmonogamous looking for a Commie Mommy to help me smash the patriarchy. Hit me up to go dancing!' Am I having a stroke?" the older woman murmured. "I don't understand a word of this."

Curtis fought back a snicker.

"Mom, give me the phone." The wavy-haired daughter snatched back the iPhone and tossed it in her bag.

With a start Curtis realized he knew her. It was Georgiana Stockton; she had been in his high school class at Henry Street ten years ago. He contemplated saying hello, but then it would be obvious he'd overheard their entire conversation.

"In my day, things were so much simpler," Georgiana's mother tutted. "You just went out with your deb ball escort or maybe your brother's roommate from Princeton."

"Right, Mom, but people my generation aren't giant elitist snobs," Georgiana said and rolled her eyes.

Curtis smiled to himself. He could imagine having the same exact conversation with his own mother, trying to explain why he wasn't going to marry her friend's daughter just because they owned adjoining properties on Martha's Vineyard. As Curtis watched Georgiana out of the corner of his eye, she suddenly jumped up from her chair.

"Oh, no! I left my Cartier bracelet in Lena's BMW and she's leaving soon for her grandmother's house in Southampton!"

Georgiana tossed her bag over her shoulder, grabbed her tennis racket off the floor, planted quick kisses on both her mother and sister, and clattered past Curtis to the door. As she swept by, her tennis racket banged Curtis's table, sloshing his coffee, dousing his poppyseed scone, and leaving him frowning in her wake.

ONE

Sasha

There was a room in Sasha's house that was a portal to another dimension, and that dimension was 1997. Here, Sasha discovered an egg-shaped iMac computer with a blue plastic shell, a ski jacket with a stack of hardened paper lift tags still affixed to the zipper, a wrinkled pile of airline boarding passes, and a one-hitter with an old yellow lighter hidden in the back of a drawer. Every time Sasha mentioned to her husband that she'd love to put her sister-in-law's high school ephemera in a box, he rolled his eyes and told her to be patient. "She'll get her stuff when she has time." But Sasha had her doubts, and it was weird living in a home where one bedroom was entirely closed off, like a preserved shrine to a lost child.

On good days, Sasha could acknowledge how incredibly lucky she was to live in her house. It was a four-story Brooklyn limestone, a massive, formal palace that could have held ten of the one-bedroom apartments Sasha had lived in before. But on bad days, Sasha felt she was living in a time capsule, the home her husband had grown up in and never left, filled with his memories, his childhood stories, but mostly his family's shit.

W hen Sasha and Cord had been in the house for three weeks, Sasha invited her in-laws to dinner. "I'll make mushroom tarts and a goat cheese salad," she said in the email. She spent all morning rolling pie dough and even walked to the fancy market on Montague for pomegranate seeds to sprinkle over baby lettuces. She vacuumed the dining room, dusted the bookshelves, and put a Sancerre in the fridge. When her in-laws arrived, they had three L.L.Bean canvas bags in tow. "Oh, you didn't have to bring anything!" Sasha exclaimed, dismayed.

"Sasha," her mother-in-law trilled, opening the closet to hang her Chanel bouclé jacket. "We can't *wait* to hear all about your honeymoon." She carried the bags into the kitchen and proceeded to pull out a bottle of white Burgundy, two flower arrangements in low vases, a tablecloth with fleurs-de-lis on it, and three scalloped Williams Sonoma baking dishes with lids. She lined them up on the counter and, like a woman at home in her kitchen of forty years, opened up the cabinet to take down a glass for her wine.

"I've made mushroom tarts," Sasha tried, suddenly feeling like the lady at the Costco free sample table, trying to sell warm cubes of processed cheese.

"Oh, I saw in your email, darling. I gathered that meant it was a French-themed dinner. You just let me know when you're ten minutes away and I'll pop my coq au vin in the oven. I also have endives Provençal, and I brought plenty, so we might not need your salad. The candlesticks are in the drawer there, now let's go take a look at your tabletop arrangement and I'll see what else we need."

Out of solidarity, Cord ate the tart and the salad, but when Sasha caught him looking longingly at the endives, she gave him a thin smile that said, "You can eat the damned vegetables, but you might have to sleep on the couch."

The agreement was new for all of them, and Sasha understood it was going to take some getting used to. Cord's parents, Chip and Tilda, had been complaining for years that their house was too big for the two of them, that it was too far from their garage, that they were tired of doing their own shoveling and hauling their own recycling out to the curb. They were investors in an apartment building two blocks away—the former Brooklyn Heights movie theater that was now five luxury condos—and they had decided to take the maisonette for themselves, moving in over the course of one week, using only their old Lexus and their housekeeper's husband, whom they paid three hundred bucks. That seemed like a quick divestment from a house they'd inhabited for four decades, but aside from their clothing, Sasha couldn't really figure out what they had brought to the new place. They had even left their four-poster, king-size bed in their bedroom, and Sasha felt more than a little weird sleeping there.

The Stocktons decided to let Sasha and Cord move into their vacant house and live there as long as they would like. Then, when they sold the place one day, they would split the money between Cord and his two sisters. There were some other pieces of the agreement designed to evade unnecessary inheritance taxes, but Sasha looked the other way for that bit of paperwork. The Stocktons may have let her marry their son, but she understood on a bone-deep level that they would rather let her walk in on them in the middle of an aerobic threesome with Tilda's bridge partner than have her studying their tax returns.

After dinner, Sasha and Cord cleared the table while his parents headed into the parlor for an after-dinner drink. There was a bar cart in the corner of the room with old bottles of cognac that they liked to pour into tiny, gold-rimmed glasses. The glasses, like everything else in the house, were ancient and came with a history. The parlor had long blue velvet drapes, a piano, and an itchy ball-and-claw foot sofa that had once belonged in the governor's mansion. Sasha made the mistake of sitting on it once and got such a bad rash on the backs of her legs that she had to use calamine lotion before bed. There was a chandelier in the foyer, a grandfather clock in the dining room that chimed so loudly Sasha screamed a little the first time she heard it, and an enormous painting of a ship on a menacingly dark ocean in the study. The whole place had a vaguely nautical vibe, which was funny since they were in Brooklyn, not Gloucester or Nantucket, and though Chip and Tilda had certainly spent summers sailing, they mostly chartered boats with crew. The glassware had ship's wheels etched in them, the place mats had oil paintings of sailboats, the bathroom had a framed seafaring chart, and even their beach towels had diagrams for tying various knots. Sometimes Sasha found herself wandering the house in the evenings, running her hand along the ancient frames and candlesticks, whispering, "Batten down the hatches!" and "Swab the deck!" and making herself laugh.

Sasha and Cord finished moving the plates to the kitchen and joined Cord's parents in the parlor, where he poured them each a small glass of cognac. It tasted sticky and medicinal and made Sasha weirdly aware of the small hairs inside her nostrils, but she drank it anyway, just to be companionable.

"So how do you kids like the place?" Tilda asked, folding one long leg over the other. She had dressed for dinner and was wearing a colorful blouse, a pencil skirt, sheer stockings, and three-inch heels.

The Stocktons were all quite tall, and with the heels her mother-in-law positively towered over Sasha, and if anyone said that wasn't a power move, they were lying through their teeth.

"We love it." Sasha smiled. "I feel so lucky to have such a beautiful and spacious home."

"But Mom," Cord started, "we were thinking we'd like to make some changes here and there."

"Of course, sweetheart. The house is yours."

"It really is," Chip agreed. "We're all settled at Orange Street."

"That's so kind," Sasha jumped in. "I was just thinking that the bedroom closet was a little tight, but if we took out those built-in cubbies in the back—"

"Oh no, sweetie," Tilda interrupted. "You shouldn't take those out. They are just the perfect thing for all kinds of bits and bobs—off-season footwear, hats, anything with a brim that you don't want crushed. You'd really be doing yourself a disservice if you took those out."

"Oh, right, okay." Sasha nodded. "That makes sense."

"What about this parlor furniture, though," Cord tried again. "We could get a really comfy couch, and if we changed out the velvet curtains we could have a lot more light."

"But those drapes were custom made for the room. Those windows are absolutely enormous, and I think if you took the drapes down you'd just be so shocked to realize how hard it is to get the right kind of thing there." Tilda shook her head sadly, her blond hair shining in the chandelier's light. "Why don't you just live here for a little bit and really get to know the place and put some thought to what might make you the most comfortable. We really want you to feel at home here." She patted Sasha's leg firmly and stood, nodding at her husband and teetering her way to the door. "Well, we'd best be off—thanks for dinner. I'm just going to leave the Le Creuset here and you can run it in the dishwasher. No problem at all there—they don't need to be handwashed—and I'll take them home next time we come for dinner. Or you can just drop them at ours. And you can keep the vases—I noticed your tablescape was a bit spare." She slipped on her jacket, ivory and pink with a hint of lavender, looped her handbag over her arm, and led her husband out the door, down the stairs, and back to their newly furnished, totally not-nautical apartment.

WHENEVER PEOPLE asked Sasha how she and Cord met she would answer, "Oh, I was his therapist." (A joke—WASPs don't go to therapy.) In a world of Match and Tinder, their courtship seemed quainter than a square dance. Sasha was sitting at the counter at Bar Tabac drinking a glass of wine. Her phone had died, so she had picked up an abandoned *New York Times* crossword puzzle. It was nearly finished—something she'd never come close to accomplishing—and as Sasha studied the answers, Cord walked up to place an order and started chatting, marveling at the beautiful woman who also happened to be an ace at crosswords.

They'd gotten together for cocktails a week later, and despite the fact that "their whole relationship was based on a lie," a phrase Cord liked to use regularly once he discovered Sasha couldn't actually complete even the Monday crossword, it was pretty much the perfect romance.

Well, it was the perfect romance for a real, functional pair of adults with a normal amount of baggage, independence, alcohol use, and sexual appetite. They spent their first year together doing all the things New York couples in their early thirties do: whispering earnestly in the corner of the bar at birthday parties, expending outrageous effort getting reservations at restaurants that served eggs on ramen, sneaking bodega snacks into movie theaters, and dressing up and meeting people for brunch while secretly looking forward to the time when they would feel comfortable enough together to spend Sundays just lying on the couch eating bacon sandwiches from the deli downstairs and reading the Sunday *Times*. Of course, they got in fights too. Cord took Sasha camping and the tent flooded, and he made fun of her for being scared to pee alone at night, and she swore at him and told him she would never set foot in Maine ever again. Sasha's best friend, Vara, invited them to opening night of her gallery show, and Cord missed it, stuck at work, and didn't understand the magnitude of his transgression. Cord got pink eye and had to walk around looking like a half-rabid bunny, and Sasha teased him until he sulked. But overall, their love was storybook stuff.

It did take Sasha a long time to figure out that Cord was rich— embarrassingly long, considering that his name was Cord. His apartment was nice enough, but normal. His car was an absolute beater. His clothing was nondescript, and he was a total freak about taking good care of his stuff. He used a wallet until the leather cracked, his belts were the same ones his grandmother bought him in high school, and he treated his iPhone like it was some kind of nuclear code that needed to be carried in a briefcase handcuffed to his wrist, or at least wrapped in both a screen protector and a case thicker than a slice of bread. Sasha must have watched *The Wolf of Wall Street* too many times, because she always thought rich New York guys would have slicked back hair and constantly be paying for bottle service at clubs. Instead, they apparently wore sweaters until they had holes in the elbows and had unhealthily close relationships with their mothers.

Cord was borderline obsessed with his family. He and his father worked side by side every day, his sisters both lived in the neighborhood, and he met them for dinner all the time, and they talked on the phone more than Sasha spoke to anyone. Cord did things for his parents that she couldn't fathom—he went with his father to get haircuts, whenever he bought new shirts he bought his father the exact same ones, he picked up the French wine his mother liked at Astor Place, and he rubbed her feet in a way that made Sasha leave the room. Who rubbed their own mother's feet? Whenever she saw it, she thought of that scene in *Pulp Fiction* where John Travolta compared it to oral sex, and she got so upset she felt her eye twitch.

Sasha loved her parents, but their lives weren't intertwined like that. They were casually interested in her work as a graphic designer, they spoke every Sunday and texted a bit in between, and sometimes when she went home to visit she would be surprised to realize they had traded in their car for something new and never mentioned it, and once had even knocked down a wall between the kitchen and the living room.

Sasha's sisters-in-law were nice to her. They texted on her birthday, they made sure to ask after her family, lent her a racket and whites so she could join in family tennis on vacation. But Sasha still felt that on some level they would prefer she wasn't around. She would be in the middle of telling Cord's older sister, Darley, a story, and when Cord walked in the room Darley would simply stop listening and start asking him questions. Georgiana, his younger sister, would ostensibly be talking to everyone, but Sasha noticed her eyes never left her siblings. Their family was a unit, a closed circuit Sasha couldn't ever seem to penetrate.

THE STOCKTONS were in real estate. At first, this made it feel even stranger to Sasha that their house was so cluttered. Shouldn't they be living in some kind of spare, *Architectural Digest* dreamscape? But it turned out their interest in real estate was less about selling single apartments and more about large-scale investing. Cord's grandfather, Edward Cordington Stockton, had inherited a modest fortune from his family. In the 1970s, he used that money to buy up property on the Upper East Side as the city teetered on the edge of bankruptcy. He spent forty-five dollars per square foot. That real estate was now worth twelve hundred per square foot, and the Stocktons were extraordinarily wealthy men. With his son, Cord's father, Chip, they bought up waterfront in Brooklyn, moving along Dumbo and into Brooklyn Heights. In 2016, when the Jehovah's Witnesses decided to divest themselves of their Brooklyn Heights properties, they jumped in, joining a group of investors to buy the famous Watchtower building, along with the former Standish Arms Hotel. Edward Cordington had passed away, but Cord now worked alongside his father, the third generation of Stockton men in New York real estate.

Paradoxically, the Stockton family had chosen to live in the fruit streets section of Brooklyn Heights, the three little blocks of Pineapple, Orange, and Cranberry streets situated on the bluff over the waterfront. For all their investment in converting old buildings to new high-end condos, they made their home in a section completely barred from significant change by the Landmarks Preservation Commission. There were little plaques on various homes in the neighborhood, signs that read "1820" or "1824." There were tiny white clapboard houses. There were leafy gardens hidden behind wrought-iron gates. There were former stables and carriage houses. Even the CVS looked like part of an English hamlet, with walls of ivy-covered stone. Sasha particularly loved a house on the corner of Hicks and Middagh streets, a former pharmacy, where the tilework on the entryway spelled out "DRUGS."

Cord's mother's side of the family was perhaps of even more prestigious pedigree. Tilda Stockton, née Moore, came from a long line of political royalty. Both her father and brother had been governors of New York, and she had been featured in family profiles in *Vogue* and *Vanity Fair*. She had married Chip Stockton when she was twenty-one, and though she had never had a proper nine-to-five job, she had earned a reputation as a wildly successful event consultant, mostly by connecting her wealthy socialite friends with her favorite party planners. For Tilda Stockton, no evening was complete without a vision, a theme, a tablescape, and a dress code. It all made Sasha want to hide under a pile of monogrammed cocktail napkins.

Sasha spent the months following her wedding trying to settle into her new Pineapple Street home. She decided that she was an archaeologist, studying the ancient civilization of her in-laws. But instead of Tutankhamen's tomb, she found an ashtray Darley made in sixth grade that looked like a malformed mushroom. Instead of the Dead Sea Scrolls, she found Cord's elementary school science paper on types of pinecones. Instead of the Terracotta Army, she found an entire drawer of free toothbrushes from a dentist on Atlantic Avenue.

Of the four bedrooms, Darley's room was the worst, but none of them was truly vacant. Cord's old room had been cleaned out when he left for college, but it still housed a silver gilt candelabra, a set of

Mandarin floor vases, and dozens of framed paintings, artwork that the family had acquired over the years but had no place to hang. Georgiana's room still held all her college textbooks and photo albums, along with an entire shelf of tennis trophies; and the primary bedroom, while emptied of clothing and jewelry, still contained the décor and furniture of the previous residents, and it was extremely hard for Sasha to achieve orgasm while the mahogany headboard that probably belonged to a congressman or secretary of transportation banged against the wall.

As she squeezed her empty suitcases into already-crowded closets, she pondered whether she might be allowed to replace the shower curtain. She would wait a few months.

CHIP AND TILDA decided to throw a housewarming party at their new apartment on Orange Street and asked that their children and spouses arrive early. It was on a Wednesday evening, because most of their friends spent their weekends at country homes and some liked to go up Thursday night. The Stockton parents' social life in the city existed only between Monday and Wednesday, before their friends scattered to the far reaches of Long Island and Litchfield County.

"What should I wear?" Sasha asked Cord, standing in front of the closet. She never knew how to dress around his family. It was like there was a mood board everyone else seemed to be consulting, but the vision eluded Sasha every time.

"Wear whatever you want, babe," Cord replied unhelpfully.

"So I can wear jeans?"

"Well, I wouldn't wear *jeans*." He frowned.

"Okay, so should I wear a dress?" Sasha asked, annoyed.

"I mean, Mom said the theme is 'upward and onward.'"

"I don't know what that means."

"I'm just going to wear what I wore to work. I'm sure most people will do that."

Cord wore a suit and tie to work, so that was about as relevant to Sasha's life as if he wore operating room scrubs or firefighter overalls. She was flummoxed, so played it safe and wore a pretty white blouse tucked into navy blue trousers, and the small diamond earrings her mother had given her for college graduation. She put on lipstick, and as she checked herself in the old mirror over the fireplace, she smiled. She felt classic, like Amal Clooney leaving the UN for dinner with George. Upward and onward, indeed.

When they arrived at the apartment, Cord's sisters were already there, Georgiana looking beautifully bohemian, her long brown hair cascading down her back, a floaty dress skimming her ankles, freckles dotting her nose, and Darley wearing a belted jumpsuit that had surely been featured in *Vogue Italia*. Darley's husband, Malcolm, was standing at her elbow, and Sasha breathed a sigh of relief. Early on she had identified Malcolm as an ally in the strange world that was siblings by marriage, and they even had a code they muttered when things got really weird: NMF. It stood for "not my family," and it exonerated them from any situation where they felt like outside witnesses to bizarre WASP rituals, like the time in July when the Stocktons had insisted on taking a professional family photo for their Christmas card and made them all wear shades of blue and white and stand in a semicircle around Chip and Tilda, who were seated in two chairs. The photographer directed them for nearly an hour, the sun baking down upon them as Berta, their housekeeper, bustled in and out setting up the grill, and the gardening staff watered the plants, carefully avoiding eye contact. Sasha had felt like part of the Romney family and was completely mortified by the whole thing, but at least she'd been able to exchange pained glances with Malcolm. Together they were foreign-exchange students, united in their understanding that they had arrived in a deeply strange land.

Berta had been preparing all day for the housewarming party, and the dining-room table was groaning under the weight of silver platters of shrimp on ice, roast beef on crusty round melba, smoked salmon on toast points, and tiny one-bite crab cakes. She had poured glasses of white wine and arranged them on a tray that she would hold near the entrance, so that guests might begin drinking immediately upon arrival. Red wine was forbidden, obviously, mainly for the sake of the new rugs, but also because red wine teeth made everyone look terrible. Tilda was obsessed with teeth.

The guests began to arrive, and Sasha recognized many of them from her wedding. The Stocktons had so many friends at the wedding that Sasha had spent the entire reception shaking hands and trying to remember names, pausing only when her cousins pulled her out on the dance floor to shake it to "Baby Got Back." It was an elegant affair.

Cord knew everyone and was soon swept off to the study to show a bald gentleman his father's collection of watches. Some were rare military watches, some vintage Patek, some Rolex with matte and gilt dials, and they had been passed down from Cord's grandfather. They were so valuable that Chip had been approached by various auction houses with offers to buy them, but he declined. He never touched them or even looked at them, but Cord said Chip liked knowing he always had money in his apartment, like wads of cash hidden under a mattress. (Sasha privately thought it might have more to do with the family aversion to decluttering.)

Georgiana was sitting on the sofa whispering with her god-mother, while Darley and Malcolm were holding court with a small group from their racket club on Montague Street, showing them iPhone pictures of their children. Georgiana often looked prettily disheveled, her jacket slung over her shoulders and her wrists stacked with mismatched beaded bracelets, but Darley looked clean and ex-pensive, her brown hair cut to shoulder length, her makeup barely there, a small gold watch and her wedding rings her only jewelry. Sasha stood awkwardly at the periphery, unsure how she might in-sert herself into a conversation. She was relieved when a woman with a helmet of blond hair made a beeline toward her and smiled broadly.

"Hi, I'd love another chardonnay, thanks so much," the woman said and handed her a glass smudged with greasy fingerprints.

"Oh, I'm Sasha," she laughed, putting her hand to her chest.

"Thank you, Sasha," the woman replied cheerfully.

"Oh, sure," Sasha recovered. She took the glass into the kitchen and refilled it from one of the bottles in the refrigerator and brought it back out to the dining room, where the woman took it with a whis-pered thanks and retreated to the table, where her husband was eat-ing roast beef. Sasha made her way into the living room to look for Cord but was intercepted by a rotund man in a bow tie who handed her his dirty plate, nodding briefly before continuing his conversa-tion. Confused, Sasha walked his plate to the kitchen and set it on the counter. This happened another four times before Sasha finally made it to Cord and glued herself to his side, nursing her own glass of wine and counting the minutes until she could go home. Could they smell that she wasn't a blue blood? Did her public school edu-cation waft from her hair as though she had spent a long day cooking on a spattering griddle? She let her eyes roam around the room, studying the women around her. They were a pack of fancy poodles, and she felt like a guinea pig shivering with nerves.

Finally, the guests departed, and Chip dragged Cord into his office to give him an article he'd clipped from the *Journal*. (Chip and Tilda still clipped articles, refusing to forward links like everyone else.)

"Did you have fun?" Darley asked, tucking a shiny lock of hair behind her ear.

"Yeah, it was really nice," Sasha tried.

"Such a cool way to spend a night out," Darley said wryly, "hanging out with old people you don't know."

"There was one sort of funny thing," Sasha confessed. "People kept handing me their dirty plates. I mean, it was fine, but did they give you their plates too?"

"Oh!" Darley laughed. "That's so ridiculous! I hadn't noticed but you're wearing the same thing as Berta! They must have thought you were a caterer—shit! Malcolm!" She called her husband over to tell him.

Everyone laughed, Cord walking up to rub her shoulders to make sure she thought it was funny too, and Sasha played along, knowing deep in her heart that she would never wear a white blouse to a Stockton family party again as long as she lived.

TWO

Georgiana

Georgiana had a problem, and it was mostly her traitorous cheeks. She had always blushed easily, but lately it felt like she had become some sort of character out of science fiction who wore their emotions entirely on their skin. She would feel the heat rising in her face, a slight prickle on her neck, and then—poof—scarlet.

What had for years been a mostly adorable trait had turned into a professional liability now that Georgiana had a real job and, problematically, an enormous, goofy, childlike, and mortifying crush. His name was Brady and she couldn't even look at him in meetings. They had hardly ever spoken—he was older than her, maybe early thirties, and a project manager who had no reason ever to even think of the small pink person frantically glaring at the floor—but whenever Georgiana passed him in the halls, sat in the same conference room, or ran into him at the copier, she had to avert her eyes like he was a solar eclipse and she needed those dorky paper glasses.

They worked for a not-for-profit and the offices were in an old mansion on Columbia Place that was still set up like a home. To get to her desk, Georgiana walked through a beautiful foyer where their receptionist, Denise, sat behind a heavy mahogany desk, up a spiral staircase, through a grand room that they used alternately as their conference room and cafeteria, then through a large bedroom where four desks were arranged for the grant-writing department, and into a tiny space that must have originally been for a maid or a wet nurse. They were all crammed in like sardines, but it was wonderfully charming. Georgiana's little two-person office had a big window that looked west over the Promenade out across the East River. The mansion's bathrooms were scattered throughout the house and decorated with maps of the various regions where they worked, and hanging over the printer, along with instructions on refilling toner, was a gilded portrait of a duchess taking a harp lesson.

The mansion belonged to their founder, heir to a pharmaceutical fortune. He had traveled the world as a young man and become aware of the lack of medical care available in developing countries and set up a not-for-profit to teach local organizations how to build sustainable health systems. They operated mostly on grants from places like the Gates Foundation and the World Bank, and also had some wealthy private donors. Georgiana was in the communications department, so her job was to suck up to the aforementioned donors, and to cull photos of their work abroad for their website, edit articles about their projects for the newsletter, and manage their social media accounts. It wasn't because she was especially interested in social media, but because she was under thirty everyone assumed she would be, and it helped her land the job to casually mention that she had eighteen hundred followers on Instagram. (Who didn't? All you needed to do was remove your privacy settings and post the occasional picture of your cute friends at a party.)

But this was the main difference between Georgiana and Brady: she was lowly support staff, fangirling the organization's successes in the field and writing it up in the newsletter, and Brady was at the center of the action. He had been to Afghanistan and Uganda, he was featured in the photos Georgiana pored over, speaking to a group of doctors in a makeshift hospital, kicking a soccer ball with adorable kids in front of a banner with information on vaccines, looking deeply into the eyes of a doctor in India as they reviewed their contraceptive distribution plans. He was the star of the play, and she was painting the sets, simultaneously desperately wishing he would notice her and dreading the moment when he might, sure her cheeks would go aflame.

It was a Friday, and Georgiana was standing at the mailboxes under the stairs sorting envelopes by destination, domestic into one bin and international into another. As she sorted, she double-checked each address to make sure it looked right—she had updated their contacts so that they could do giant mailings without having to enter the addresses individually, but it was still a slightly imperfect system. She was puzzling over an envelope, lost in thought, when a voice startled her.

"You okay?" It was Brady. He leaned past her to retrieve his mail from a box with his name below it.

"Yeah, just trying to figure out if this one is addressed correctly." Georgiana held the letter out so that he might see it. They were standing so close she could have kissed him if she lurched fast enough. *Oh my God, why would I lurch-kiss this person?* She briefly hated her own brain.

"It looks fine. What's the problem?" Brady asked.

"But is it domestic or international? It doesn't have a country on it," Georgiana replied, perplexed.

"United Arab Emirates," Brady read slowly, pointing to the bottom line of the address. Was the envelope shaking? Georgia felt like it was shaking.

"Right, but shouldn't there be a country under that?" she asked.

"United Arab Emirates is a country."

"Oh, I just—" Georgiana stopped talking.

"It's on the Arabian Peninsula by Saudi Arabia and Oman?"

"Yeah." Georgiana had literally never heard of it in her life.

"Dubai is one of the cities there."

"Right, with those Palm Tree islands you can see from outer space." Georgiana nodded her head vigorously. She knew Dubai. "And the shopping malls and sports cars."

"Yeah. But that's not the part where we're trying to provide health care."

"Right, right, no, no," Georgiana agreed. Was it possible she had ever sounded like a bigger idiot? She wasn't sure.

"Anyway, the envelope is good to go." Brady smiled—or maybe he was laughing?—and gave her a quick nod before he walked off with his mail.

Georgiana tossed the envelope into the international bin and felt her cheek. Blazing.

That night Georgiana went to a birthday party in Williamsburg and woke up Saturday morning with a hangover so intense she could feel it in her teeth. She texted Lena a series of skull emojis and Lena wrote back and told her to come over. Kristin was already there, and they opened up the pullout couch in Lena's living room so that they could convalesce together horizontally. They ordered grilled cheese and French fries and a side of onion rings from

Westville, because though they all claimed to not really like onion rings, they might as well have a few since they were on their death-beds. They watched rich ladies fight on Bravo, and at three, when Lena's boyfriend came home from the gym, he laughed at them, lying there like three vodka-soaked degenerates.

Georgiana loved going out, but hangover days with Lena and Kristin were kind of the best. Sometimes they went to movies and fell asleep and missed the whole show, sometimes they decided to sweat it out and went to a barre class and spent the entire hour bitch-ing and moaning and getting dirty looks from the instructors, and sometimes they gave up and went to the diner on Clark and ordered Bloody Marys, saying "hair of the dog, hair of the dog" until they were drunk again and had to go home and nap.

Georgiana, Lena, and Kristin had gone to high school together and had promised to all live in a big apartment when they were grown up. They hadn't ended up as roommates, but they lived in the same neighborhood, and having three different apartments to hang out in actually made it even better. Lena was an executive assistant for a rich hedge fund guy who loved her so much that he was willing to overpay her in exchange for her promise never to quit. It wasn't the career Lena had dreamed of when she graduated with a degree in art history, booking flights and making dinner reservations, but she was earning three times what she had been offered at Christie's, so she stayed. He regularly transferred his mileage points to her ac-count, and at this rate she'd never have to fly coach again, which seemed like a fair price to pay for one's dreams. Kristin worked for a tech startup and mostly hated it, but she never had to go to the gro-cery store, eating breakfast and lunch in the work cafeteria and fill-ing a lunchbox with salad and grilled salmon to bring home after work. Since they went out five nights a week, Kristin was always carting her Tupperware bar to bar, and they teased her pitilessly for looking like some weirdo who was going to break out a five-course meal in the middle of Sharlene's on Flatbush.

As they lay on the pullout with their onion rings, Georgiana told them about the mailbox debacle with Brady. They had spent more time than Georgiana would like to admit talking about her crush, so even though this was the least cool story she had told in a while, she felt it was her obligation to give her friends the update now that something real had happened.

"George, how the fuck did you not know that the UAE is a country?" Lena asked, sitting up and giving her a despairing look.

"Well, I'm not like, a *scholar* of international boundaries! I majored in Russian literature!" Georgiana defended herself.

"It's really bad, dude," Kristin agreed. "But at least he talked to you? I mean, he offered to help you, so that's a positive." She was trying to be supportive, but Georgiana hadn't given them much to work with, she understood. They spent the rest of the afternoon discussing how she might recover her standing with Brady, coming up with conversational gambits that ranged from the boring to the absurd: "Did you know that the poverty line in the UAE is about twenty-two dollars a day?" "I've heard falconry is really big in the Emirates." "Is it true Emirates Airline has the best free pajamas in first class?" Her friends really were useless at this sort of thing, but she liked that they all got to say Brady's name a lot as they conspired.

Georgiana couldn't tell for sure, but after that she started feeling like she was seeing more of Brady, spotting him behind her in line at the coffee cart and offering a quick wave, passing him in the back hall on her way to the library as he came out of a meeting. He usually ate lunch with two other project managers from the first floor and she had eavesdropped on them talking about Premier League soccer and someone's home brew project. People in their office didn't really eat at their desks; they mostly brought food from home or ran out for a salad or sandwich and ate it at the big table at the top of the second-floor stairs, and Georgiana had never given much thought to whom she ate lunch with. Sometimes she would read her phone or a magazine while eating leftover fried rice or a slice of pizza, sometimes she would chat with whoever happened to be at the table at the same time. When Brady and one of his first-floor friends sat down across from her at the table one afternoon, she was eating a salad and reading ESPN on her phone. They nodded hello and she continued scrolling, now completely incapable of focusing on the words in front of her face but desperate to appear busy.

"What's going on this weekend?" Brady started, unwrapping a sandwich and popping open a can of seltzer.

"Going to Philly to see the wife's family," his friend replied. "What about you?"

"I think some college friends are going to be in town, so we'll be at the Long Island Bar Saturday night," Brady said before taking a bite. Georgiana looked up at him, and he caught her eye and smiled. Was he saying that for her? Did he want her to come and meet him? No. That was delusional. He was having a conversation about his weekend plans like a normal person and she just happened to be sitting there, and he smiled at her because he was not psychotic or a total misanthrope.

She dotted the corners of her mouth with her paper napkin, closed the lid on her salad, and mumbled, "Bye, guys," before returning to her desk. She couldn't just sit there and pretend to eat.

Just being near Brady made her feel like she'd taken nine shots of espresso and her hands were shaking.

Lena and Kristin didn't have a read on the situation. Was he just making conversation, or did he want her to meet him? Either way, she lived in the Heights, she occasionally went to the Long Island Bar on Atlantic Avenue, and it wouldn't be weird if she happened to be out at the same time, so on Saturday night she dressed carefully, spent an extra ten minutes drying her hair, and wore the boots that kind of hurt her toes because they looked really great with jeans. Lena, Kristin, and their friend Michelle walked over to the bar with her. They got there at eight and ordered tequila sodas, and by the time they finished them Brady still hadn't arrived. Kristin and Michelle had another party they wanted to go to, so they left, but Lena stayed to hang out. They had another drink and gossiped about Lena's sister, who was engaged to the most boring man on the planet, then about their old high-school teacher, who had run away with the squash coach, and Georgiana's mother, who refused to whiten her teeth because she thought it would be bad for her, but now drank red wine through a straw at home so as not to stain them further, resulting in her drinking twice as fast and twice as much, which had to have equally deleterious health results. At midnight Brady still wasn't there, so they left, hugging goodbye on the street corner. Georgiana let herself into her apartment, used a wipe to take off her careful makeup, and flopped on the bed in an old basketball T-shirt. She felt lonely and pathetic, but she knew that all across the city there were girls just like her who had spent their Saturday nights waiting for something to happen, nursing a drink or reading a paperback in a coffee shop or scrolling endlessly on their phones, alone and biding their time until their real life would begin.

In the morning, Georgiana dressed in tennis whites and met her mother at the Casino, their club on Montague Street. They hit for an hour, and with each swing of the racket she felt her frustration pounding out. Georgiana was a strong opponent, she hit hard, and she had been taking lessons since she was four, but her mother was a backboard. She was nearly seventy, but her footwork was so practiced that she never had to run; her shots weren't hard, but she got a racket on everything; and her form was so impeccable that she had Georgiana sprinting all over the court chasing the ball. Playing tennis was and always had been the cleanest line of communication between Georgiana and her mother. Tilda was hard for her to talk to; she was of a generation that despised difficult conversations, and shut down at the slightest hint of conflict or unpleasantness. When Georgiana was a teenager, she found this infuriating, every venture at true closeness put on ice. But tennis had saved them. When they couldn't talk, they played. Her mother cheered her on, complimented her best shots, gave her strategic pointers, and marveled at her agility. In the years when Georgiana wasn't sure her mother even really liked her, she knew that at least she approved of her game.

In an alternate universe they would have gone to a gossipy brunch after tennis, and Georgiana would have confessed her humiliation at the Long Island Bar. She would have told her mother all about Brady, the way other project managers looked up to him, the way she swore she sometimes felt him looking at her, the crush so powerful she dreamed about him regularly and woke up simultaneously thrilled to have been with him and devastated that it was only in her sleep. Instead, she zipped her racket into its case and followed her mother out the big swinging doors of the Casino and down Henry to their new apartment, where her mother set out a lunch made by Berta, served on her favorite flowered china with matching napkins, and they ate while looking at the newspaper and not speaking except to occasionally read interesting bits aloud.

It was weird seeing her parents in their new home. Georgiana had lived in the house on Pineapple Street since she was a baby, and every piece of furniture, every scar in the wooden banister, every speck in the granite countertops felt essential to her family, like the very place had leaked into their DNA and they had leaked right back. They were meant to live in a drafty old limestone, meant to creak and age along with their antiques, and seeing her mom and dad puttering around a glossy marble kitchen island sometimes felt like watching Ben Franklin using a Nintendo Switch.

Even weirder than seeing her parents in their new apartment was thinking about Cord's new wife living in her childhood home. Georgiana had been open to Sasha at first, but two things happened that soured any possibility of a warm and fuzzy sister-in-law relationship. The first happened a month before Cord's wedding, when he showed up drunk at Darley's house with swollen eyes because Sasha had refused to sign the prenup, had left his apartment and not come back. At some point, a week later, Sasha had reappeared. Cord wouldn't speak of it again, and neither Georgiana nor Darley knew the details. The second thing happened the night of the wedding. Georgiana and Darley joined all the younger guests at a bar on Stone Street for the after-party. Sasha's cousin Sam had been snorting coke all night and had become wildly indiscreet. He buttonholed Georgiana at the end of the bar and asked her bluntly just how loaded her family was.

"What?" Georgiana had replied, laughing in disbelief.

"Your boy, Cord, obviously has fuck-you money. Just the way you guys talk and all the clubs. It tracks that Sasha would marry a rich guy. She changed when she moved to New York. Now here she is, locking it down with a prep-school Republican."

"Cord is a registered Independent," Georgiana replied defensively, as though that addressed anything Sam had just said. But when she thought about it alongside Sasha's negotiations over the prenup, it rubbed her the wrong way. And now Sasha lived in Georgiana's house.

Even though it was a Sunday, Georgiana's father was working in the second bedroom, where he had set up his office. After she finished eating, she made a cup of English breakfast with milk and two spoonfuls of sugar and quietly tapped on the door. Her father was reading an old, yellowed back issue of *The Wall Street Journal* with a magnifier, his glasses lying discarded on the desk. She set the tea down at his elbow and gave him a kiss on the cheek.

Georgiana liked to think that she and her father had a special relationship. While Darley and Cord were only two years apart and had each other as best friends, Georgiana was a decade younger. (Georgiana teased them by calling them "geriatric millennials," while she was on the cusp of Gen Z.) It was almost like being an only child, both Darley and Cord off to college when she was in the third grade, and since her parents knew she was their last baby (Tilda mimed an alarming scissor motion whenever she made that declaration), they coddled her and made sure to do all the things they had felt too busy to do when the others were small: taking her to Paris at ten, bringing her along to weeknight restaurant dinners, coming to as many of her high school and college tournaments as they could.

"How was the tennis, George?" her father asked, refolding the paper and leaning back in his chair.

"Oh, it was all right. I need to be running more, I don't think I'm as fast as I was when I was playing every day." In college at Brown she was on the tennis team, and without that exercise regimen, Georgiana was five pounds heavier. It didn't bother her really, except that she was worried her mother might start beating her.

"And how is work?"

"It's good. I have a newsletter deadline this week, but I have all the stuff I need—I just have to edit and do the layout." Every month Georgiana solicited information from project managers in the field about what they were doing and then Frankensteined their slapdash responses into articles.

"Bring me a copy when you're done so I can read it." He smiled.

Georgiana was pleased. Her parents had been really supportive of her decision to go into the not-for-profit sector after college. While Cord had followed in her father's footsteps and worked alongside him, neither Georgiana nor Darley had any interest in real estate investment. It was probably for the best, since it would be a neat transition when their father retired. All their associates already knew Cord, most of them were comfortable speaking to him about even the thorniest of issues, and it was expected that he would take over all their holdings eventually. Their father had already been enjoying the perks of having Cord at his side, delegating "relationship management" of the most difficult people to his son.

"What's this?" Georgiana asked, lifting a newspaper clipping off the desk. Her father had written her name on a yellow Post-it stuck to the clipping.

"Oh, it's a book review I thought you'd find interesting. A do-gooder after your own heart," he chuckled.

Georgiana skimmed the review. It was a biography of a Roman heiress in the year 408. Melania the Younger was a daughter of one of Rome's senatorial families who had converted to Christianity and wanted to remain a virgin. Unfortunately, her parents married her off at the age of fourteen, but Melania managed to make a deal with her husband: If she provided him with two children, they could have a celibate marriage thereafter and devote their days to Christian works. When her father died, she inherited his vast estate, land, fortune, and fifty thousand slaves. In service to God, she decided to give away her inheritance, but it proved harder than she would have expected: The slaves refused to be freed. They didn't trust her intentions, and worried that she would no longer protect them from Barbarians and famine. It turned out they were right, and many of them starved to death.

"Wow, Dad, what made you think of me? Are you planning on marrying me off against my wishes?" Georgiana teased.

"Well, I've been trying to get someone to take you off my hands, but so far no luck." Chip raised an eyebrow.

"Thanks, Dad." She kissed him on the top of his head. It amused her that he thought of her as a "do-gooder," when she knew that freeing fifty thousand slaves and typing newsletters for a not-for-profit were fairly different levels of beneficence.

Georgiana said goodbye to her mother and carried her racket back to her apartment, where she showered and spent the rest of the day lying in bed, reading a novel, and texting Lena and Kristin. Apparently, the party Kristin had been to after the Long Island Bar had gotten pretty wild, and their crazy friend Riley drank so much bourbon he fell asleep on the subway and woke up in Canarsie.

The next morning, Georgiana packed herself an avocado-and-cheese sandwich, got dressed, and arrived at the office before nine. She combed through the mess of photos for her article and

picked the four best. She took the seven hundred words of free association about the project in Uganda and managed to pull together a
coherent and rather moving piece about a local maternal health clinic.
Nearly 2 percent of women in Uganda die from obstetric causes and
only half receive any sort of care after giving birth. By offering a safe
and clean place to stay, the clinic was able to teach new mothers
about breastfeeding and cord care while also administering the
medical attention they need. The photos of the women holding their
newborns, smiling through their tired eyes, touched Georgiana in a
way she hadn't expected.

It was funny, Georgiana had always considered herself fairly well
traveled for someone her age. She had been to France, Spain, and
Italy; she had been on a safari in Kenya and seen the glaciers in
Alaska; she had even walked along the Great Wall of China with her
high school class. But her work had made her recognize how little of
the world she had actually seen. She had been to tourist spots, rich
cities and towns made for the entertainment of the wealthy. She had
never witnessed actual poverty; she had never contemplated how
people truly lived in the parts of the world where *Condé Nast Trav-
eler* failed to list the best restaurants.

At one thirty she was starving, so she grabbed her sandwich out
of the refrigerator and made her way to the large dining table. Everyone else had come and gone, so she sat alone and spread her napkin on
her lap. When the chair next to her pulled back, Georgiana startled.

"This seat taken?" Brady asked.

"Please," she replied. They had the whole entire table to themselves, and yet he was sitting right next to her. She had left her phone
charging at her desk, so she had nowhere to look, nothing to pretend
to be absorbed by while eating.

Brady opened a cardboard container and took out a grilled

cheese, a small puff of steam escaping from the box. "Late lunch?" he asked.

"Yeah, I'm pulling together a newsletter and lost track of time." Georgiana retrieved a rogue piece of avocado from the ziplock bag.

"Is it about the outstanding work we've been doing on the Palm Tree islands?"

Georgiana looked up at him with a start, while he pretended to study his sandwich with an innocent expression.

"No. It's actually about our plans to provide free nose jobs to the poor debutantes of Monaco," she replied.

Brady let out a surprised bark of laughter and Georgiana smiled.

"Pretty funny," he said. "So, how was your weekend? What did you get up to?"

"Played tennis, went out with some friends, nothing wild. How about you?"

"Well, it was kind of a bust. I was supposed to get together with some college friends and go out Saturday, but at the last minute my buddy sprained his ankle, so I ended up spending the evening with him at urgent care trying to get an X-ray."

"Oh, that stinks."

"Yeah, I was really looking forward to a night out." He looked at her meaningfully. "At the Long Island Bar."

"I like that place," Georgiana murmured.

"Yeah." He shook his head slightly. "Where do you play tennis?"

They spent the next twenty minutes talking about sports in the city—which public courts checked your Parks Department tennis pass, the supervisor at the Fort Greene courts who would save you a spot if you brought him a bacon, egg, and cheese. They talked about Brady's basketball league, a bunch of guys who sometimes got so carried away that they threw elbows and had to go back to work as partners at white-shoe law firms with black eyes.

They had both finished their sandwiches and reluctantly crumpled up their paper napkins when a nearby meeting let out, and a pair of double doors opened and the room suddenly filled with colleagues marching back to their desks. Brady cocked his head and smiled before scooting out his chair. "See you around." He scooped up her trash along with his own and headed off down to the first floor, as Georgiana floated back to her tiny maid's room office, unsure whether she'd be able to write another word of the newsletter or would spend the next three hours staring out the window and replaying every single thing they had said and feeling her face get warm with pleasure over and over again.

THREE

Darley

Darley's children were obsessed with death. They were five and six, and everyone said this was developmentally normal, but Darley secretly worried it meant they were tortured souls who would get face tattoos as teenagers. It was late afternoon, and they were at the Brooklyn Bridge playground, near the slides. Darley had found a sunny spot on the stone steps and was half watching her children run and half scrolling on her phone, filling up her cart for an online grocery order. Some of the kids' classmates were there too, with their nannies, and the adults had nodded at one another, but instead of chatting they had all happily retreated into their little glowing screens.

The children had been trying to climb up the twenty-foot slide, all five of them in a line, boosting one another in a rare show of cooperation. Poppy was the ringleader, bossing the other children in her tiny, shrill voice, sounding more seagull than human, and Darley wondered briefly if it was wrong to hate the sound of a child's voice. She focused on her phone, methodically shopping for dinner items— salmon for herself, mac and cheese for the kids, pork chops for

Malcolm. She was debating the likelihood of Hatcher eating chicken that had been touched by rosemary when she noticed the children had all congregated under the slide. They seemed to be looking at something, and she watched as Poppy went to the edge of the playground to grab a long stick and run it back to the group. The afternoon was warm, and she smelled the ocean. The river was just on the other side of the trees, and Darley could hear the ferries blowing their mournful horns, could hear birdsong, and felt sweet contentment. There were days in New York when she was desperate to escape, desperate for the beach, for a garden, for a glassy lake, but then there were days like today when the leafy park felt perfect, when she wondered how she could ever contemplate any other life.

Suddenly Poppy was upon her, Hatcher right behind. "Mommy, can you fix it?" she asked. She was holding something for Darley in her outstretched arms, and it took several seconds for Darley to register what it was she had. Was it a sweater? Was it a paper bag? Was it? . . . It was a pigeon. And the pigeon was dead.

That night Darley's mother came to dinner along with Georgiana, Cord, and Sasha. As Darley poured the wine, Poppy sat straight in her chair, a chicken nugget speared on her fork, and announced to the table, "Mommy was not pleased with me today."

"Why, Poppy, dear? What happened?" her mother asked, ready to jump to Poppy's defense.

"I found a pigeon under the slide at the playground and I picked it up. I don't know if a dog bit it or if it had a sickness, but it died."

The table was momentarily silent. "What did you do with it?" her mother asked, aghast.

"Mommy took it and put it in the recycling," Poppy said sadly, gnawing on the nugget like she was eating a candied apple on a stick.

"The recycling? You didn't just put it in the garbage?" Sasha asked with alarm.

"Of course I put it in the garbage. Then we came home, and I boiled her hands, and I am never letting the children out of the house again," announced Darley, filling her wineglass to the rim. That was the thing about Sasha; she could always be counted on to say the most annoying thing in any given situation. It was a talent, really.

After dinner, her mother and siblings left, and Darley gave Poppy and Hatcher a long soak in the tub. She made it the bubbliest bubble bath, squirting as much soap in the water as she could without risking the children getting UTIs or eye pain. She scrubbed their hair until it squeaked and then toweled them off and slicked lotion on their legs and backs before sending them off to find their pajamas. Malcolm was working late, and so she read to both kids in her bed, book after book about tooth fairies and trolls, magic school buses and treehouses. They were still young enough to frequently be confused about the differences between real and pretend. They both believed in magic, and Darley was often torn about when she should intervene with the truth and when she should let them dream. Hatcher had been asking her lately to build him a shrinking machine, so they spent long afternoons taping together cardboard boxes and drawing on buttons and knobs, but the play sessions always ended with him inconsolable, devastated that the machines never really shrunk anything. Poppy talked about the tooth fairy incessantly, counting the days until she would lose her first tooth. Darley had once arbitrarily told her daughter that she would lose her first tooth when she was seven, and Poppy had taken it as gospel, outraged at the unfairness when a classmate lost a tooth at five and a half. When Poppy asked what the tooth fairy did with all the teeth, Darley had lied quickly, saying that the fairy gave them to babies who needed teeth, and this started a long and convoluted series of falsehoods about how the fairy got the teeth in their tiny mouths and how that was probably the reason babies were so fussy all the time.

After Darley finished the fourth book, she walked the children to their room and tucked them into bed. As she helped pull the sheet up under Poppy's chin, her daughter looked at her, suddenly wide awake. "Mommy, what happens when you die?"

"Well, honey, it's like we always talk about. We don't really know what happens after we die, but in some ways, we stay part of the world forever. Our bodies go into the ground and become part of the earth, and then plants and grass and flowers grow, and we become part of those plants and maybe an animal comes by and eats those plants and we become part of those animals and it goes on like that forever." Darley stroked Poppy's hair off her forehead and watched her child frowning lightly in concentration.

"So the bird that died today?"

"Yes, honey?"

"Since you put the bird in the garbage it will be part of the garbage forever?"

"Oh, well, no. Someone will bury it in the ground," Darley lied. "I love you so much, honey. Sleep well." She turned off the light and backed out of the room, full of the understanding that her children were going to be totally fucked up.

DARLEY AND MALCOLM had two sets of wedding vows: The ones they said in church in front of God, their friends, and family, and the ones they whispered later that night in bed, holding hands and giggling at the false eyelashes still stuck to the pillow like spiders, the bobby pins Darley kept discovering lodged deep within her mop of sprayed hair. Holding hands, their wedding bands catching the light, they whispered: *I promise I will never expect you to pack my suitcase, I promise I will never hide in my office and pretend to work when our friends are over, I promise I will never sit in the back seat while you drive me like a chauffeur, I promise I will never sleep with anyone but you.*

Darley had friends, she had cousins, she had a vibrant social life filled with dozens of people she could call for a cocktail, for a tennis match, a manicure, or even, possibly, a kidney—but she didn't trust anyone like she trusted Malcolm. Her husband was, without a doubt, the best person she had ever met. Together they had a marriage unlike that of any of her friends in that they never, ever lied. It was stunning how casual lying was woven into most married life. Her friend Claire had a bank account she'd never mentioned to her husband. Her godmother hid shopping bags behind the study door and waited until her husband was out to put the new clothes in her closet, cutting the tags and shoving them deep in the trash. Her best friend occasionally snuck off to get a haircut or a facial and told her husband she had a meeting, not because he would even mind, but because she said she just wanted to have something for herself.

Darley didn't get that at all. She could never function in a relationship full of cavalier deceit, and she knew Malcolm felt the same way.

When they decided to get married, Darley couldn't ask Malcolm to sign a prenup. The entire thing felt like arranging for their eventual divorce and drew a thick line between what was hers and what was his. She didn't feel the money belonged to her anyway. It belonged to her grandparents and her great-grandparents. She had done nothing but act as a drain—private school and vacations and clothing and death by the thousand cuts that was raising a child in the most expensive city in America. The family lawyer explained to Darley that she had two choices: She could have Malcolm sign the prenup and agree to some paltry sum that would be given to him each year after their eventual divorce, or she could lock the account away, refuse the money, and have it all pass directly to her children when they were adults. She consulted Malcolm, and he said it was ultimately her decision. He would sign it, or she could have her trust skip her entirely, and they could use their very expensive educations to make their own way. So, Darley did it. She locked herself out of her own inheritance and bet all her chips on love.

Malcolm was already earning more money than most Americans could even dream of. He was not only a genius but had the sort of obsessive intellectualism that is rewarded in the financial sector. He was fascinated by airplanes and had been since he was a child. As a teenager he started a blog about the different features of various plane models that was so thorough that Boeing had linked to it on their website. He studied flight routes and identified inefficiencies, posting them on his blog and emailing airlines with his findings. He enrolled in business school, and after he graduated he earned his pilot's license in his free time, using weekends to dart up and down the East Coast, often landing just to eat a sandwich near the airport before getting back in the Cessna. Darley went with him, a copilot in seating arrangements only, content to wipe the windshield and check the oil levels and otherwise stare out the window as New England spread out below. Once, they packed sleeping bags and slept on an airfield in West Virginia, rising with the sun to buy matching base-ball caps at the airport convenience store before climbing back in the plane to be home for lunch.

Malcolm was hired right out of business school to work for Deut-sche Bank's Global Industrials Group. He knew more about aviation than any of the other associates did, hands down, and quickly built client relationships that went far deeper than those of his peers. Deutsche Bank moved him to the Aviation Corporate and Invest-ment Banking Group, where he continued to rise quickly. Unlike the rest of banking, where pedigree mattered intensely, Aviation was in-ternational, all business conducted in English, a sector where depth of knowledge mattered more than connections. Malcolm traveled all the time, flying ten hours just to attend one pitch meeting and then taking a flight home that very same night—the boomerang. For most people this travel would be crushing, but for Malcolm it was flying—sure, he was a passenger instead of the pilot, but this entire world thrilled him. Unlike typical bankers who had to travel to Molina, Illinois, or Mayfield Heights, Ohio, where their industrial clients were based, airline bankers had clients in the best cities in the world—London, Paris, Hong Kong, and Singapore. Plus, with the secret status hat trick he had—ConciergeKey on American, Global Services on United, Diamond 360 on Delta—travel was never the soul-crushing experience it was for the hoi polloi. He breezed through security, he carried his laptop to the lounge, he walked onto the plane last and slid his bed into the lie-flat position. He didn't care about champagne or hot towels, he just wanted to work on his computer with a minimum of annoyance, then wake up refreshed in time to find the uniformed driver holding his name on a sign at the other end.

This left Darley alone with the children, but she was never really alone. Malcolm texted her at takeoff and landing, in the car to the hotel and after the meeting. She knew where he was at every moment, from Brisbane to Bogotá, and they would FaceTime from his near-identical hotel rooms. He brought her home airline pajamas from so many flights that she had an entire section in her closet filled with unopened plastic pouches.

Malcolm had coworkers who used their business travel as a sort of international sex buffet, activating Tinder wherever they landed. A guy on his team had girlfriends in Sydney, in Santiago, and in Frankfurt, and he visited the same ones over and over. Did these women think their American boyfriend was going to fall in love and bring them back to New York? Or was it just consistent sex from a handsome, rich guy who breezed into town and bought them dinner and gifts? Darley didn't know what the man's wife knew, and it didn't concern her. While he was off drinking pisco sours with pretty young strangers, Malcolm was in the hotel room on the phone with his wife.

Darley and Malcolm met in business school, married the summer after graduation, and somehow ended up pregnant right away (not "somehow," it was the usual way, but always sort of a shock). When Darley got pregnant again a mere six months after Poppy was born, it felt like a bomb went off in the middle of their youth. While she had been an associate at Goldman Sachs and had managed to have a baby and a career, it was impossible to work eighty-hour weeks with two under two. She quit her job so Malcolm could keep his, but Darley never would have survived it without Malcolm's parents. The Kims were everything the Stockton family was not. Soon-ja and

Young-ho Kim had moved to the United States from South Korea in the late 1960s; the Stocktons came over on the *Mayflower*. The Kims had made themselves from scratch, Young-ho earning his PhD and making a successful career as a chemist; Darley's father had inherited both his fortune and entire business from his father. The Kims were also communicative, loving, and functional. After their wedding, Soon-ja and Young-ho insisted that Darley call them by their first names, something Darley felt hesitant to do at first. She'd grown up calling all her parents' friends "Mr." and "Mrs." She had heard that Korean families were usually even more formal, so for the first year of marriage Darley mostly called them "Um," to avoid saying any name at all. They showered Darley with gifts, never arriving at her apartment without an eighty-dollar candle purchased from a department store or beautiful cloth napkins with a Provençal print. When Poppy was born, Soon-ja moved into their apartment the day the baby nurse left and slept on the sofa for six months, taking turns with Darley overnight, feeding Poppy bottles of expressed breast milk so that Darley could sleep, giving the baby baths and trimming the tiny crescent moons of her soft fingernails. Poppy and Hatcher were as much her babies as they were Darley's, and any sense of formality between them had long disappeared into that vortex of time filled with naked breasts and milk stains and cream for the scar that ripped across her abdomen.

AFTER THE PIGEON, after the bath, after Darley had spent the better part of an hour ordering birthday presents for the nine children with parties in the coming weeks, Darley changed into her pajamas and crawled into bed. Malcolm came home at midnight, letting himself into the apartment and moving silently through the kitchen to the back bathroom, where he showered and brushed his teeth before carefully peeling back the blankets to join her. Half asleep, Darley found him and wrapped her body around his. While she slept alone more often than not, she slept most soundly with their legs intertwined. In the morning, the children treated Malcolm with the reverence usually reserved for astronauts or Olympians, showing him drawings they had made at school that week, performing songs they had learned on the bus, telling long and convoluted stories about someone named Kale, whose older brother had been to a birthday party at a bounce house in Queens where there were more than fifty trampolines.

Malcolm made pancakes from scratch, which created a huge mess, a funny choice when Darley had a bakery box of blueberry muffins from Alice's Tea Cup, but she sat at the table with a big smile on her face, sipping coffee and watching Hatcher drip syrup down his chin. After breakfast they took their scooters to soccer practice on the plaza, where a dozen kindergartners wore matching red T-shirts and constantly forgot what they were doing and picked the ball up with their hands. Darley had a hundred errands to run, knew she should use this time for a yoga class or tennis with her mom, but she wanted to be with Malcolm, so she snuggled up next to him on the bench and whispered with him about the other parents—the mom who hosted a dinner party at her ten-million-dollar apartment in Cobble Hill but never paid her share for the teacher gift at Christmas; the couple down the street who got a city permit for a block party, but instead of telling the neighbors, invited all their friends and blasted music until two a.m.; the unassuming lawyer who wore Green Bay Packers jerseys all weekend with his kids but then appeared on the front page of *The New York Times* alongside a Supreme Court justice.

After soccer they took the kids to lunch at Fascati, to the library to check out a dozen books, then to the Broken Toy playground, where they pushed around discarded bicycles. That night Darley fell asleep wrapped around Malcolm and barely moved when he slipped out at four, off to finish a presentation at the office before catching a flight to Rio that night. When Darley's alarm went off at six, she registered that she felt exhausted. She wanted to stay under the covers, her head thick and heavy, but she forced herself out of bed to make coffee and pack lunch for the kids. She woke them and laid out their clothing, she made their breakfast—avocado toast for Poppy, peanut butter toast for Hatcher, coconut yogurt for Poppy, strawberry yogurt for Hatcher. She pulled on jeans, a loose gray T-shirt, and a baseball cap, snapped helmets under the kids' chins, and carried both their backpacks as she half walked, half jogged down the sidewalk as they scootered to school. At the gate she checked them in with the security guard and parked their scooters along the wall, dozens and dozens of colorful Micro Minis lining the stone facade like decorations on a gingerbread house. There were plenty of neighborhoods in Brooklyn where you wouldn't want to leave a scooter outside and unlocked for six hours, but in Darley's little enclave of the Heights, she felt like she could probably lose her wallet every day for a week and still get it back each time.

At home she tried to rally for the gym, but nothing felt right. Her arms and legs hurt, her neck ached, and even walking from the front door to the kitchen felt like a march through snow or waist-deep slush. She sat down on the sofa and she must have slept, because suddenly she woke and ran to the bathroom and vomited. She lay on the floor, not caring that she was in the kids' bathroom, that she was lying on top of a spiky Buzz Lightyear action figure, that the yellow bath mat clearly had some pee on it. For the next hour she intermittently vomited and lay dazed and feverish. When she gathered the strength, she hauled herself to her bedroom, where she stripped off her jeans and pulled a trash can next to the bed. At noon she called her mother.

"Darley, I'm just running out, can I call you back?" her mother answered.

"Mom, I think I have the stomach flu. Malcolm is traveling. Can you pick the kids up from school?"

"Oh sweetheart. We'll figure it out. What time?"

"They get out at two forty-five."

"Okay, darling, two forty-five."

At three o'clock, Darley was dozing, sweating and freezing in her damp sheets, when she heard the front door open and close, heard backpacks hit the floor with matching thuds, heard the singing and yelling and clamor that always seemed to surround her children. Knowing they were safely home, Darley drifted back to sleep and dreamed she was in a strange house, walking through room after room, looking for someone, anyone. She woke and vomited again. The clock said seven thirty. As she wiped her mouth with a tissue and tried to decide if she had the strength to walk to the bathroom for water, there was a gentle knock on her bedroom door.

"Come in, Mom," Darley called out weakly.

"Darley, it's Berta," her mother's housekeeper called out tentatively. "I'm sorry, but I have to go home."

"Oh, Berta!" Darley sat up, forgetting that she wasn't wearing pants. "Thank you for being here. Where is my mom?"

"Mrs. Stockton had a crisis with one of her table arrangements. The birds' nests they sent for her 'Flights of Fancy' dinner party had bugs in them, and they ruined all the fruit bowls, but it's fine. I gave the children pasta and broccoli for dinner, but they are not tired for bed."

"Thanks so much, Berta." Darley tried to stand, but another wave of nausea overtook her.

"I'm sorry, but I have to go home for my grandkids." Berta's daughter was a nurse who often did late shifts and counted on her mother to fill in.

"Of course, Berta. I'll call my brother or my sister. Thanks so much for coming over. Can you just turn on a movie before you leave?" Darley knew that if a movie was playing her kids would leave her alone for at least an hour and a half. She couldn't face them, she worried she'd frighten them (their death obsession didn't help), or worse, get them sick.

Berta nodded and closed the door softly. Darley shut her eyes. Georgiana had work in the morning. Cord and Sasha had work in the morning. Darley's mother, well, Darley's mother had already shown what she was willing to do. She picked up the phone.

"Soon-ja?"

"Darley, my love, how are you and my babies?"

"I'm not great, Soon-ja, I think I have the stomach flu. I'm vomiting and Malcolm is heading to Brazil for his deal . . ."

"I'll be right there. I'm getting in the car now. I should be there by nine at the latest. You hang in there, my love, and don't worry about a thing."

Darley fell back against her pillow, the sound of cartoon characters singing in high creepy voices seeping into feverish dreams of birds' nests and pigeons.

In the morning, Darley woke to see the sun already peeking through the blinds. She could hear Soon-ja in the kitchen making breakfast. Her stomach and throat were raw, her eyes felt scratchy with sand, and she was pretty sure she smelled worse than the class hamster they had taken for spring vacation. But she was better. Until she flipped her phone over on her nightstand and saw the text from Malcolm: I've been fired.

FOUR

Sasha

On birthdays and holidays, special occasions when the wine was flowing, the family would linger over dinner and reminisce, telling stories of bad behavior and shenanigans over the years. Cord would talk about the time he and his high school friends got drunk, then lost, in Paris while they were supposed to be sketching at the Louvre on a class trip. Georgiana would talk about sneaking out after dark down at their club in Florida. They delighted in their flirtations with deviant behavior and cackled away, even when they all knew the stories by heart after dozens of retellings. Sasha loved hearing them, even the ones that were familiar, and she laughed and laughed, but she never contributed her own. She knew better than that. It was because her family stories made their craziest misadventures seem like a night sipping O'Doul's at math camp.

The truth was, Sasha came from a very wild family. Her cousins were infamous in the small beach town outside Providence where she grew up, and most of them had only avoided mile-long rap sheets because her uncle happened to be the chief of police. For the most part, their antics were met with slaps on the wrist or warnings. But her cousins drunkenly stole Boston Whalers for joyrides, they stayed up all night snorting coke on houseboats in the bay, they crashed weddings at the mansions in Newport, and they claimed to drive better drunk than sober, an assertion countered by their dented fenders and broken fence posts. While Cord may have suffered a broken arm from a ski accident, Sasha's cousin Brandon suffered a broken arm from falling off a second-floor balcony wasted on Jameson and NoDoz. It was just a different level of bad behavior. On rich people these exploits looked funny, but on Sasha's family she knew they just looked trashy.

After the disaster that was Sasha's engagement party—her older brother, Nate, was thrown out of the Explorer's Club for trying to feed the stuffed polar bear a leg of lamb—she made her father read the entire family the riot act before the wedding, reminding them that their uncle was *not* the chief of the New York City Police, and that while they should feel free to act like complete buffoons and degenerates in Providence, they would be embarrassing Sasha in front of her new family with that sort of behavior at her wedding. The lecture was greeted with general merriment among her cousins— they loved nothing more than being reminded of outrageous past transgressions—and they proceeded to be utter lunatics at her reception, dismantling a floral arrangement to drink champagne out of a giant vase.

In spite of her family's behavior (or, truthfully, partially because of it), Sasha loved her wedding. It was grand, it was elegant, and it was just wild enough to make sure nobody would ever forget it. The celebration was held at the Down Town Association, a private club on Pine Street founded by J. P. Morgan as an all-men's club for bankers. Cord had lunch there several days a week, and they had attended champagne tastings and lectures there in the evenings—once even an Italian-themed dinner with wine pairings that was so boring

Sasha accidentally got hammered on Barolo just to survive. The club was three floors of old-fashioned New York glamour, with sky-blue ceilings, dark wooden railings, a walk-in cigar humidor, and a massive marble barbershop in the back of the men's room, where they filmed the Jodie Foster movie *Inside Man*.

Cord and Sasha fed each other cake, he swung her delighted mother around the dance floor (all those cotillion lessons as a boy paid off), and Sasha gamely tried to keep up with her father-in-law, who led her in a waltz to Katy Perry's "Firework." Malcolm and Darley cut loose for once, Malcolm putting his tie around his forehead like a character in *Animal House*, and when a friend of the family got turned around on his way out of the men's room and walked in on Cord's business school roommate feeling up Sasha's cousin in the barbershop, he laughed and told everyone it was the best party he'd been to in a decade.

Since Cord's family paid for the wedding (a breach in tradition), Sasha insisted on paying for the honeymoon. She found a deal online for a resort in Turks and Caicos, a place right on the beach, where every suite had its own hot tub overlooking the ocean. She had briefly fantasized that they might get some kind of royal treatment as honeymooners, upgrades and rose petals on pillows, but when the resort van picked them up at the airport she quickly realized the entire place was full of couples like them. As they planned their wedding Cord had rolled his eyes at the "wedding factories," complaining about the places that pumped through reception after reception, creating cookie-cutter celebrations that were no more special or individual than a suburban prom. Now she worried he would be turned off by a place that was so clearly a factory extension, but he was happily leafing through the resort booklet, planning tennis matches, bike rides, and dinner reservations.

While they had gone to a zillion friends' weddings together, they hadn't actually traveled much, and Sasha quickly realized they had entirely different views of what it meant to be on vacation. For Sasha, vacation meant putting on her swimsuit at dawn, walking to the beach, and moving only to get the occasional cold drink or salty snack. Cord apparently felt that vacation meant moving constantly, like a human Roomba, bouncing from one activity to the next. He chartered a boat to Middle Caicos so they could stomp through dark and gummy caves full of bats. He hired a pilot to take them for a noisy loop above the island in a helicopter. He drove them to the famous conch fritter restaurant and they downed the chewy fried lumps with icy bottles of Turk's Head beer. On the last full day, Sasha begged Cord for the chance to just lie on the beach, and while he brought a mask and snorkel and explored the tiny reef out beyond the sand, she flopped on a warm towel and did absolutely nothing, letting her mind clear until it felt baked clean by the sun.

They had two bottles of champagne chilling in their suite and meant to drink them before they left. After roasting on the beach until sunset, they made their way back to the room, and on their way they stopped in each of the half dozen hotel pools for a dip. They were taking their final soak in a warm-water pool, an oversize Jacuzzi surrounded by hot pink bougainvillea, when another couple appeared through the flowers. They nodded hello and slipped into the water at the other end. They had just gotten married (of course) and were visiting from Boston. After five days alone, Sasha and Cord were feeling sociable, and soon it was dark and they were having so much fun talking that they invited the other couple back to their suite for drinks. They dripped their way from the giant resort Jacuzzi to the smaller one on the screened-in porch off their bedroom. Cord popped the champagne with a knife, a party trick he'd learned to do with a saber, and they all experienced the rapturous head high that comes from drinking bubbly on an empty stomach with borderline sunstroke. It was somewhere toward the end of the second bottle that the guy from Boston removed his wife's bikini top and everything got weird. How had Sasha not realized what they had done? They had invited another couple to hang out, drunk and near naked, in their hotel suite and somehow *not* realized they were initiating a sex party? Cord, who possessed a mastery of handling awkward social situations rivaling that of a foreign diplomat, hastily mentioned dinner reservations, provided the topless wife with a bathrobe, and whisked them out into the warm evening. Alone, Sasha and Cord fell down laughing and swore to tell any friends who asked that they had survived their honeymoon with their marital vows intact, and no one need know more than that.

SASHA UNDERSTOOD that Cord loved her, but he didn't need her, and that might have been the most attractive thing about him. He was restrained in his expressions of affection—sure, he loved sex and he was unfailingly kind—but he didn't say "I love you" every time they hung up the phone, he didn't bring her flowers or presents without occasion, he didn't tell her that she was the best thing that had ever happened to him. And that was the way Sasha wanted it. After all the heartache of her first love, she was done with grand romantic gestures. She had seen the tumultuous underbelly of such passion.

Sasha had fallen in love in high school. His name was Jake Mullin but everyone just called him Mullin. They had known each other

since they were eleven, placed in the same gifted and talented program at their public school, a classroom in a trailer near the parking
lot. He made her nervous, and she spent years giving him a wide
berth. It seemed like he was barely looked after. He never wore a
jacket, and even in the snowy winter she remembered seeing him
standing on the edge of the playground wearing a black Metallica
T-shirt. His family lived across from the wharf in a peeling green
house with iron railings, and while Sasha's own mother packed her
lunches with hearts drawn on napkins and plastic baggies full of
popcorn made in the air popper, Mullin never seemed to have anything. He didn't even carry a backpack. Sasha was older before she
realized he ate the free lunch, lining up at the cafeteria turnstile
holding the small, laminated card at his side.

Mullin could draw. She'd never noticed, never paid attention,
but one day in high school she walked by his desk and saw a bird so
realistic she gasped. Though Sasha could draw almost as well, it was
because she took art seriously, spent all her free time in the school's
art studio, built all her electives around painting and ceramics classes.
Mullin would spend English class carefully shading the detailed
veins of a leaf and its stem and then, at the end of the period, crum-
ple the paper in the trash.

They got together the summer before junior year. There was a
reservoir someone had discovered in the next town at the end of a
long dirt road just before the highway. The gate was locked, but if
you parked, then hiked ten minutes along shady paths, you came to
a breathtaking lake with a stone tower at the center. Sasha and her
friends spent the whole summer with a big gang of kids, drinking
beer and smoking pot on the edge of the water, skinny-dipping and
jumping off the tower. She didn't know exactly how it started, but
over the course of two hot months she became increasingly aware of

when he was swimming, when he was stretched out on a rock in the sun, and she wanted to be wherever he was. Their first kiss was out by the tower as they were treading water. When he pulled away, he laughed and said, "I'm probably going to drown if we don't move this to the shore."

After that they were never apart. Her brothers and cousins loved Mullin. He had a landscaping job and had saved up some money for a boat, a Boston Whaler. He took them out whenever they wanted, picking up a case of Coors Light and bags of chips so they could spend entire days anchored out by the sandbar drinking and swimming. Whatever that darkness was that had kept Sasha at bay when they were younger had dissipated, and they were inseparable during their junior and senior years, her parents even allowing him to sleep over at her house. It was unspoken among them that Mullin sometimes needed to get away from his own family. His father drank and his brother was a cokehead. Mullin shared a bedroom with his brother and would sometimes arrive at school looking exhausted and strained.

Mullin had less than she did but was generous to a fault. He always insisted on paying for things, sandwiches or drinks or gas when she stopped to fill the car. When he came for dinner at her house, he brought her mother gifts: three pounds of steak from the butcher shop, a paper sack full of corn, a white bag of apples. Sasha knew it was unusual that her parents let her boyfriend sleep over, so she tried to honor that kindness—they never had sex under their roof, instead sticking to the back of her car, the boat, the beach at night.

When Sasha got into art school, he took her to dinner to celebrate. They went to the nicer of the two pizza places in town, and since Mullin's dad was friends with the waitress, she quietly slipped them two glasses of sticky red wine in heavy goblets. Sasha would be going to Cooper Union in New York, the best art school in the country, famous for having no tuition. Mullin hadn't applied to art school. He wasn't interested in drawing or painting; it was just something he did when he was bored. Instead, he would be going to the University of Rhode Island in the fall. He would live at home and commute, keeping his job at the landscaping company. He hadn't applied anywhere else.

As the summer arrived and Sasha's move to New York loomed, Mullin became increasingly irritable with her. They went to the movies one night, and Sasha ran into a guy from her French class who was working the concessions. She ordered popcorn and he replied in French that the popcorn was disgusting and sat in the glass case for weeks. She laughed and took it anyway. Mullin was silent for the whole movie, and when it was over, he marched back to her car without a word. As they drove home, he wouldn't speak to her until, five miles from her house, he demanded she pull over. He screamed at her for flirting with someone in front of him, slamming his hand against the glove compartment. He got out and started walking home. Sasha drove alongside him for a while but finally gave up and left him to walk. Two days later he came by late at night, crying, and she forgave him.

He did the same thing when he came to visit her freshman fall. A guy on her hall dropped by to say hello, and Mullin freaked out that she was cheating on him. He punched the wall in her bathroom, breaking a tile and getting blood all over the floor. He left and then a couple days later started calling her to apologize. He called her over and over and over until she had to turn off her ringer. He went to her house and talked to her younger brother, Olly, who called her sobbing the next day. Her family was all on Mullin's side. "You know he had a fucked-up home life," they said. "He just loves you and you left him."

He showed up at her dorm the next weekend, and she broke up with him, but he wouldn't take it. He was intent on winning her back. He mailed her gifts, he had flowers delivered, he bought her a diamond promise ring that she knew he couldn't afford. Sasha wanted to be done with him, wanted some space to move on and make friends and start a new life, but she couldn't. She loved Mullin in spite of everything, and she also knew that she was all he had. When she pictured him sleeping in his bedroom, his brother awake and blasting music, his father trashed and knocking into the furniture, her heart broke. She had left and he had nowhere to go. They spent that winter fighting and making up, Mullin going into jealous rages and then wallowing in remorse. Sasha's friends grew to hate him, her mother thought it best she end things, her brothers and cousins still even more committed than she was to making it work. When Mullin hit a guy for talking to Sasha at a party and she was caught in the scuffle, she was taken before the Cooper Union disciplinary committee and Mullin was barred from campus. For her that was the final straw. She was doing something she loved, she was set to graduate free of debt, and Mullin was fucking it up for her. She hardened her heart against him. It was over.

Her family couldn't forgive her. They still saw Mullin all the time, still went out on his boat, still joined him for beers at the reservoir and the sandbar. When she was home for holidays, her brothers made a point of letting her know they were going out to meet him at Bluffview for dinner, at the Cap Club for drinks. When she brought home a new boyfriend two years later, they gave the guy the cold shoulder and, because he had hair past his ears, referred to him as "the hippie" to his face. When the guy broke up with her a few weeks later, she could hardly blame him. Who would want to get involved with a family like hers?

Ten years later, Sasha still saw Mullin when she was home visiting her parents. He was still best friends with her brothers, still came over to watch the Super Bowl, took them out on his boat—now a bigger and better Whaler. He had his own landscaping business, he was doing well for himself, but instead of moving on he clung to Sasha's family as if it were his own. Sasha didn't know if his father still lived in the peeling green house. She made a point of never asking. Mullin had irrevocably changed something between her and her brothers, but also in how she thought about love. She had seen what all-consuming passion looked like, how it felt to ride the currents of intense adoration and fury, and she didn't want it. She wanted someone stable, someone easy, someone who loved her but not enough to lose himself entirely.

FIVE

Georgiana

Georgiana knew that between millennials and their therapists her contemporaries had figured out how to blame their parents for all sorts of life problems, but when it came to Georgiana's pathetic dating history, it really was her parents' fault. They sent her to a private school down the street, where everybody knew everybody else's business and had all been friends since they were four, and so by the time they hit puberty they were all basically siblings and the idea of dating felt downright perverted. They sent her to an all-girls summer camp until she was twenty, where everyone burped and let their leg hair grow long. They made her take ballroom dancing classes at twelve, where the boys wore white gloves, and her assigned partner, Matt Stevens, kept time by exhaling forcefully through his nose, directly into her face. It was no wonder she arrived at college a virgin, a fact so humiliating she lied about it to everyone, including her freshman-year boyfriend, Cody Hunter, who happily but unknowingly deflowered her in a single, extra-long bed that smelled of Axe body spray and lacrosse pads.

She had plenty of friends who were guys, but whenever she was interested in anyone, she avoided them rather than face the embarrassment of her blushing and social awkwardness. This meant that at the age of twenty-six she had had a total of three boyfriends, two sexual partners, and the romantic confidence of a tadpole.

As much as she wanted to build on her one great lunchtime conversation with Brady, she found herself unable to re-create the situation. When she saw him in the halls she smiled and said hello, but it seemed one of them was always with another colleague or on the way to a meeting starting momentarily. They overlapped at lunch a few more times, but there were always others at the table picking at plastic containers of Thai takeout or salad.

Lena and Kristin were endlessly indulgent, willing to discuss even the smallest hallway interaction and parse it for meaning, but even they agreed that if Georgiana wanted to make Brady her fourth boyfriend/third sexual partner, she was going to have to find a way to talk to him again. It turned out, though, that Brady took care of the issue himself.

Georgiana had a weekly tennis match on Monday evenings, so she changed into her skirt and top in the second-floor office bathroom, the one papered with maps of Laos and Cambodia, and slung her racket and bag over her shoulder, heading down the spiral staircase, out past the mailboxes and reception, and into the warm evening. As she was about to cross Montague, she heard a voice behind her and turned.

"Hey, Georgiana, wait." It was Brady.

"Oh, hey, what's up?" She smiled, her stomach immediately flipping like a fish.

"You walking to the tennis courts?"

"Yeah, I have a match at six."

"Oh cool, I'm going that way too." He smiled. The walk sign illuminated, and they crossed together, along with a sea of joggers, bicyclists, commuters carrying laptop bags, and mothers pushing strollers.

"Who are you playing?" Brady asked.

"Oh, today I'm playing this girl June Lin. It's annoying because our matches are supposed to be entirely five-fives, but she's definitely a five-oh. She's just not great, but whenever we play I get annoyed and end up trying to force her to run and then get sloppy."

"So you're really slumming it by playing down to her level, huh?" he teased.

"I mean, I'm not trying to be a brat, but there is a different circuit for five-ohs. I don't understand why she wants to lose all the time."

"So you always beat her?"

"Well, no, because I get frustrated and screw up!" Georgiana laughed.

"So maybe she is going along, beating all these five-five players, and it's just convincing her further that she's a five-five?" Brady asked, faux innocently.

"I mean, that's exactly what's happening! It's a vicious cycle!"

"I gotta tell you, Georgiana, you come off like a nice person, but underneath you're a competitive beast! I was going to ask if you wanted to play sometime, but now I'm not so sure," he teased. The light breeze was ruffling his hair, and he had rolled his shirtsleeves up his forearms. Georgiana was suddenly aware of how close they were, how easily they had fallen into step, how little goose bumps were now covering her bare legs. She shook the thought away before she became fluorescent red and ruined everything.

"I'd love to play. Let's do it," she said.

"Cool, are you free after work tomorrow? Or is that too much tennis two nights in a row?"

"There's no such thing as too much tennis for us five-fives. But I'm not going to go easy on you. And if you're not at least five-oh I'm going to be a real snot about it," she warned.

"I wouldn't expect anything less. And just so you know," he tilted his head at her, squinting his eyes, "I think you're actually a ten." With that he turned and walked back the way they had come, and Georgiana died forty-seven deaths inside. It was the cheesiest, best thing any man had ever said to her, and she immediately pulled out her phone to text Lena and Kristin. They had been waiting on the shore, searching the seas for signs of hope, and finally, their ship was coming in.

The next evening they met on the front steps of the mansion and walked together to Atlantic Avenue. Brady had on athletic shorts with a small, clear sticker still affixed to the leg, and his tennis bag looked brand-new. They warmed up at the net playing mini tennis, volleying the ball back and forth. She could see he held the racket comfortably, had a nice swing, and moved with the ease of a practiced athlete. They backed up to the service line and rallied. He was strong—Georgiana always liked playing against guys—and they took turns walloping the ball cross-court, neatly placing their shots in the same spots over and over. When they started playing for points, Georgiana realized that she was indeed much better than he was, but that he was a fun competitor. He played fast and hard but occasionally hit one crazy shot that was so wildly misplaced they had to chase it onto the adjoining courts, yelling apologies to their neighbors and stifling their laughter. They played for an hour until the whistle signaled the end of their session and the next pair sauntered onto the court, stretching ostentatiously, unwilling to miss even a second of their allotted time. Tennis players were notoriously intense.

Georgiana and Brady began playing once a week, usually on Tuesdays. At work they maintained a professional distance, exchanging quiet nods and grins in the halls, sitting at opposite ends of the lunch table. But on the walks to and from the courts they talked. They talked about Brady's travel bug; about the year after college he spent in the Peace Corps, stationed in Uganda; the time he attended a wedding there and they slaughtered a goat and asked him to take the first bite even though he had barely met the bride and groom and the idea of goat made him queasy. His parents were international aid workers, and he'd grown up traveling with them, had a passport full of stamps by age ten. Georgiana told him about the safari she took as a child, her grandmother so bored by the entire thing that she read a novel in the back of the Jeep while drinking gin from a tiny flask; and the time her brother climbed Kilimanjaro with his college roommate and ended up getting so sick he lost fifteen pounds. (Cord quickly gained it back on a steady diet of corn chips and salsa.) With each story told, Georgiana was horribly aware of the differences in their lives. While Brady had struck out on great adventures, had seen so much of the wide world, Georgiana had lived as a coddled rich girl, and, if pressed, would admit that most of her great adventures involved a sleepaway camp that cost twelve thousand dollars a summer or college trips to the Caribbean or Mexico that passed in a haze of mezcal and cerveza.

When Brady went away for two weeks, traveling to a malaria conference in Seattle, Georgiana felt her days go flat. Gone was the bubble of expectation she felt each morning walking down Hicks Street to work, eager to spy him at the printer or mailboxes. Gone was the happy swagger she felt thwacking the tennis ball at him, knowing he was spending an entire hour facing her, waiting for her to dictate his next move. She felt her life was on pause, and fourteen days stretched before her like an eternity.

To pass the time, she met her brother for dinner at the Ale House on Henry Street after work one night. She hadn't really spent any time with him one-on-one lately, and so they took a booth in back and ordered pints of Sour Monkey, burgers and fries, and a plate of calamari. Much to their mother's horror, Georgiana and Cord were absolute garbage disposals, eating anything and everything. When she was eleven and Cord was home on college break, they would hold contests to see who could eat the most chicken tenders, who could eat more hot dogs. It was disgusting, but they loved it, and their mutual enthusiasm for junk food was a bond between them.

"So, we haven't even really talked about your honeymoon. How was it?" Georgiana asked. "And please don't tell me how many times you boned."

"Well, we boned a lot." Cord nodded seriously. "Mostly doggy style."

"Shut up." She rolled her eyes.

"No, it was awesome. Turks is beautiful, we did tons of hiking and swimming and snorkeling, and we got massages and did all the romantic crap."

"Sounds like an episode of *The Bachelor*. Cool."

"It was unabashedly cheesy. Literally everyone at the resort was on their honeymoon. It was all couples and rose petals and people holding hands and feeding each other strawberries and champagne."

"I wouldn't have thought that was your style, but okay."

"Aw, are you jealous because you don't have anyone to get a couples massage with?"

The waitress came by and dropped off the platter of calamari, and Georgiana set about squeezing lemon all over the crispy mess.

"First of all, couples massages are just weird. I think they're designed so that people who hate each other can do something romantic and not talk."

"Hot take, okay."

"And secondly, maybe I do have somebody."

"Ooooh, that's exciting. Anyone I know?"

"Nah, a guy I work with."

"That's tricky. Do people at the office know about it?"

"No way. We're keeping it quiet."

"That's smart. I slept with my boss once and now it's all anyone at work talks about."

"Cord, your boss is Dad."

Cord cackled and grabbed one of the big, gross calamari pieces with all the frilly legs and shoved it in his mouth. He really was the best brother, happy to give her valuable life advice and eat all the scary bits of squid.

Without Brady at work, Georgiana was actually incredibly productive. She cranked out new copy for the annual report, she sorted through photos, she ate lunch in record time, proofreading her own work at the table while her colleagues talked animatedly and unappetizingly about digging new latrines in Mali.

On the Sunday of Brady's second week away, Georgiana was hungover (Lena's boyfriend had hosted a single-malt tasting), but she dragged herself out of bed to meet her mother at their racket club, the Casino. They had an eleven o'clock court time and they would retreat to the apartment for lunch afterward. As they began to hit, Georgiana could feel the difference all her extra playing had made. Not only had she doubled her weekly tennis, but she'd started running a bit more often, wanting to keep herself fast on the court.

"Georgiana, you've lost weight," her mother said approvingly. She was always the first to notice even the most infinitesimal of fluctuations in Georgiana's figure. "Do you have a new beau?"

Georgiana was startled by her mother's guess. They rarely spoke about her love life, and when they did her mother usually referred to men as Georgiana's "friends" with barely a wink.

"Well, there is a guy I've been playing tennis with," she admitted, her cheeks, already pink with exertion, growing ever pinker.

"That's nice. Don't forget to let him win sometimes, dear."

Classic mom, Georgiana laughed to herself. Georgiana would never let anyone win on purpose, not even if they had a broken leg. When Cord was getting ready to hike Kilimanjaro he had received six inoculations in one arm and could barely swing his racket, and Georgiana still played her heart out and spanked him royally. He would have fallen over with shock if she'd done anything less. Competition was their family love language.

At noon they walked back to Orange Street, where Georgiana's father was at his desk with a stack of newspapers and Cord and Sasha were unpacking a bag of bagels and smoked salmon on the kitchen table.

"Oh my God, bagels from Russ and Daughters!" Georgiana exclaimed, making a dive for the bag to grab a poppyseed.

"Put it on a plate, dear, you'll enjoy it more," her mother admonished as Cord laughed. Sasha was carefully arranging silverware and napkins on the table as though Kate Middleton or the cast of *Queer Eye* were coming by shortly to judge her. Georgiana just wished

Sasha wasn't there. It was exhausting being around someone who tried so hard all the time.

As they ate, Sasha broached her favorite topic: what of their family memories she might throw in the garbage. "Georgiana, I know you really don't have a lot of storage in your apartment, but I was wondering if you might want to take your tennis trophies? And there is that wooden animal I think maybe you made? The tail goes up and down? Do you want that?" she asked in a hopeful voice, carefully spreading the thinnest layer of cream cheese on a plain bagel.

The "animal" was a beaver and a great source of private shame for Georgiana. When she was in the sixth grade they had taken a woodworking class at school and been instructed to choose different projects. One girl made a small game where a seesaw launched a ball on a string through a hoop. Another made the base for a lamp that would flick on and off using a system of pulleys. Georgiana found instructions for making a ten-inch beaver that rolled on four uneven wheels, causing its wide, flat tail to thump up and down. She spent weeks on it, sanding the wheels and covering it with varnish, making a pretty crosshatch pattern on the tail. It wasn't until they shared their final projects that someone realized what she had done.

"You made a *beaver*, Georgiana? You know what that means, right? You literally made a beaver!" The laughter was endless. She was a nice girl—Georgiana had never spoken about her vagina, never mind learned slang for it. Somehow everyone else seemed to get the joke, though, and it was the highlight of the year for most of the class, cementing Georgiana's reputation as utterly asexual. Every time she looked at the beaver she felt a pang of humiliation. She knew she shouldn't care anymore, but over time it had come to symbolize her romantic failures and deep lack of maturity.

"I'll come take a look, but I really don't have much space," Georgiana hedged. She wasn't sure why, but she couldn't bear to imagine Sasha throwing the stupid beaver away. She had spent weeks making it and putting it in the garbage just felt wrong. And she was secretly proud of the tennis trophies even if they were from high school and college.

After they finished lunch, after Georgiana went and kissed her father hello and goodbye, after she agreed to go with her mother to a philanthropy-themed luncheon the following week at the University Club, she followed Cord and Sasha back to their house. Sasha gave her an empty Fresh Direct bag for her to pack her things, and she made her way up to her childhood bedroom. She admired the trophies lining the shelves, but then realized there was actually a lot more stuff still there. She had books and photo albums, a crystal Tiffany dish that once held her earrings, a tin of dried rose petals she had brought home from her grandmother's funeral, a drawer full of old glue sticks and gummy bottles of nail polish. She sorted through it, leaving the junk and piling the things she felt nervous about Sasha throwing away into the bag. Someone had swapped Georgiana's favorite marigold coverlet for a plain white quilt, making the room look like a sterile hotel. She found the marigold one folded in the bottom drawer of the dresser and, just to make a point, spread it back on the bed where it belonged. When she finished, she realized the beaver was still sitting on her desk. She didn't actually want it in her apartment. She poked her head out her door and looked around. Cord and Sasha were in the kitchen making coffee, so she buried the thing in the back of her closet.

GEORGIANA HAD once woken up in bed with a naked couple. It was her senior year of college, and she'd driven to Amherst to visit Kristin. They had gone to a Chinese restaurant and had scorpion bowl races, where they ordered two giant vats of red punch for the table, divided into teams, and sucked out of straws to see who could finish first. They then went to a bar where Georgiana didn't know a soul but had a wonderful time drinking buckets of Bud Light and playing "I never," which Georgiana was very good at since she had never really done much of anything. They went back to Kristin's off-campus house, where Georgiana was assigned the bed of another girl who was away visiting her parents in Boston, but when she got up to pee in the night, she ended up slightly turned around in the dark and climbed back into the wrong bed—the bed where Kristin and her senior-year fling were passed out. They woke up six hours later, wildly hungover, only to realize that Georgiana was in the wrong bed, and while she was wearing a navy T-shirt that said HENRY STREET TENNIS and a pair of leggings, the other two occupants were completely buck naked. Luckily, they thought it was totally hilarious, and they told everyone at brunch in the dining hall, where Georgiana ate four waffles before she realized she was still drunk and had to sleep it off before getting in her car and driving back to Brown.

To this day that was only the third penis Georgiana had ever seen, not counting the end of *Boogie Nights* or *The Crying Game*. (Movies didn't count. Neither did porn, not that Georgiana watched any. She was very afraid of her phone getting a virus.)

———

Georgiana wanted to wake up next to Brady. She wanted to eat waffles with Brady. She definitely wanted to see Brady naked. When he came back from his two-week trip, they resumed their Tuesday tennis dates. Brady's hair was slightly longer, and he had gotten some color on the bridge of his nose. Georgiana teased him that he'd actually lied to everyone and taken a beach vacation instead of hanging out in government conference rooms. Nobody looked this good after talking about malaria and flying cross-country in coach.

After they played for an hour, they were both sweaty and thirsty. It was a warm evening and Georgiana took a big swig from her water bottle while Brady changed out the tape on his racket grip.

"Did you cheat on me while I was gone?" joked Brady. "I see you got that nice underspin on your backhand. Who'd you play with?"

"I know! I figured out what I was doing wrong! My mom and I were playing over the weekend and suddenly it clicked." She threw her water bottle back in her bag and pulled her hair out of her ponytail.

"That's so cute you and your mom play together," Brady said, and Georgiana promptly felt about twelve years old.

"She's nearly seventy, so I go easy on her. She actually told me I should let you win."

"You talk to your mom about me?" Brady asked, bumping her shoulder with his own.

"She asked who I was playing tennis with!" Georgiana said mock-defensively. "I didn't say we were, like, lovers!"

"So that's it then? I'm just someone you play tennis with?" He bumped her shoulder again but left it there so that they were leaning against each other, his whole arm warm on her side.

"I guess so far." She leaned back against him and she could feel their closeness with every inch of her body. He reached for her face and tucked her hair behind her ear. She lifted her chin and he kissed her, his lips soft and warm. They looked at each other and laughed. She felt lightheaded with happiness.

"Come on." Brady grinned, tossing the grip tape into his bag and zipping it closed. Georgiana grabbed her stuff and together they walked the path out of the park, simultaneously pretending nothing had happened and knowing that everything had changed.

The next week they made plans to play after work, and since the courts were a ten-minute walk from Georgiana's apartment, she cleaned her place ahead of time and left a bottle of wine and a six-pack in the fridge. In the morning she moisturized her arms and legs carefully, she washed her hair even though it was going to get sweaty, and she debated for a solid ten minutes about her underwear. White cotton underpants were obviously not sexy, but she couldn't fathom playing sports in a lace thong so she settled on a light pink bikini pair that were at least small enough to be cute.

Georgiana played like garbage that evening, too anxious about what might happen after their game, but Brady played even worse. Since the courts were by the East River, his crazy shots went flying off into the water, and even though they started out with six tennis balls they ended with only four. They hit like such idiots Georgiana was pretty sure people thought she was a three-five and she would have been mortified if she weren't so busy thinking about how Brady's chest looked in his shirt.

After they finished, they both smiled at each other, flushed and uncomfortable as they delivered their lines. "My apartment is just down the street, want to come over for a beer or a drink?"

"Oh, sure, that would be cool."

They barely talked as they walked, and when Georgiana unlocked the door to her place she held her breath, suddenly afraid he would change his mind or that she had left, like, a giant teddy bear in the middle of her bed. Once they closed the door they didn't even pretend to look for a drink. Brady kissed her and she kissed him back. They kicked off their shoes and pulled their shirts over their heads and fell on the bed, tangled up and sweaty and laughing, and when they finished Brady lay on his back looking at the ceiling with a silly smile on his lips.

"You know how they say you can tell how good someone is at sex by watching them dance or play sports?" Georgiana asked. "Well, the great news is that you are much better at sex than you are at tennis."

"Oh, thank God," Brady laughed. "I don't even want to know what the sexual equivalent of hitting two tennis balls in the river might be."

"I think that would be like, breaking a bone or a piece of furniture."

"I mean, breaking furniture could be fine. I bet some very prominent sexologists have broken a bed."

"I think sexologists are the people who study sex, not the ones who are really good at doing it."

"You think they learn everything from books? I don't think so. I think they probably need to log field experience to get certified. Like how a hair stylist needs to give student haircuts."

"What would be the bigger risk then? Letting a student sexologist sleep with you or a student stylist cut your hair?"

"I'd pick the haircut," Brady said. "I'm not vain, but I am very picky about who I have sex with."

"Me too," Georgiana said seriously. She sort of felt like she should confess how inexperienced she was, how few boyfriends she'd had, how little she knew about this whole thing, but at the last minute she bit her tongue. It was going so well, why screw it up by admitting that? She was just so happy.

While they remained formal at work, they fell easily into a routine outside the office: they met for tennis and sex every Tuesday, then sex without tennis on weekends. They didn't only have sex—sometimes they went for a run through Brooklyn Bridge Park, around the piers and down into Red Hook, where the Statue of Liberty seemed impossibly close, where tugboats were moored along the docks, where they ran past warehouses with open doors and could peer inside and see glassblowers and welders and artists working. They played basketball on the courts at Pier 2, where teenage boys blasted music as they waited for their turns, spitting and leaning against the cement wall. Then they would go back to her apartment and shower—or not—and fall into bed hungry and exhausted.

Sometimes it felt like the extreme physicality of their relationship was all tied up with their intense connection. They were two bodies who loved being alive in their bodies. They were not just mouths and hands and breasts, they were quads and hip flexors and biceps, they were muscles to stretch, to ice, and their sweat was part of everything they did. Georgiana felt most like herself when she was moving, and she could tell that Brady was the same way. When she was running, she never worried about who was looking at her or what she should say; the butterflies and knots in her stomach were replaced by the pleasant burn in her lungs and her legs, knowing that the only thing she needed to worry about was moving, pushing forward, that she belonged entirely to that moment.

Brady didn't seem interested in meeting her friends or family yet, and she didn't push to meet his. It was natural to keep their relationship a secret at work, with him being so much more senior, and a decade older; maybe it made the spark even brighter, to know that they existed in a place outside of normal life. Georgiana didn't need to be his girlfriend; she didn't need to stake that claim, because she knew, completely and positively, that everything she felt for Brady was reciprocated, that they could call it friendship and he would still look at her in a way that made her insides go hot and electric. They were friends with benefits, and for Georgiana that benefit was that she was sleeping with someone she loved completely.

SIX

Darley

Darley liked to think that she was easygoing: She ignored foot faults in family tennis, she never sent back food in a restaurant, and she even gritted her teeth and smiled when Malcolm lay down on the couch wearing the same germ-encrusted clothing he'd worn on the plane. There was one thing, however, that made Darley insane with annoyance. White moms at the playground, older squash ladies at the club, even, horrifyingly, some of Darley's own extended family: they said, "Half-Asian babies are so cute." Or "I wish I could have a half-Korean baby!" Or "Your kids are so lucky to have such an exotic look." It made a vein pulse in Darley's temple. The thought that Poppy and Hatcher were so different from all the other kids these women saw, or that they were "exotic" like lychee nuts imported from the tropics, filled her with fury.

For Darley it was a painful reminder of how very white her world had always been. Although they lived in Brooklyn, their entire apartment building was white. Their circle of friends was nearly all white, their Florida club was all white, and when she looked around Cord and Sasha's wedding, she could count the guests of color on one hand. While Darley's parents had loved Malcolm from day one, there were still moments when it was painfully obvious that they only ever hung out with white people: When Tilda pronounced "BIPOC" as "BIP-ock," when Chip called anything with salsa "ethnic food," when they referred to R&B, hip-hop, or pop music as "gangster rap."

When Poppy turned one, Darley and Malcolm threw her a party at the Casino. For Malcolm's family, the first birthday, the dol, was basically a bigger deal than their wedding. The Kims insisted on paying for the entire thing, hiring caterers and buying Poppy a beautiful traditional Korean outfit, red silk with light green sleeves. They served steak and salmon, they passed the baby around for everyone to hold, and then they put her on a big blanket in the middle of the room for the doljabi. The doljabi was a tradition meant to symbolize the child's personality. Typically, one would lay out an array of objects, including thread, a pencil or book, and money, illustrating longevity, intelligence, and wealth. Whichever item the child crawled to would represent their prospects. For fun, they also laid out a tennis racket, a toy airplane, a test tube, and a calculator. When Poppy crawled toward the test tube, Malcolm's father cheered—another chemist in the family! The cheering startled Poppy and she burst into tears, and Darley ran to pick her up. They tried again, but she just sat there and chewed on her sleeve. They scooted the tennis racket closer, zoomed the toy airplane around her head, waved the calculator to get her attention, but she was uninterested. They finally gave up and changed Poppy back into her smocked dress before giving her a piece of cake. Darley, six months pregnant and starving all the time, ate her own and then her daughter's and hoped nobody was thinking what she was: *Oh, Poppy is going to take after her mother and do nothing.*

THE MORNING Darley saw Malcolm's text, still weak and possibly delirious from the stomach flu, her first instinct was denial. There must be some mistake. Nobody would fire Malcolm. She took a shower, dried her hair, cleaned the bathroom, and opened the windows to get rid of any sick smell. She dressed neatly in a navy tank dress, pinched her sallow cheeks, and went out to the kitchen to thank Soon-ja for everything she'd done. Soon-ja made her dry toast and tea, setting it all out on a pretty place mat with a tiny bud vase. As Darley crunched and sipped, they talked quietly about the kids, about the apartment. Darley's mind was spinning, but she wouldn't say a word to Malcolm's mother. She needed to know the whole story first, needed to speak to her husband. She would wait until Malcolm was home so they could talk about it in person. But the fact was, Malcolm was the child of Asian immigrants in the old boys' club that was banking, and while Darley didn't know exactly what had happened, she couldn't stop thinking about his friend Brice and feeling a knot in her stomach.

The previous summer, on a warm Saturday in July, Darley and Malcolm had piled the kids in the car and driven out to an exclusive golf club in Greenwich, Connecticut. For six months, Malcolm had been working back and forth between New York and London, and he had become close friends with another managing director in the Mergers and Acquisitions team, an American named Brice MacDougal, who lived in Greenwich. Brice was also married and had children around the same age, and so, on one of the rare stretches where they were both home, he and Malcolm had made plans to get their families together.

Darley hadn't been to this golf club before and was immediately startled by how green and manicured everything looked. The suburbs certainly had their appeal. Malcolm had driven the car through stone gates along neat green fairways, long stretches of rolling hills dotted with the occasional golf cart. They parked and Brice met them in front of the dining room and led them out to the pool, where his blond wife was attending to two children in matching light-pink swimsuits.

Darley wasn't much of a golfer, so she and Brice's wife had planned to go swimming with the kids while the men played, all meeting up for lunch afterward. The pool was basically empty aside from a few teenagers hanging around the other end, so the kids could splash and scream without disturbing anyone, and Darley had felt herself relax. Brice's wife was friendly, and once Darley realized she didn't work either, she was able to enjoy herself. As they stood in the waist-deep water fixing leaky goggles and throwing dive sharks, they chatted about how much their husbands had been gone, how desperately they were looking forward to sending the kids to sleepaway camp, the relative merits of city and country living. Darley hated to admit it, but she had started feeling inadequate around women her age who were managing both kids and careers. It made her feel like she needed to explain herself, to justify spending all that time and money on grad school. With stay-at-home moms it was easier.

When it was time for lunch, Darley had hauled her kids into the pool dressing rooms to change them into dry clothes—a dress-code mandated polo shirt tucked into shorts for Hatcher and a sundress and sandals for Poppy. She herself had a flowy blue-and-white dress that made her feel like she was on vacation in Greece.

They met Malcolm and Brice outside the dining room, where they had staked out a table on the deck under a striped awning. A waiter handed them all oversize menus and Brice talked them through the best choices—the lobster roll, the salmon burger, the BLT with avocado. As they chatted, Darley looked around and felt a strong sense of well-being. The deck was crowded with happy people eating lunch. Yes, they were all in club attire—collared shirts tucked into pants, and yes, they were mostly men—it was a golf club after all—but as she studied the crowd, she realized why it looked so different to her. So many of the faces at the lunch tables were Black, so many of their shirts fruit-punch pink and lime-green. It stood in stark contrast to lunchtime at their various New York clubs, where most of the time the only Black or Brown faces were those of the servers. Was Greenwich just a more progressive place than Brooklyn Heights?

The children all drank lemonade out of cups with plastic straws, they demolished all their French fries and mostly ignored their hamburgers, Darley sipped a glass of white wine, and Brice told them all a funny story about walking into the wrong hotel room in London and accidentally catching their boss in his towel. (How could a key card work for a different room? It terrified Darley to imagine it.)

There was a new analyst on their team at work, a twenty-two-year-old named Chuck Vanderbeer, who was also a member of the country club. Brice had been there the first time Chuck came to see the golf course. There had been an accident the previous summer—an older gentleman had suffered a heart attack at the wheel of his Volvo and crashed his car into the dining room, where it burst into flames and injured three people. Since then, the club had decided it was unsafe to have cars quite so close to the building, so they had blocked that part of the driveway with a chain and asked members to park in the lot and walk the fifty paces to the entrance along the stone path. When Chuck Vanderbeer arrived in a black SUV, his driver paused by the gate, climbed out of the car, removed the chain, and drove Chuck right up to the door. And yet, somehow, he was still voted in by the membership committee. His family was so well connected he had at least seven sponsors in the club.

At the bank he had quickly distinguished himself, not with his work, but by nicknaming himself the "Rock Star" and arranging lunches with all the division heads—Malcolm's and Brice's bosses. Rumor had it that he'd been thrown out of Deerfield for setting off fireworks, but his father, a big shot in private equity, still got him into Dartmouth. The thing was, the kid was a complete zero. He left a deal book on a plane—an offense that would render anyone else unceremoniously fired, and he was barely reprimanded. He took an Ambien on a flight and was still visibly drunk from it when they walked into their meeting in Dubai. Malcolm had once caught Chuck staring at himself in the mirror of the men's room, smoothing his hair and smiling like a psychopath.

Brice and Malcolm agreed the kid was a total liability and hated that they were saddled with him on the team. They were stuck in the middle of a nepotism sandwich, their bosses pleased to have a Vanderbeer on the roster, but privately happy not to manage him directly.

Darley had laughed at Brice's stories and ordered a second drink. It was the perfect Saturday afternoon, a million times more fun than most gatherings with her husband's colleagues, and it made her hopeful. Maybe they could spend more time together with Brice's family. Maybe they could even consider moving out to Greenwich. She wondered if she had been wearing blinders, always feeling like Brooklyn was the best home for them, like Brooklyn was more liberal and diverse than the suburbs.

They were finishing lunch when a microphone squealed and a sunburned man in a pale-yellow polo took the stage. "Good afternoon, golfers. We're about to get going with the brief program here in just a few minutes."

"Oh, sorry guys," Brice apologized. "It's going to be annoying to listen to this. Maybe we can finish up and go hang out by the pool for a bit."

"What's going on?" Darley asked.

"Oh, it's Caddy Appreciation Day, so they're doing an awards ceremony."

"Caddy Appreciation Day?"

"Yeah, they invite all the caddies to join them for lunch and give out funny prizes."

"Oh." Understanding washed over Darley. One by one the Black men at each table got up to receive awards, shaking hands with the man in yellow before returning to their seats. They weren't members of the club at all. They worked there. The club was just as white as her own.

WHEN MALCOLM got home from the airport it was almost lunchtime. He walked into the apartment, dropped his laptop on the counter, and poured himself three fingers of Tanqueray without uttering a word.

"Hey, love." Darley came up behind him and wrapped her arms around his middle. His button-down shirt was creased, and he smelled slightly of sweat after two nights on planes. Malcolm didn't say anything, and Darley pressed her face against his back, felt him swallow and shudder slightly. "What happened?"

"Some absolute bullshit is what happened," Malcolm replied quietly. He put his glass in the sink and let Darley lead him into the living room to talk.

Thirty-six hours earlier Malcolm had flown to Rio to make the final board presentation to Azul, a Brazilian airline based outside of São Paulo. The presentation would be followed by a signing with American Airlines, whereby they would purchase 10 percent of Azul, giving them a stronger foothold in South America. When Malcolm arrived at JFK and reviewed his flight itinerary he sighed. The plane was a 767-300ER, an old model with narrow flatbeds, no seatback TV, and, worst of all, no wi-fi. It was annoying that the route he'd flown dozens of times in the past year had the worst planes. He said hello to the check-in agent, who asked after Darley and the kids. The flight attendant working the business-class cabin gave his shoulder a little squeeze hello. Malcolm spent so much time at JFK he basically considered the flight attendants, lounge attendants, and gate agents his colleagues.

As the plane lined up on runway 31L, Malcolm listened to the twin engines spooling up, and in spite of himself, he felt his heart skip happily, even after all this time. He took a final glance at his in-box, then at the wallpaper on his phone—Darley and the kids at the U.S. Open—and powered it off for the flight. But when he landed ten hours later and turned his phone back on, his whole world changed.

Malcolm had called it from day one that Chuck Vanderbeer

would be a disaster; he just hadn't realized that the self-proclaimed Rock Star of Deutsche Bank Aviation Group would also pull him down as he crashed and burned. Chuck worked side by side with Malcolm, Brice, and their team putting together deals, pitching mergers between international airlines, privy to the most sensitive financial information about these companies and their futures. He then, unknown to anyone in his professional life, spent his nights drinking at the bar at Papillon in Midtown and bragging to bored young women about the deals he was landing. Unfortunately, the woman who seemed utterly fascinated by the Rock Star's tales of banking derring-do happened to be a financial reporter for CNBC and produced a story about the likely investment by American Airlines in Azul. As soon as the story hit cable news, Azul killed the deal and left Deutsche Bank holding the bag.

Malcolm had more than three hundred emails, a dozen frantic voicemails, and sixty-five text messages, mostly from Brice. He staggered down the jetway in Rio, scrolling through message after message. The deal he had worked on for nearly a year was dead. The American Airlines management team hadn't even bothered boarding their connecting flight from Miami. Any chance Malcolm had at damage control was long gone. Both Chuck and Malcolm were fired, Chuck for leaking the story and Malcolm for standing too close to the little fool.

"But you didn't do anything wrong!" Darley cried indignantly. "Chuck was the leak! You had nothing to do with it!"

"I was unreachable," Malcolm said with a grimace. "When the news broke, I was in the air with no wi-fi. The entire deal was crumbling and I was lying on a flatbed eating warm mixed nuts."

"This is completely unfair," Darley vented. "What about Brice? Is Brice being fired?"

"No, Brice is fine. While I was offline, Brice was on the ground managing the narrative. He protected himself."

"Why? He was on the same team! He knew Chuck even before you did!"

"Brice has more friends in the organization than I do. He has the banking pedigree." Malcolm kicked the leg of the chair.

"Brice should have fought for you too!"

"Well, he didn't."

"That little shit. They are *both* little shits," Darley spat.

"I just can't believe they all let me take the fall." Malcolm shook his head.

"It's their loss, Malcolm. We'll be okay. You'll make some calls and set up some interviews. You'll be working again in no time."

"Maybe." Malcolm looked broken, like a dishonored gladiator in defeat.

"They're idiots for letting you go." Darley curled up in Malcolm's lap and buried her face in his neck. It made her so upset that she wasn't able to protect him. That the Brices of the world had scores of family friends to vouch for them and Malcolm didn't have anyone. Sure, her father was connected in the real estate world, and if you wanted to throw a Moroccan-themed dinner for fifty at a moment's notice her mother had the hookup for a caterer and a florist, but that wasn't going to do Malcolm any good.

The whole thing reminded Darley of the time her high school friend Allen Yang applied to be a member of the Fiftieth Club. He had the sponsors, he had the letters, he certainly had the money, and when he went in for the faux-casual interview to drink scotch with the membership committee in the club lounge, he felt like he'd nailed it. Then his application was denied. Darley knew it was racism. There was no possible other reason. But nobody had explicitly said it, so Allen had to let it ride. How much of Malcolm's ousting was because he was in the wrong place at the wrong time, and how much was because he wasn't an old boy with a last name like Dimon, Moynihan, or Sloan? Nobody said, "We're firing you because you don't have a white dad to stick up for you," but to Darley it was clear as day.

M alcolm spent the next few weeks inviting old business school friends to lunch, reaching out to colleagues from his early investment banking days, and taking meetings with anyone who'd see him. While Chuck Vanderbeer quickly failed up, his private equity father securing him an analyst position at Apollo, it was evident Malcolm's name had been dragged in the dirt. As far as banking was concerned, Malcolm was radioactive. His friends and acquaintances would order their steak, always rare, and before even taking their first sip of iced tea asked, "What the hell happened with that Azul deal?" Everyone knew, and somehow they thought it was his fault. It didn't matter that he hadn't done anything wrong; he was tainted and was unceremoniously thrown out of the Masters of the Universe club.

When headhunters started calling, Darley was optimistic. "See, doll? Lots of people want you."

But the positions they offered were at third-tier firms, horrible banks where he'd have no hope of getting back into aviation. Malcolm just couldn't stomach the thought, couldn't go from being a highflier to a serf. If he took one of these jobs, he'd be spending the majority of his days commuting to and from Midwestern industrial cities, connecting through Chicago, sitting in economy class, spending his nights in Red Roof Inns where the beds' polyester linens were designed to hide stains.

Darley comforted him, pointing out how many bankers became briefly infamous for far worse—the twenty-six-year-old kid who lost his company $500 million in unauthorized trades only to do the same thing again a year later. He somehow still had a job. (It didn't hurt that he was descended from several first families of Virginia.) The guy who hid $2.6 billion in losses on copper futures from his bank in Tokyo. The rogue trader who bankrupted Barings Bank in 1995.

"You're not making me feel better," Malcolm complained. "Those guys were idiots."

"You're the smartest person I know," Darley told him. She meant it. "You'll land a better job."

"If I were so smart, I wouldn't have missed Poppy and Hatcher's childhood to make money for a bank that kicked me to the curb," he said glumly.

WHEN PEOPLE ASKED DARLEY how she and Malcolm met, Darley simply said "at business school," and that was enough for most people, but the truth was that she had sought Malcolm out, had wanted him before she'd even laid eyes on him. Darley had spent two years as an analyst at Morgan Stanley between Yale and Stanford. An associate had shown her Malcolm's blog about airlines, and when she realized he was also going to be enrolled at Stanford too, she felt the way Kate Middleton must have felt when she realized that Prince

William had switched from the University of Edinburgh to St Andrews. He would be hers. That was because Darley had a bit of a side gig of her own. Through perfectly legal means she had managed to figure out the algorithm for JetBlue ticketing and had been trading airline stocks based on their consumer volume year over year. Every month she bought a ticket at 12:01 on the first and then 11:59 on the thirtieth or thirty-first. Their numbering system was stupidly straightforward, and in that way she could figure out how many tickets they had sold. She wasn't playing with big money; she was day-trading for fun and just to prove that she'd cracked it. When she confessed this to Malcolm over tacos and margaritas on their first date, it was as though she had told him she had been Bo Derek's body double or could do a split, it was that sexy. She had already been factoring in the fluctuating costs of fuel, but with Malcolm they managed to also consider cost savings and expenditures based on routes and jets leased to other airlines. Although JetBlue changed their ticketing codes a year later and Darley's loophole closed, the deal was done: Malcolm had met his equal, a partner for life who loved him for exactly who he was, and Darley had bagged her Prince William.

SEVEN

Sasha

Georgiana was a wolf marking her territory, peeing around the perimeter of her den. When Sasha peeked through the door of Georgiana's bedroom following her visit to "clean out her trophies," she audibly gasped. "Cord! Come look at something!"

Cord ambled down the hall, holding a flaking croissant in one hand and a pack of polyester tennis strings in the other.

"Look." Sasha gestured grandly at the floor, where a pile of old pens and crumbling erasers had been unceremoniously heaped on the rug. "And she didn't take a single trophy! It looks like she burgled herself!" The drawers of her dresser were half open, hair ties were scattered on top along with several old ChapSticks. "She trashed the place."

"It's not trashed," Cord said mildly. "It's mostly little stuff."

"But it's pretty rude, right? To come over and make a mess?"

"She's just kind of a slob." Cord shrugged.

"Look, she went and found that old orange bedspread and put it on top of the white one I bought. It's like she's telling me it's still her room."

"Here," Cord offered, scooping up the pens and dumping them into the desk drawer. "Her room was always a disaster, don't take it personally."

"I'm kind of starting to take it personally, Cord." Sasha was honestly fed up. You could only be treated like an interloper for so long before you had to say something. "I'm not sure what I did wrong, but I just feel like your sisters don't like me."

"What are you talking about? That's not true." Cord patted her back and tried to leave the room. He was a WASP through and through, deeply uncomfortable with conflict.

Sasha pushed on. "They basically roll their eyes whenever I'm talking." It was more than that, but it was hard to explain. How did you articulate how it felt to have someone constantly turn their back, wrinkle their nose, look away?

"Darley is distracted being a mom. And George is a kid. She only cares about tennis and partying with her friends. She's on a different page right now. Just try to meet her where she is." Cord winced as though this conversation was causing him physical pain.

Sasha saw the wince. She didn't mean to punish Cord. She softened. "So I just need to start drinking White Claw and talking about the French Open and she'll stop being so rude?"

The relief on Cord's face was plain. Sasha would let it go. "That's how I get women to like me. I pretend to care about things they care about." He grinned. "Now—unrelated—let's go drink wine, look at art, and throw away my high school stuff."

Sasha laughed and followed him down the hall, closing the door to Georgiana's room behind her. She grabbed a pinot grigio and two glasses and carried them to Cord's bedroom, where she set them on the floor—there wasn't any other clear surface. His single bed was piled with discarded treasures, mostly things from his grandparents' apartment. When Cord's paternal grandparents, Pip and Pop, passed away, the Stockton family decided to sell their brownstone on Columbia Heights. They took out half of the art and decor so the photographer could make the place look bigger, moving much of the stuff to Pineapple Street. The place had sold quickly, and nobody had time to deal with getting an appraiser to look at the antiques, so the limestone was overflowing with expensive castoffs. On Cord's bed there was a Baroque-style giltwood mirror, a twenty-four-inch mantel clock with a base made of ornate bronze covered in gold leaf, an orange leather box containing a dozen fountain pens from Montblanc, and a stack of framed watercolors, mostly of boats. His bookshelf was stuffed with two layers of tattered old hardcovers, their scuffed brown and navy spines peeling and ragged. The desk was laden with file folders and newspaper clippings; Sasha had never seen a family more archival—they clipped newspaper articles daily, and Tilda read the morning paper with a small knife at her place setting, ever ready to slice away a piece of interest. All along the floorboards paintings in heavy frames stood four deep.

"I have a fun game for us to play," Cord suggested, his eyes twinkling. "It's called 'By Birth or By Marriage.' You have to guess who was a Stockton and who married into the family."

"Okaaaay," Sasha agreed, grinning and taking a swig of her wine.

"Number one: this fellow." Cord lifted up an oil portrait of an older gentleman in a suit, posing formally with an Irish setter at his feet. He had Cord's same dark eyes and brow, the same elegant nose.

"Birth." Sasha rolled her eyes.

"Correct! That's my grandfather, Edward Cordington Stockton. Okay, two: this lady." Cord pulled out a smaller portrait, this one of a young girl, maybe eight, wearing a blue dress with a Peter Pan collar and a bow in her hair. She had Georgiana's cascading curls, Georgiana's pretty pout.

"Birth." Sasha laughed.

"Ding! Ding! My grandfather's sister, Mary. All right, this lady." Cord pulled out a big painting in a gilded frame. The subject was fair, smiling coquettishly and holding a book in her lap. Sasha couldn't see Darley or Chip or any of the Stocktons in her round cheeks or upturned nose.

"Marriage?" Sasha ventured.

"No idea," Cord laughed. "I've never seen this one in my life! I think Pip must have bought it on eBay."

Sasha pursed her lips. If you weren't related by birth your name wasn't worth knowing. Got it. She picked her way over to the desk to look at the file folders. Through the cloudy plastic Sasha recognized a face. She unwound the bit of twine and flipped the file open. It was Darley and Malcolm's *New York Times* wedding announcement, clipped from the paper. They looked perfectly glamorous in their small, cropped headshot, Darley wearing a pair of glittering diamond earrings, Malcolm in a suit and tie. She skimmed the write-up. "Darley Colt Moore Stockton, daughter of Mr. Charles Edward Colt Stockton and Mrs. Matilda Baylies Moore Stockton, will be married this Saturday . . ."

"What's that?" Cord peered over her shoulder.

"It's Darley's wedding announcement."

"Oh." He wrinkled his nose.

"You didn't want one," Sasha reminded him. She had mentioned it once when they were engaged, and he had immediately dismissed the idea.

"It's just so gross and snobby." Cord peered down at the photo of his sister. "So-and-so's rich parents work in investment banking and so-and-so's rich parents work in private equity and they are all just going to marry their children until they're as inbred as King Tut."

"Cordington Stockton, son of the New York real estate Stocktons, marries Rhode Island girl descended from barflies and fishermen," joked Sasha.

"The service will be conducted at the Cap Club bar by the train station, and the bride's brother, drunk on Narragansett, will officiate."

"The reception will feature all-you-can-eat quahogs for those who know the proper way to pronounce the word for a water fountain."

"It's a *bub-lah*! And clam *chow-dah*!" Cord hollered.

"Hmmm, should we raise our kids to speak Rhode Island?" Sasha mused.

"Nope, Tilda would cut them out of the will." Cord kissed her.

"We can't throw any of this stuff away, can we?" Sasha took one last dismayed look around Cord's room.

"We definitely cannot. Sorry. But now that we've had some wine and done some cleaning, we get to do your other favorite thing . . ." Cord batted his eyes playfully and took Sasha's hand. She relented. Maybe she'd sneak some of the clippings into the shredder while he was at work. With that, Cord led her down the hall to their bedroom, to the four-poster bed she would always think of as his parents'.

SASHA HAD a pregnancy scare her freshman year of college. She and Mullin had been teetering on the cusp of another breakup, and things were tense between them. She was coming home for Thanksgiving, and she hoped that it would be easier where everything was familiar. She couldn't shake the feeling that New York put Mullin on edge, that he somehow felt insecure or uncomfortable around the sophisticated and often rich kids she'd met at school.

It was tradition for everyone in town to go out to the Cap Club that Wednesday night—college kids who had moved away were home for the long weekend, eager to show off how well they were doing outside the confines of their little town. The Captain's Club was nothing fancy—it was a long brick building across from the train station, where they served beer and cocktails and, if you really wanted it, a glass of wine that tasted like vinegar and probably had bits of cork in it. There were red leather stools along the bar, booths in the back, a jukebox, and a dartboard. Her cousins were there, the fact that most of them were under twenty-one politely ignored by the bartenders, who were all friends of the family. That was the thing about living in a small town—you got away with less, but you also got away with more.

Mullin was in a weird mood, laughing too loudly and drinking fast. Her younger brother, Olly, was wasted and being an idiot, wearing a T-shirt that said EAT PUSSY, IT'S ORGANIC, trying to light a cigarette inside and complaining when Sasha pushed him out into the alley to smoke. There were other kids from their class there too—kids who were at school in Boston, in Maine, in Connecticut. Sasha could tell it embarrassed Mullin that he still lived at home. He was smarter than nearly anyone in there, but instead of living in a dorm in New Haven or Princeton, he was sharing his childhood bedroom and driving back and forth to classes, mowing lawns in the early mornings and cleaning up the empty bottles his father left in the kitchen. She slung an arm around his waist and whispered in his ear, "Let's go find a place we can be alone. I miss you."

She had only had half a beer, so she drove them out to the causeway, where they parked on the gravel and looked out at the ocean. It was too cold to get out, so they kissed in the car, moving to the back seat to peel off their clothing. "I don't have condoms, do you?" she asked.

"Nah, but I won't finish," Mullin promised. They started having sex and at first it felt wonderful, but then Sasha began to worry. "Don't forget to pull out," she whispered, but Mullin moved faster and faster. He came inside her with a groan and she shoved him off her body.

"What the fuck?"

"Sorry, sorry. You felt so good." He pushed his hair out of his eyes.

"Mullin, I'm not on the pill."

"It'll be fine. Don't worry. I'm sorry."

Sasha yanked her clothing back on, angry at Mullin and angry with herself. As she lay awake in bed that night, having dropped Mullin at his own house, she wondered if it really was an accident or if Mullin wanted her back home, wanted to find a way to keep her here with him.

When her period was two days late, she went to campus health for a pregnancy test. It came back negative, and she cried, great heaving sobs, the sobs of exhaustion and anger and relief and probably also hormones, because her period came the next day.

Of course, she never told anyone in her family that story. Her mother would be furious with her for having unprotected sex; she would ban Mullin from the house. She had no idea how her father and brothers would react, but part of her suspected they would find her at fault. And it was her fault. She trusted someone who didn't have her best interests at heart.

———————

While it hurt Sasha that her family seemed unable to accept her breakup with Mullin, she was also moved by the way they made room for him. They saw his own family was lacking, and so they folded him in, setting out a stocking for him at Christmas, keeping the pantry full of Corn Chex and Pop-Tarts, foods only he ate. Sasha had initially thought that was what married life would be like—that she would marry Cord and his family would fold her on in. But they didn't. Her own family was a restaurant booth—you could always scoot in and make space for one more. Cord's family was a table with chairs, and those chairs were bolted to the floor.

A month before her wedding, a man in a suit rang the bell at her apartment. Sasha was home alone, eating a yogurt and working on her computer, designing layouts. She had been hired by a small contemporary art museum in Manhattan to design their new signs, shopping bags, and advertisements. She peered at the security screen and knew it wasn't FedEx, so she scampered down the hall to put on a bra before opening the door.

"Are you Sasha Rossi?"

"I am," she said with a confused smile.

"I'm a lawyer for Fox Allston, and we manage the Stockton family trust. We've prepared a prenuptial agreement for you to sign. I suggest you retain your own lawyer and he or she can be in touch to negotiate."

"A lawyer?" Sasha asked, bewildered.

"You should always use a lawyer for this kind of agreement. I wish I could recommend someone, but unfortunately, you'll need to retain a different firm. Give a call if you have any questions." With that, the man handed Sasha a manila envelope and gave her a nod before trotting down the hall to the elevator bank.

"What the fuck?" Sasha carried the envelope to the kitchen and called Cord at work. "Cord, the weirdest thing just happened. A lawyer just showed up at the door and handed me a prenup! Like, I got served!"

"Hey, can we talk about this later? We're in the middle of some stuff here," Cord said.

"Oh, sure, yeah, tonight." Sasha hung up. But that night, after dinner at his apartment, Cord had no interest in talking about it.

"Just get a lawyer and let them sort it out," he said, shrugging.

"I mean, I will, but were you going to mention it to me?" she asked.

"What's there to say? It's paperwork. They'll figure something out, you'll sign it, we'll move on."

"I mean, for starters you could be like 'I love you honey and I never want to get divorced.'"

"You can have your lawyer add that part." Cord rolled his eyes.

"Ouch," Sasha replied, offended.

"Look, it's not up to me. Everyone signs them. It's how marriage works. Marriage is a legal arrangement. This is part of it. Don't make it a big deal."

"Maybe in your world this is how marriage works, but not in mine. Do you think my parents have a prenup?"

"I don't understand why you're trying to make me feel so bad about this!" Cord said.

"Because it makes me feel bad!"

"It shouldn't matter!"

"If it doesn't matter, why didn't you tell me about it?"

"Because it's not a big deal!"

"You *know* it's a big deal. I'm trying to build a life with you and you're making it clear that you want to have an escape hatch. That no matter what, I'll never really be part of your family."

"We're getting married. What else do you want from me?" Cord asked coldly.

"What else do I want from you? I want you to put me first. I want to be the most important person in your life. I want you to tell me that no matter what happens you will always be on my side. That you'd choose me over your family."

"That's a ridiculous thing to ask. I would never choose anyone over my family." Cord walked into the bedroom and closed the door. Sasha stumbled out through the lobby and slept in her own apartment that night, getting up early the next morning and driving home to Rhode Island. She couldn't stand to look at Cord, couldn't imagine climbing into bed with yet another person who put her needs last.

When she told her parents what had happened her father was outraged. "He had a lawyer show up with papers like you were some parolee? That's just wrong. If that's how rich people act, you don't want to be one anyway."

Her mother was more sympathetic. "I had wondered if something like this might happen, sweetheart. These families can be very strange about who they marry. You have to assume this is coming from the parents, not from Cord."

Sasha wasn't sure, though. Maybe it came from Cord. Maybe it came from Chip and Tilda. But either way, she felt humiliated that they had talked about it, that they had made a plan against her, that rather than welcoming her with open arms they were shielding themselves from her infiltration.

She called her friend Jill, who was a lawyer in Providence, and they met for coffee. She passed her the manila envelope and Jill looked it over, nodding her head and making a few small notes on a pad with a pencil. "It's a pretty generous prenup, Sasha. There are a few things that we would customarily ask for, but as these things go it's on the nicer side of standard."

"How standard is it, though? How often do people get prenups?"

"I think it's something like five or ten percent among the general population, but obviously really common among people with means."

"It's hard not to feel offended by it. Like he thinks I'm trying to steal his money."

"I'm sure for his family it's as routine as getting braces or piercing your ears—just a step on the road to adulthood. Try not to read too much into it," Jill said. Sasha wanted to believe her, wanted to let it go, but on nights she couldn't sleep she still heard his voice, low but plain with honesty: "I would never choose anyone over my family."

NONE OF Sasha's art school friends lived in Brooklyn Heights. As a rule, they lived in neighborhoods that required a subway transfer or a bus ride to visit, neighborhoods where the bodegas stocked spicy chips that were shaped like little cones and hurt your tongue to eat, neighborhoods where the water in the canal had a vaguely lavender tint. Sasha's freshman-year roommate, Vara, chose to move to Red Hook, which, even though it was just a ten-minute bike ride from the limestone, felt like a hundred miles (or a hundred years) away. Vara's big artists' loft on Ferris Street was a stone's throw from the waterfront, where a sugar refinery and shipyard crumbled prettily into the

Buttermilk Channel. Big cranes moved shipping containers around the lot next door, graffiti covered the sidewalk, and the neighboring warehouses were rented out every weekend for hipster weddings.

On Wednesday nights, Vara hosted a Drink and Draw, offering terrible wine and a nude model to any former classmate with ten dollars to spare. Cord was working late and Sasha missed her friends, so she strapped on her helmet and coasted her bike down the hill. She got there five minutes early and threw a ten in the coffee can by the door, claiming a stool and an easel in the middle, right near Vara, so that they could gossip as they drew.

Vara was dressed outrageously as usual, wearing a canvas smock over a crop top and high-waisted pink silk pants. Her long black hair curled down her back, and she had on a pair of gold glasses that Sasha hadn't seen before.

"Hey babe, let me see those." Sasha reached out to snatch them from Vara's face.

"No, no, I'm blind without them, don't." Vara ducked her head and danced away.

"Those are fake, right? You don't need glasses."

"I desperately need them, get away!" Vara squealed.

"Hmm, okay, so from now on every time I see you, you'll have them on?"

"Well, probably not *these* glasses," Vara hedged. "It depends on the outfit."

"Mm-hmm, okay." Sasha grinned.

A good group had already assembled for the Drink and Draw: Vara's girlfriend, Tammie, puttered around opening bottles of red and white, sniffing the corks and making a terrible face. Simon, a painter with a shaved head, kissed Sasha hello and dropped his money in the can. Zane, with floppy hair and skateboarding shoes, worked at a foundry designing typefaces by day. Allison had brought her dog, a sleepy old Lab who immediately settled in by her feet to snooze. Sasha poured herself a big tumbler of white wine, took a sip, and shivered. It really was horrible, but maybe that was part of the charm of the evening.

As more and more of their classmates arrived and claimed easels, Vara checked her phone again and again, frowning with annoyance. "Ugh, I hired a new model tonight and he's not answering his phone. I have no idea where he is."

Sasha groaned. On nights when the model didn't show, one of their classmates had to sit instead. They got half the money from the coffee can, but it was in no way worth it, spending an hour and a half frozen in the same position, muscles screaming, foot asleep. Last time Sasha had been stuck modeling she had a crick in her neck for a week.

At a quarter past seven, Vara gave up on the model and put a dozen paintbrushes in a jar, one of them marked with a blue tip. The loser would sit for the group. One by one they picked paintbrushes blindly, Sasha sighing with relief when she pulled a regular brown one. Zane pulled the blue brush and swore. "I got the fucking blue brush in February. This is bullshit," he complained as he shucked off his long-sleeve shirt and pounded the rest of his wine. He stalked to the center of the room and unbuttoned his jeans, letting them slide to the floor. He was in a mood and Sasha fought back a grin. Nothing like staring at someone fume and pout butt naked for ninety minutes. Just then the door burst open, and a big, tattooed guy rushed in, dropping his bag and apologizing bashfully. The model had made it.

"Yes!" Zane hollered, yanking up his jeans, darting back to his stool, and pulling on his shirt. Everyone clapped and Vara patted him on the shoulder. It was funny, Sasha mused. She had seen most of her friends naked at some point in drawing class, and yet it was the least sexual thing in the world. But she still preferred it when they had a professional model. Often they were actors, and they brought specific energy to their poses, or they were significantly older, their bodies so different from Sasha's own that she could get completely lost in studying the way the light moved on their skin. She loved drawing men with big muscles or low bellies, women with scars or thick, powerful calves—anyone who looked different, any-one who made her truly pause and see the shape of the human form anew.

Sasha set her plastic cup aside and started to sketch. Within min-utes of the first pose the room was quiet, the sounds of pencils scratching interrupted only by the occasional murmur or the rustle of paper. As she drew, she amused herself thinking about how for-eign her world would seem to Cord's family. She wondered if Tilda ever saw a naked body beside her husband's—or if she ever even saw his.

As she biked home later that night, slightly tipsy, she thought about her hometown. Maybe she loved Vara's neighborhood because of the way it reminded her of Rhode Island. Unlike Brooklyn Heights, which was swarmed with tourists and bougie young parents, Red Hook was a decidedly blue-collar part of the city. It just made sense to Sasha in a different way.

Back in Rhode Island, there was a little scrap of shoreline along the river by Sasha's parents' house where Mike Michaelson kept his dinghy. Sure, most people kept their dinghies in their yards or paid to chain them to the dock, but Mike Michaelson was at least eighty years old, and nobody expected him to lug the thing a block to his house—he'd always kept it there. Then one year a new family bought the giant house across the street and claimed that the grass along the water's edge belonged to them—that it was included in their deed. They posted a small sign that said PRIVATE PROPERTY. NO BOATS ALLOWED. Mike Michaelson's dinghy stayed and the next day another appeared beside it. The day after that yet another. Soon there were thirty dinghies all piled on the shore, and everyone who went by the docks on their way to their moorings snapped pictures and cackled. The new owners took down the sign.

The more Sasha tried to fit in with Cord's family the more she thought about those dinghies. Every society had traditions, institutional knowledge, their own innate sense of how things should be done. If you grew up in a snowy climate you knew to pop up your windshield wipers before a big storm. On Lower Road if you shoveled out your car you put a beach chair in the spot to make sure it was there when you got back. When you took your boat back up the river you kept the red buoys on the right and watched your wake around the little boats. At the bar, a coaster on top of a pint glass meant the seat was taken and the drink was still good. These rules were so deeply ingrained in Sasha that she barely had to think twice about them, but suddenly, with Cord, she was subject to an entirely different array of social niceties: You cleaned the lines on the clay tennis court after a match; you never wore denim to the club; you didn't show up with wet hair; you said "Nice to see you," never "Nice to meet you," even if there was no conceivable way you'd ever crossed paths before in your life.

Sasha felt wrong-footed 90 percent of the time but also simultaneously felt she was Molly Ringwald in an eighties movie and everyone else was the preppy villain. Cord's world was full of pearl girls, all wearing their grandmother's earrings with crisp button-downs and loafers, as interchangeable as they were sexless. Sasha often had the sneaking suspicion that if she saw them naked, they would have bodies as smooth and flat as Barbies. She swore to herself that the day she tied a cable-knit sweater around her shoulders would be the day she died.

When Cord had suggested they move into the Pineapple Street limestone after their wedding, Sasha hesitated. Sure, it was big and nice, but she never felt comfortable there. Sasha loved her own apartment, a glass box in a doorman building in Downtown Brooklyn. The windows stretched floor to ceiling, and she could see all of Manhattan spread out across the river. It was new construction, all white walls and chrome appliances, and Sasha loved the modern spareness. She kept it neat as a pin—she tucked away her books and pretty vases, didn't even put art on the walls, loving the feeling of giving her eyes a break after a day of working on her computer in Photoshop.

The Pineapple Street apartment was anything but spare—sometimes Sasha felt the clutter was going to send her into an epileptic fit, overwhelming her like a strobe light. "How about instead of the limestone we move into my apartment after the wedding?" Sasha tried to entice Cord.

"Your apartment is a one-bedroom, and we want kids. We'd outgrow it in a year. This is a no-brainer, Sasha. My parents are *giving* us a four-story house to live in."

She could tell he really wanted to live there, she could tell he loved the place, so even though it killed her to leave her glass box in the sky, she said yes.

Right away she sensed it caused tension with Darley and Georgiana. She couldn't tell if they were mad that Chip and Tilda had moved out or that she, an outsider, had moved in, but there was a decided chill in the air whenever they talked about the move. At first Sasha was sympathetic, but it started to wear on her. Yes, they had grown up there, but they each had an apartment of their own. They had their country house on Spyglass Lane. Now they had the maisonette on Orange Street. Through Chip and Cord's company they owned half of Downtown Brooklyn and Dumbo. The family was lousy with property, and they were going to put up a stink about her living in a place that felt like an expensive mash-up of *Antiques Roadshow* and *Hoarders*? They were spoiled. There was no other way to say it.

She didn't resent them for growing up with money—Sasha had led a lucky life herself. She had never skipped a class field trip, she had taken piano lessons and gymnastics and played softball in the town league. But she also vacuumed her own bedroom, loaded the dishwasher after dinner, took out the trash on her night. Cord never even wiped out the sink after he shaved, so sure someone else would be along to do it. As a teenager, Sasha also worked jobs after school and in the summers. She sold trees at the garden supply store, she answered phones at the electric company, her brothers had paper routes and delivered boat parts to the marina. Meanwhile Cord and his sisters played sports, went to summer camp, and then graduated to internships. Their summers were designed to enrich their minds and bodies, while her summers were meant to pay for college.

The weird thing was, though, Sasha wouldn't have traded places with them. She loved working at the garden store (the electric company was less picturesque), and even when it sucked, it had taught her how to work. Sasha wanted to be successful, and she understood that if she wanted to do anything of significance it was on her to make it happen. She had a career as a graphic designer, she could support herself, and she did it all on her own. And yet, here she was, living in the limestone on Pineapple Street, feeling like an interloper, watching Georgiana pile dinghy after dinghy on her tiny scrap of shoreline.

Sasha pushed her bike up the steep hill from Dumbo, and when she reached the house she carried it down the steps to the basement and locked the door behind her. She dropped her keys on the table in the parlor, fighting a strange mood that had overtaken her. But she heard quiet jazz music playing. She could smell garlic and tomatoes in the kitchen and realized that she was starving. Cord came out of the kitchen holding a fistful of silverware, and when he saw her his eyes lit up. "My little Van Gogh!" he cried, wrapping her in his arms. "How is the ear?" He pretended to examine her as he kissed her neck. It wasn't home, it wasn't Red Hook, but as Cord fed her pasta and then took her to bed, it wasn't a blue paintbrush either.

EIGHT

Georgiana

I f Georgiana's mother had one weakness it was for clothing. And wine. And for hitting to the alley when she played doubles. And repression. And gossip. And for buying things late at night on the computer. And once Georgiana had seen her try to take a puff on a cigar at a party, and it was like watching a blowfish try to whistle, but that was neither here nor there. The point was that her mother had an absolutely humongous collection of clothing, and whenever Georgiana was invited to a costume party she headed straight to her closet.

From the depths of her mother's walk-in Georgiana had exhumed the following looks: "Yummy Mummy" (a white bandage dress piled with candy necklaces, a baby-bump pillow shoved down the front), "Sexy Pope" (a gold pashmina tied like a bandeau and paired with flared white trousers and a hat made from a King Arthur flour sack), and "Ruth Baby Ginsburg" (her mother actually *had* a lace collar for some unimaginable reason, but the pacifier came from CVS). When Georgiana heard that the theme for her high school friend Sebastian's birthday was Oligarch Chic, she was nearly overwhelmed with the possibilities. Her mother owned more fur than the Bronx Zoo, had multiple dresses with feathers, and even had a tiara in a box. (She had tried to make Darley wear the tiara for her wedding but was unceremoniously shut down.)

Georgiana invited herself over after work on Wednesday to rummage through her choices. Her parents were home, Berta was cooking duck with jasmine rice, and her mother poured them each a glass of red wine while she supervised the pillage of her wardrobe. (Tilda offered her a straw so Georgiana might avoid tooth staining, but she preferred to slug it like a heathen.) There was a floor-length black sequined gown that would have been perfect had it not been so warm. There was a cropped white rabbit-fur jacket that was so soft she couldn't stop petting it. There were even diamond earrings in the shape of panthers that were so wonderfully gaudy Georgiana would have made fun of them if they hadn't been real and worth the cost of a midpriced sedan.

"Will your friend be at the party?" her mother asked nonchalantly, pulling out a white silk jumpsuit and laying it on the ottoman.

"No, it's just people from school. Lena and Kristin and everyone." Georgiana slithered into a leather dress and immediately started sweating. People talked a lot about white shoes after Labor Day, but leather dresses after April Fool's Day were even less practical. She shucked it onto the floor and rummaged through the sequined dresses in back. She wore a bra and underwear, aware of being mostly naked in front of her mother. It was funny to think about how similar their bodies were, while also how different. She knew from watching her mother on the beach, watching her mother try on clothing, how she would look in forty years. They had the same frame, tall with the same slim hips, broad shoulders, the same small breasts. Her mother's stomach was soft and wrinkled; the place where three babies had grown looked slightly puckered, while Georgiana's was flat, any softness from drinking too much beer on weekends. Georgiana was stronger, but she knew her mother was in remarkably good shape for her age, and the fact that she was still so trim was an act of sheer will, mostly motivated by her refusal to give up a forty-year collection of clothing.

She finally settled on a low-cut gold dress, studded strappy heels, big Chanel sunglasses, and a leopard-print hat. She wanted to borrow some jewelry—there was a ring with a ruby the size of a gumdrop—but her mom had limits on her generosity.

Sebastian had everyone meet at his apartment in the East Village before the dinner so that they could ride out to Brighton Beach in a party bus. They were going to a Russian dance hall, and Georgiana had to admire her friends' commitment to the theme. The guys were wearing shirts unbuttoned to reveal half their chests, layers of thick gold necklaces on display. The women wore all manner of fur and leather, heat be damned, but somehow Oligarch Chic had morphed into a more general nineties club look, their eyes winged with liquid liner, their hair huge, their heels five inches high.

There was a bar in the back of the bus with vodka, mixers, and big magnums of champagne, and when the driver turned on flashing colored lights Georgiana felt like she was wasted at seven p.m., the road bumping beneath them. Along with Lena and Kristin, Sebastian had invited their usual circle plus his freshman-year roommate, Curtis McCoy. Georgiana didn't know Curtis well, but she remembered visiting his family home on Martha's Vineyard with Lena once and realizing that they owned an entire gated compound, that the

Clintons and the Obamas had spent summers in houses on their property. He was next-level rich. Curtis's father was the CEO of a defense company and that had somehow always made her feel nervous around Curtis, like the fact that his family made Tomahawk missiles gave him an inherent dangerous power that she should steer clear of.

When they arrived at the dance hall, they spilled out of the bus and into the grand foyer. Georgiana suddenly felt like they were crashing a wedding, seeing the big groups of families, teenagers in suits, and middle-aged women in ruched satin dresses. A man in a starched white shirt led them to a banquet table in the center of the hall, and a swarm of waiters set about pouring them vodka and delivering massive platters of pickles and smoked fish, pancakes dotted with piles of chilled pink roe, sliced beef, and blintzes stuffed with cheese. Sebastian and his friends skipped the food and set about drinking with single-minded dedication, but Georgiana knew she'd end up a sloppy mess if she weren't careful, so she made herself a plate of blintzes and pickles.

There must have been three hundred people in the hall, eating and drinking and mostly ignoring the two women in Jessica Rabbit cocktail gowns standing on stage and singing a duet to Miley Cyrus's "The Climb." As the evening progressed, more and more performers came onto the stage and groups made their way to the dance floor. The guys, now fully drunk, took selfies with the towers of empty vodka bottles stacked atop their table. Lena and Kristin wanted to dance, so Georgiana followed them out to the floor, happy she'd skipped the fur coat as she joined the sweaty crowd. It was like a bat mitzvah on steroids, like being onstage for the Super Bowl halftime show. The fact that every other partygoer was Russian and lived an hour from their part of New York set them free to dance like maniacs, to let sweat pour down their temples, to feel their careful makeup washing away.

Georgiana had to pee and left the dance floor to find a restroom, climbing a marble staircase to a beautiful lounge filled with puffy chairs and gilded mirrors. She used a paper hand towel to blot her face, and she fixed her makeup in the powder room vanity. She had long ago abandoned her hat and had her big Chanel sunglasses pushed up like a hairband. Her feet ached and she was dying of thirst, so instead of returning to the dance floor she followed the maze of carpeted halls back to the banquet table, where she saw Curtis sitting alone at the end. Slightly buzzed and feeling friendly, Georgiana grabbed her water and pulled out the chair beside him.

"Hey Curtis, having fun?" she said, smiling.

"Not particularly, no." He frowned, glancing at her briefly before looking off over her head.

"What's wrong?"

"The fact that you have to ask that means that it's not worth discussing," he said.

"What?" Georgiana asked, completely confused. Why was he being so rude to her?

"Do you not see how fucked up this whole thing is? I can't believe I'm here."

"How fucked up a birthday party is? No, I guess I don't see it," Georgiana replied, annoyed.

"You think it's cool that a bunch of rich white kids who met at private school are dressed in costumes to ridicule an immigrant group in their own neighborhood? That seems fine to you?"

"It's Oligarch Chic. It's making fun of rich people. And Russians are white," Georgiana said with a frown.

"As I said, the fact that you had to ask meant it wasn't worth me discussing it with you. Nice sunglasses." Curtis turned away from her and picked up his phone.

"Fuck you, Curtis. You don't know me."

"Of course I know you. You're a rich real estate brat living off your trust fund, only dimly aware that an entire world exists outside the coddled one percent."

"Oh, so you live in Zuccotti Park? You went to the School of Hard Knocks? Didn't you go to Princeton?"

"Oh, so you *don't* live off a trust fund?"

"I work for a not-for-profit providing health care for developing countries," Georgiana said icily.

"And who pays your rent?"

"I own."

"And your rich parents bought that apartment."

"My grandparents left me money, not that it's your business."

"And how did they make that money?"

"Well, some of it they inherited—"

"So your family got rich off being rich."

"No, my grandfather worked hard."

"And what did he do?"

"Real estate investment."

"Gentrification." Curtis nodded smugly, as though this had proved his point.

"You are an ass."

"I probably am. But at least I am self-aware enough to know it. Have fun ridiculing people who didn't come over on the *Mayflower*." And with that Curtis shoved back his chair and stalked out of the banquet hall. Georgiana's cheeks were aflame, and to her horror she felt a tear rolling down to the corner of her mouth. She wiped it quickly and picked up a random glass from the table and filled it with vodka before taking a gulp. What a prick.

That night, as the party bus rumbled along the Belt, Georgiana looked around her. Of course her friends were lucky, of course they had completely unfair advantages, but she knew them and they were good people. Lena and Kristin would lie down in the street for her. They voted Democratic, they gave to Planned Parenthood, they had museum memberships. Their families sat on boards, they paid for tables at benefits, they tipped generously. Her own parents had even paid for both of Berta's kids to go to college. Curtis McCoy was a pompous hypocrite. But their conversation still left Georgiana shaken, and in the morning when she woke, stinking of pickles and booze, she couldn't tell how much of her hangover was physical and how much was left over from Curtis's casual cruelty.

She couldn't manage to shake the mood. All day Sunday she walked around in a state, feeling like she had just been delivered some terrible news, like her apartment had burned down or they had discovered avocados caused cancer. It was stupid, honestly. A billionaire jerk whose family sold bombs to the government called *her* a bad person. It was laughable, really.

Georgiana walked over to Pineapple Street that evening and dropped her mother's silk dress off at the dry cleaner. The rule was that she could borrow whatever she wanted as long as she returned it clean, but Georgiana had discovered a loophole: the dry cleaner had her mother's credit card on file and delivered to her door, so as long as she dropped the clothes off with them, it was as good as done.

Cord and Sasha were hosting family dinner at the limestone, and Georgiana momentarily thought about stopping at the wine store to pick up a bottle, but she knew her mother would bring plenty for everyone. She still had a key to the house, so she let herself in and took off her shoes by the door.

"Cord! Darley! I'm here!" she called, wandering into the kitchen. Sasha was spinning in circles, pulling a roasted chicken from the oven, sprinkling slivered almonds on a salad, emptying a pot of steaming rice into a bowl. Her mother was stationed over her Le Creuset, guarding what looked to be a leg of lamb and a ragout while Darley carefully placed fish sticks on the foiled sheet in the toaster. It was hot and busy, and Georgiana could sense the discord like an invisible force field that repelled her instantly back out of the kitchen and down the hall toward her father in the parlor. Malcolm was hiding in there as well, Poppy and Hatcher fighting over who got to be the dog in a game of Monopoly.

"Hi Daddy, hi Malcolm, hi guys." Georgiana kissed everyone hello and flopped down on the floor next to her niece and nephew. She half-heartedly listened to her father try to teach them the rules of the game, and as she played with the fringe on the Oriental rug she let Curtis's words run through her head: *So your family got rich off being rich.* Of course, it was true. Her father couldn't be faulted for it, though. He wasn't lazy, he wasn't selfish; he was a real estate investor, and he helped make places for people to work and live. What was he going to do? Let old buildings go to seed? It was his job to move the city forward. He cared about his partners, he worried about them when the market turned, he worked until late at night, he was up early every morning. It was personal for him; he knew that it was within his power to make the city more beautiful, and he left his mark. It was easy to say that money was the root of all evil, but so many of the things money could buy provided dignity, health, and knowledge.

Georgiana looked at her brother-in-law playing with his children. Malcolm hadn't inherited in the same way, but his father was an analytical chemist, he grew up in comfort, and he worked in finance now. He wasn't saving people's lives every day—he worked for a bank— but his knowledge and research helped keep the airline industry functional, helped smooth the mechanics of a sector that essentially connected people around the world. There was honor there. And nobody could question how hard Malcolm worked. As far as Georgiana could tell, Malcolm was always either working or spending time with Darley and the kids. He lavished his family with his love. He was maybe the nicest man Georgiana had ever met, and if he weren't married to her sister she'd be half in love with him herself.

This was the kind of marriage Georgiana wanted one day, that both she and Darley wanted for Cord, so it killed them a little that Sasha had behaved so badly over the prenup, that she would never be a real sister, would never have the level of trust that Malcolm had earned in the Stockton family. They had started calling Sasha "the Gold Digger" or "the GD" for short after she moved into the Pineapple Street apartment. It wasn't kind, but it seemed fair.

When Cord announced that dinner was served, Georgiana had to laugh. Nothing went together; there were tiny portions of twelve different things, the tablescape was pathetic, and everyone seemed tense and grumpy about the whole affair. Tilda looked particularly piqued. Georgiana served herself with an eye to politics, making sure to take a big helping of lamb and only a small piece of chicken, complimenting her mother loudly on the ragout. The kids each ate one fish stick and then slithered under the table before vanishing off to one of the bedrooms to play.

As they ate, they talked about the Icelandic singer Björk, who put her Henry Street apartment on the market for nine million dollars (she and her ex, Matthew Barney, had been parking their big black yacht in the East River); her mother's tennis partner (Frannie had hurt her wrist and there was a chance she'd have to miss a few weeks on the court, rendering Tilda bereft); and the weird tunnels that connected so many of the former Jehovah's Witnesses' properties in the neighborhood (the tunnels made sense when they were all part of the same organization, but what were you supposed to do when there was a whole underground lair full of laundry rooms and storage cages connecting your apartment building to a stranger's?). When they asked Georgiana about Sebastian's birthday party, she told them about the dance hall, about the music and the food, but she held back on mentioning anything about Curtis.

"I do wonder, though," she mused. "The theme was Oligarch Chic. Do you think that's offensive?"

"When I was a junior, a couple of students got called to the disciplinary committee because they had a Cinco de Mayo party with sombreros," Cord said, cutting a bite of chicken. "I feel like it was a little much to take disciplinary action, but I wouldn't host that party now."

"Freshman year they had a Pimps and Hos party, and everyone dressed up in tank tops and hoop earrings, and the guys tried to give all the girls money to kiss," Darley announced with wide eyes. "Nobody even thought about reporting it, but I am so horrified every time I think about it."

"Did you go?" Sasha asked.

"I went, but I didn't go in costume," Darley said, biting her lip. "I think I wore a sweater from Brooks Brothers."

"But, like, do you think Oligarch Chic is offensive?" Georgiana pressed.

"I think maybe it's like if the party was Mobsters and Mob Wives or something," Malcolm ventured. "Like, it's not so much about offending the mafioso or the oligarchs, it's more about perpetuating harmful stereotypes of Italian Americans or Russian Americans."

"That makes sense," Georgiana agreed, privately mortified that it was the one person of color in their family who had to explain ethnic stereotyping to her. The conversation veered off from there, onto *The Sopranos* and *The Americans* and then, as every conversation about film and television eventually must, to her father describing to everyone why he never thought Woody Allen was funny in the first place, like his lack of a sense of humor had meant he had intuited the director's misdeeds through some great omniscient power rather than just not liking *Annie Hall*.

Georgiana was rolling her eyes with Cord when Poppy came running into the room screaming. "Hatcher is throwing up!"

Darley was off like a shot, and they all stampeded through the apartment up to Darley's bedroom, where Hatcher was on his knees on the floor, crying pitifully over a puddle of clear vomit with a white stone glistening in the middle.

"What on earth is that?" Tilda asked.

Darley, now a mother and immune to the horrors of most bodily fluids, reached into the puddle and held the white stone to the light. "It's a tooth."

"A tooth?" Malcolm asked with alarm, patting Hatcher's back. The kids were five and six and had not lost any teeth yet. "Let me see, buddy. Which one was it?" He peered into Hatcher's open mouth. "I can't see anything."

"Here, take my flashlight." Georgiana swiped the flashlight on her phone and they shined it into Hatcher's mouth to find the spot where a tooth had been.

"None of his teeth are missing." Malcolm frowned.

"We found it in the drawer," Poppy whispered.

"You found what in the drawer?" Darley asked. "Which drawer?"

"We thought it was a bag of gum. In there." Poppy pointed to a dresser drawer that was slightly ajar. Malcolm reached in and pulled out an ancient plastic baggie full of something white.

"Are these teeth?" he asked in horror.

"Oh." Darley bit her lip with embarrassment. "Those are my baby teeth."

"Oh my God." Georgiana felt a laugh building deep inside her and fought to contain herself. "Your son found your thirty-year-old baby teeth in a bag and thought they were gum and ate them and then threw up. Oh my God, Dar, this is *amazing*." Unable to control herself any longer, she dissolved into peals of laughter, her anxiety evaporating into the air. As she looked around at her family, Poppy and Hatcher giggling uncertainly, Malcolm and her father looking mildly disgusted, and Darley mortified, she caught Sasha's eye. The GD looked absolutely victorious.

ON TUESDAY as she and Brady walked to the tennis courts, she told him all about her weekend—about the dance hall and Curtis's remarks, though not about the tooth. The tooth was too disgusting to share with a man she hoped to continue to have sex with.

"So my friend Sebastian had a birthday party this weekend out in Brighton Beach and he invited this guy, Curtis McCoy." Georgiana paused at the traffic light and Brady leaned over and took her heavy bag off her shoulder. He was always doing that—carrying her stuff or paying for her coffee—and each time it made her stomach flip happily. They didn't say "I love you," not even close, but she knew she loved him without a doubt, and she was starting to think he might love her too. "Curtis is this total asshole. His family lives in Wilton and has, like, horses. His father is the CEO of one of the country's biggest defense contractors. They own half of Martha's Vineyard and—"

"Um, George? Are you trying to make me jealous here? Telling me about the handsome billionaire you hung out with this weekend?" Brady teased.

"No!" Georgiana swatted him on the arm. "I'm trying to say that the guy basically grew up as Prince Harry wearing Nazi costumes and is acting like he's Prince Harry married to Meghan."

"I think I lost you there," Brady laughed.

Georgiana didn't feel like getting into the whole oligarch appropriation issue, so she simplified. "This guy Curtis grew up richer than anyone I know, and he was being grumpy at dinner, and when I asked him what was wrong he totally went off on me. He accused me of being a trust-fund brat who was profiting off the little guy. He made it sound like I was Marie Antoinette!"

"Your friends sound really fun," Brady deadpanned.

"He is *not* my friend." Georgiana pouted. She wasn't sure what she'd been hoping to get out of this conversation, but reminding

Brady that she was a privileged child and that her friends sucked wasn't exactly it.

"Look, if he can't see what an amazing person you are, then even better for me. I won't have to worry about you running off to join him on his horse farm or his half of Martha's Vineyard." Brady playfully bopped Georgiana on her bum with his racket.

There was still something eating at Georgiana, something she needed Brady to understand. "I want to be an amazing person, but it's hard, right? Even just to be a mostly good person? I mean our job is one thing. We all work in nonprofits because we want to do good in the world."

"Not me." Brady frowned.

"Not you what?"

"That's not why I work in global health."

"Okay, why do you? Why not be a corporate lawyer or investment banker?"

"I grew up this way. With my parents. Traveling to different countries, meeting people, moving around, it seems normal to me. We lived in Ecuador for three years when I was a kid, we lived in Haiti for two, we lived in India."

"Were you homeschooled?"

"No, most of the time we went to the local school. In Ecuador my dad would put us on the back of a four-wheeler and we'd literally drive through a river to get to school. Kind of hard to get excited about taking a school bus after that."

"That's amazing," Georgiana said.

"It was. I mean, there were bad parts. We got a pretty disgusting skin infection once and it took weeks for the pharmacy to get in the right antibiotics. And there were scary moments. I remember one time my mom had taken us kids to a waterfall in Haiti. I don't remember what my dad was doing that day. We were getting ready to leave in the Jeep when two women came up the path with their kids, and they had machetes strapped to their waists. We figured they just wanted a ride—everyone hitchhikes there—but instead they wanted our clothing. They didn't pull out the knives, they didn't have to, but we all took off our shirts and handed them over, our backpacks, our hats and sunglasses. Mom was cool about it, acting like she was happy to be giving them a gift, but my brother and I were kind of freaked out."

"Did it make you want to come home?"

"Not really. I mean, every kid that grew up in New York in the eighties got mugged at some point. It was probably the same."

Georgiana laughed.

"Anyway, it just seems like a normal job to me. Plus, I like to travel. I get bored easily." Brady shrugged.

Was he being modest? She saw how hard he worked—she'd spent more time than she'd admit reading about his role at local hospitals, looking at photos of him out in the field. When Georgiana and Brady got to the tennis courts, they changed their shoes and started to play, but all the while Brady's words echoed in her head: "I get bored easily."

PART OF GEORGIANA'S JOB was arranging the company's presence at the Global Health Conference in Washington. She had never traveled for work, and in the weeks leading up to D.C. she managed to work the phrase "I'm going on a business trip" into casual conversation so many times her friends began to tease her.

"Yeah, you're adulting superhard, George. Cool," Lena laughed. Lena traveled for work all the time with her boss and even kept a little bag of toiletries under her bathroom sink that she could just throw into her carry-on.

Georgiana had actually been working overtime to pull together the company booth. She had shipped signage to the convention center, she had reserved the space, she had sent updated literature to the printer, and had even made huge, glossy blowups from new photos of their work in the field, only one of them featuring Brady's face. (She privately wondered how weird it would be if she stole the sign and kept it in her apartment.)

Because they were a not-for-profit, the entire conference had to be planned with an eye toward savings and so everyone attending, from the lowliest newbie (Georgiana) to the CEO, had to partner up with a colleague to share a hotel room. Georgiana would be sharing with Meg from the grant-writing team. Meg was only a few years older than she was, but an incredibly intense person who kept an industrial-size jar of Advil next to her computer and ostentatiously took three every afternoon because of the overwhelming stress of her deadlines. Meg wore slacks, flats, and button-downs every day, her fluffy blond hair pulled into a no-nonsense ponytail. She didn't wear makeup, she rarely smiled, and she carried herself as though she might one day run for president but could be thwarted with a single typo or verbal trip. To Georgiana she seemed like the love child of Tracy Flick and Ann Taylor.

Brady was going to D.C. as well, and Georgiana had elaborate and nerdy daydreams about them racing up the steps of the Lincoln Memorial, laughing, and taking selfies at the top with the Mall spread out behind them. In reality, she wasn't sure she'd see much of him, never mind humongous Lincoln. She would be stuck at the booth the entire time, handing out pamphlets and directing people to their panels, while Brady was attending speeches on leadership technique, policy challenges in different regions, and best practices learned from other sectors. Brady was even giving a talk one day, part of a small panel on overcoming language barriers in medical care. It was sexy stuff, really.

The weekend before the conference Brady came over after their run and saw her carefully packed suitcase sitting on the floor. "You literally packed a full four days before the trip?" he asked, laughing.

"It's my first business trip!" she said defensively, feeling embarrassed.

"Are you going to write that on your name tag for the conference, or just tell everyone you meet?"

"Oh, I was assuming they would have some kind of ceremony for me, was I wrong?" Georgiana pulled off her sweaty T-shirt and swatted him with it. "Or maybe a cake at the booth that said 'Baby's first conference'?"

"Yeah, I'm not sure that's in the budget. A cake could run you at least fifteen bucks, and we're watching every cent." Brady caught the sweaty shirt from Georgiana's hands and tossed it at the hamper.

"I can't believe people have to share rooms. It's so weird. I wish you and I could share a room." Georgiana pulled Brady's shirt up over his head.

"Well, I'm sharing with Pete, and he might leave after his panel, so there is a chance I'll have my room to myself the second night. You could ditch your slumber party with Meg and join me. Unless you guys had big plans to give each other pedicures and do face masks."

"I don't think robots have toes," Georgiana joked. "This will be so fun! A cute meetup in DC! I love it." She kissed him and they didn't bother spraying the sweat off before climbing into her bed. Love was often gross, really.

When she arrived at the convention center on Tuesday, dragging her perfectly packed suitcase behind her, she was relieved to see that her new posters had survived shipping and the booth was put together just as her binder had promised. She worked alone, building the plastic displays and filling them with trifold pamphlets, arranging books on the tables, and tacking the blowups to the cork board. She honestly had no idea what she was doing, but the guy who had the job before her had made her a detailed instruction manual, and she followed it faithfully and hoped for the best. When she finished, she felt sticky and disgusting from the train and the exertion, so she headed to the hotel to change and find the rest of the team.

Meg from grant writing was already in the room when she got there, unpacking her rolling bag and hanging her suits and blouses in the small closet.

"Hey, roomie," Georgiana trilled, plonking down on the bed by the window.

"I've only taken half the hangers so that you'll have plenty of space for your stuff." Meg glanced up briefly from her unpacking. "Also, I like to shower at night so you can have the bathroom in the morning, or we can decide who will go first."

"Oh, great. I actually got super sweaty down at the booth, so I was going to grab a shower before dinner. Do you know if people are going out?"

"Gail and I are going to meet with some counterparts from Peace Works, but I'm sure someone will be in the hotel bar later." Meg frowned as she dusted the top of a tasseled loafer before placing it carefully on the closet floor.

By the time Georgiana got out of the shower Meg was gone, so she threw on jeans and an embroidered blouse and brought her book, a biography of Roger Federer, down to the bar. She ordered a vodka soda and a turkey club and alternately read and people watched as she ate. It seemed like most of the guests in the hotel were here for the conference too. There were a lot of white women in saris, a fashion choice that was rampant at her office, everyone coming back from India with reams of silk that they wore around New York with clogs, their hair either gray or tinted with henna. Georgiana's own mother would sooner wear a bathrobe to the Colony Club than a sari and clogs.

By nine she had finished her sandwich and drink and didn't particularly feel like hanging around by herself in a hotel bar, so she went back to her room, changed into her pajamas, and read in bed until Meg came home at ten and bored her to death talking about all the really excellent contacts she had made at dinner. If this was business travel, Georgiana didn't see what the fuss was about.

The next day at the booth passed in a blur, Georgiana feeling much like an airline hostess as she repeated the same lines over and over, a fixed smile on her face as her feet ached from standing on a thin layer of carpeting barely cushioning the concrete floor below. The conference center even felt like an airport. There was no sense of time, people rushed to and fro like ants, sipping bottles of water and wearing lanyards with laminated cards around their necks. But unlike an airport there were no bars, and Georgiana would have killed for a shot of vodka to dull the tedium.

She didn't see Brady all day, but at five he sent her a text:

Pete gone. Room 643 at 10p?

She texted back a thumbs-up and her feet hurt a little less. In the room that evening, Meg dressed for dinner, swapping her blouse and slacks for a nearly identical set. Georgiana was looking at her phone, trying to decide where to go get food before meeting Brady, when Meg swore loudly.

"SHIT! I'm getting a pimple! Really professional." She was peering into the mirror over the dresser, scowling at her chin.

"Oh, I have some cover-up if you want it," Georgiana offered, reaching for the makeup bag by her bed.

Meg turned to her, looking guiltily intrigued, as though Georgiana had offered her bath salts. "Can you do it for me?" she asked.

How Meg had made it to the age of thirty without ever covering up a pimple Georgiana did not know, but she obligingly pulled out her concealer and dabbed it on the pink spot, blending it carefully with her index finger. "There you go, all set."

"Wow, you can't even see it," Meg marveled, admiring her reflection.

"There's a reason makeup is big business."

"Well, this was only because it's a professional dinner," Meg snorted. "I'm not about to go rubbing chemicals all over my face regularly." She slipped on her sensible shoes and was out the door.

Georgiana took a piece of hotel stationery and scribbled a note: "Staying with a college friend, don't worry about me!" and left it on Meg's bed. It was much easier to lie on paper. She put some chemicals on her face, changed into a long, flowing green dress, and strolled to a bookstore café where she passed a pleasant two hours drinking wine and eating artichoke pasta with her book before heading back to the hotel to meet Brady.

In the morning Brady woke at seven to catch an early train back to the city. Georgiana had to disassemble the booth and ship everything home, so she returned to her own hotel room to change into jeans and sneakers. When she quietly tapped on the door, she found that Meg was up, packing her suitcase and drinking coffee from a paper cup.

"Where were you last night?" she asked, folding a suit jacket in half and tucking one padded shoulder into the other before stacking it in her bag.

"Oh, I stayed with a college friend," Georgiana said breezily, taking out her earrings and slipping them into her makeup case.

"Just be careful, Georgiana," Meg said, looking at her for the first time. She held her gaze and they were silent for a moment. Did Meg think she'd been out hooking up with some random person? Or was it somehow against company policy to visit a friend in your off-hours on a trip?

"With what?" Georgiana asked frowning.

"With Brady," Meg said. "He's married."

Georgiana felt the shock as though she had been slapped. "Okay," Georgiana whispered, breaking her gaze and pulling her sneakers out from under the bed.

"Are you all set with the booth? I'm going to try to make it back to the office for the World Bank call this afternoon, but are you all by yourself today?" Meg asked.

"Yeah, but it's easy. I have the binder," Georgiana trailed off, her mind still spinning.

"Okay, I'll see you at the office, then." Meg nodded and pulled her wheelie bag out the door, leaving Georgiana stunned and alone.

NINE

Darley

D arley didn't think she would do well in prison. She would miss her latte maker, for one thing. And the kids. But after Malcolm's American Airlines deal fell through, she knew someone would swoop in to partner with the Brazilian airline Azul. She spent an afternoon examining the competition and decided it was going to be United; they didn't have the same stake in South America's market and needed to catch up. She checked the stock price. In her mind, she made her move and took a big position. A week later on CNBC they announced that United had paid $100 million for a 5 percent stake in the company. The stock price jumped. Darley's imaginary wallet fattened.

The thing was, as bad as Malcolm getting fired looked, being investigated for insider trading was decidedly worse. Malcolm had a three-month tail on his contract with Deutsche Bank. Even though he didn't work there anymore, he couldn't trade in the airline sector, which meant Darley couldn't either. They would pay him three months of salary plus his deferred compensation from bonuses, and then after that, nothing. She and Malcolm were on the clock, counting on him getting a new job before the taps were turned off.

inally, his relentless networking paid off, and he had landed an interview with the private equity firm Texas Pacific Group. It was a prestigious job, one he would be far more pleased about taking than the subpar banks the headhunters had been lobbing his way, but after the first round of interviews it became clear that if Malcolm were hired it would be to work in the Dallas office.

"Would you move to Dallas?" he asked Darley, biting at his thumbnail, his nervous tell. She knew he had absolutely no desire to move to Texas, to uproot his kids and live that far away from his parents.

"We'll live wherever you live, my love," Darley promised. He needed a job, and she needed to support him. He flew out on a Thursday morning for two days of interviews and a weekend of golf with a business school friend at the firm, and Darley wished him luck, not sure what she even really meant, or how hard to cross her fingers.

THAT SUNDAY Darley began to run the kids at dawn: they went to soccer practice on the plaza, they marched to the bagel store for a second breakfast, they visited the carousel in Dumbo for two-dollar rides on the antique horses, and then demolished a giant plate of mac and cheese that Darley bought for sixteen dollars at the Time Out Market because it was made with Gruyère and lardons, two facts entirely lost on her small voracious charges. Her children behaved best when exercised within an inch of exhaustion, so instead of bringing them home after lunch, where they would inevitably beg to watch cartoons on their iPads, rendering them cranky zombies, Darley took them to her gym to continue the Iron Man–like marathon that was a weekend without child care.

Her gym was inside the Hotel St. George, what had once been the biggest, most glamorous hotel in all of New York City, hosting American presidents and famous celebrities from Frank Sinatra to Cary Grant. The hotel stretched an entire city block; in its heyday the massive saltwater pool had mirrored ceilings and waterfalls, the ballroom held weddings, and the hotel employed more than a thousand people. By the 1980s, it was sold to developers, sliced and diced, and the famous pool was drained. Part of the building was turned into student housing, the tower was transformed into luxury condos, the lobby became a bodega, a butcher, and a liquor store, and the vast section in the middle of the building—the place where the pool used to be—became Darley's gym. Ghosts of the original remained, the green balconies that once overlooked the swimming pool were now home to a series of elliptical machines where old people and college students climbed to nowhere, earbuds screwed into their ears. Lavish carpeting covered a strange waiting area by the squash courts, and the path to get from the locker room to the tiny new swimming pool required a series of stairs and doors, twists and turns that made Darley feel like she was walking through the underbelly of Penn Station in a wet Speedo.

In the women's locker room, Darley and the kids pulled on their suits, L.L.Bean one-pieces for the girls, trunks and a long-sleeve swim shirt for Hatcher, who was so skinny he turned blue and started chattering if he didn't wear a layer in the pool. Poppy was so accustomed to seeing Hatcher in a shirt that the first time she saw a man in the pool bare-chested she started screaming, "Mommy, that man is NAKED," and caused a minor scene with the attendant.

They shoved their sneakers and clothing into lockers, stepped into flip-flops, wrapped up in thin, white gym towels, and began the long trek to the pool, Darley bringing up the rear with a bag of goggles, noseclips, diving sharks, and bathing caps. They went through the women's showers, past the steam rooms, through a back door, and down a set of stairs with flaking green tile, along a snaking chilly hall to the pool, where the air was twenty degrees warmer and thick with chlorine. The children threw their towels down and jumped in immediately, ignoring Darley as she asked them to wait for her. They were both excellent swimmers, and she often marveled that their spindly arms were actually strong enough to motor them around so quickly. They looked like little spandex eels, wriggling with pleasure in the bright blue water.

There were a handful of other swimmers, all parents and children, and Darley lowered herself in from the ladder, observing the unspoken pool etiquette, allowing a few feet of distance between them and herself, nodding hello to the parents as they dragged their tiny offspring around on chewed-up foam kickboards. Poppy and Hatcher had no such sense of decorum and lunged gleefully along, darting between parents and children, diving for toys at the knees of strangers, kicking up giant splashes that drenched everyone near them. Darley looked around the place, surprised anew at just how run-down her gym was. The tiles of the pool were cracked in places, a strange showerhead with a chain was positioned in the middle of the room, prison style, and a hot tub filled with old people burbled over near the lifeguard. Since the building next door housed apartments for the elderly, the gym was crawling with octogenarians, and as she watched them soak in the Jacuzzi she often felt she was watching outtakes from the movie *Cocoon*.

Darley had climbed out to fetch the kids' goggles when the life-guard blew her whistle. "Up! Up!" Darley looked over in a panic and Hatcher was floating facedown in the pool. She started to run toward him, but he heard the whistle and quickly lifted his head, flipping over onto his back.

"Hatcher, what are you doing?"

"It's the dead man's float, mom," he laughed.

"Well, it's confusing for the lifeguard so stop doing it."

"Okaaaay," he giggled and squirmed his body to the side of the pool to grab his goggles.

Five minutes later the lifeguard blew her whistle again. Poppy was facedown. Darley grabbed her and flipped her over. "*Stop it,*" she hissed, and Poppy laughed. They played this game three more times before the lifeguard asked them to leave.

Humiliated, Darley marched them back out into the hallway, thin towels draped around their shivering bodies. She usually dried them off by the pool and wrapped them in fresh warm towels for the journey, but she was pissed. "What is up with you guys? Why did you keep doing that even after the lifeguard asked you to stop?"

"Aiden says that drowning is the worst way to die," Hatcher explained seriously, his voice echoing in the long, tiled hallway.

"He says your lungs fill with water," Poppy agreed.

"You guys know how to swim. That's why we taught you. So that you won't drown. Is that what you're afraid of? Are you afraid you'll drown? Because you won't."

"No, we're not afraid."

"We just wanted to feel what it was like. To die." Poppy smiled sweetly.

"You're not going to die until you're a hundred," Darley said firmly, ushering them up the final stairway and into the showers, blasting the warm water and scrubbing their heads with shampoo before sending them into the locker room to dress themselves. As Darley peeled off her wet swimsuit, she let the warm water cascade down her face. If her kids got her thrown out of Eastern Athletic, she would be seriously annoyed. The only thing more embarrassing than belonging to the most decrepit gym in Brooklyn was being exiled from it for antisocial behavior.

When Darley emerged from the shower, the children were sitting on a bench, fully clothed, staring at the naked old women newly released from aerobics class. The women chatted about their instructor, about a classmate who was hosting family from New Jersey, about someone whose husband was ill and whom they would visit with cake and flowers. As they chatted, they folded their damp tops into plastic bags, they stretched shower caps over their fluffy white hair, then bent low to place their sneakers under the benches, exposing naked buttocks. Darley averted her eyes, mildly horrified. Sure, she had given birth to two babies and her body looked nothing like it had six years ago, but when she saw these wrinkled women, their breasts low on their chests, their thighs marbled with cellulite, varicose veins and puckered scars tattooing their skin, she couldn't imagine ever possibly looking so ancient. Or being willing to appear naked in public if she did.

"Don't stare," Darley whispered, and her children snapped their eyes to her, as though woken from a trance.

"Are they almost a hundred?" Poppy asked loudly.

"Shhhh." Darley died a thousand deaths inside. "I don't know. Why don't you guys watch Netflix on my phone while I get our stuff." Having children was possibly the most mortifying experience of her life.

THERE WERE HOURS to go until dinner, so Darley fetched the children's scooters from under the gym stairwell and herded them to the playground on Pierrepoint. She found an empty bench and retreated into her phone, while Poppy and Hatcher set about exploring the grossest corners of the park, the pile of damp sticks by the door of the public restroom, the discarded plastic baggies in the drain by the water fountain, the half-broken ginkgo fruits at the base of the tree, releasing their stinky smell. She would have to give them a second bath when they got home, but it was worth it to spin the hands of the clock, to arrive at another Sunday night, an entire week of school and freedom before her.

She was torturing herself by reading her class alumni notes when she noticed her sister-in-law sitting on a bench on the other side of the iron fence. "Sasha!" she called, waving her over. Sasha startled and then gathered up her papers and let herself into the playground. She was wearing what looked like men's jeans and a black T-shirt, and while Darley knew that outfit would make her look like a Johnny Cash impersonator, somehow on Sasha it all worked. She had shiny auburn hair cut to her ears, pale freckled skin, pretty pink lips, and a petite, slim build that would have made her a great squash player. Darley couldn't help it. Years of living with her mother and sister had turned her into the kind of person who evaluated a woman's build based on her ideal athletic endeavors. It was insane, really.

"Oh, hi!" Sasha laughed. "I didn't even see you guys arrive."

"We were just thrown out of the Eastern Athletic swimming pool for pretending to drown." Darley cringed.

"You should probably stop pretending to drown. Sets a bad example for the kids."

"It's just swimming is so hard when I've been day drinking." Darley snickered and patted the bench next to her for Sasha to sit. Sasha seemed a little surprised, but Darley was desperate for adult conversation so she smiled her most welcoming smile. They looked out across the playground, where Poppy and Hatcher were crouching over the drain by the water fountain, taking turns dipping long sticks through the slots and pulling up dank piles of scummy leaves.

"What were you up to?"

"Oh, I was messing around with my sketchbook." Sasha gestured at a spiral-bound pad.

"Can I see?"

Sasha handed the notebook over and Darley leafed through it. The drawings were mostly portraits of people. She flipped past an old man playing a trumpet on a park bench, a couple cuddling on a stoop, a lady smoking out a window. She turned the page and saw her brother, his feet slung over a chair as he read a book. It was uncanny how well she had captured the funny thing he did with his mouth when he read, the way he seemed to hold a book as though he were about to drop it. How strange to see a person she loved so dearly through the eyes of someone else.

"These are incredible, Sasha. You went to Cooper Union, right?"

"Yep. And now I spend my days arguing with clients over which photo of a pillowcase will look sexier in their Christmas catalog. I'm really putting my degree to use."

"I got my MBA so that I could broker corporate acquisitions, and instead I spend my days arguing with children about whether chicken nuggets and chicken fingers represent two different food groups," Darley said. She felt the way she always did whenever she mentioned business school: proud she had gone, embarrassed she had done nothing since then. She wasn't sure why she was volunteering this to her sister-in-law, of all people.

"I mean, they kind of do," Sasha said. "Nuggets are for school lunches and chicken fingers are for eating at the sports bar when you realize you're drunk and it's only halftime."

"Mmm, yes, the five food groups: drunk, sober, hungover, school lunch, and bar food."

"I feel like you're missing the Monday food group."

"What is that?"

"The healthy one where you make everyone eat rice and broccoli and salad because you feel so gross from eating pizza and donuts all weekend."

"Oh, right, the Monday food group. That's the saddest food group, full of baby carrots and regret." Darley looked out across the playground, laughing quietly. "This girl I know posts her daily caloric intake on Instagram alongside pictures of slimy chickpeas and plain chicken breasts."

"That's so embarrassing," Sasha said, horrified.

"I know! I literally had to screenshot it and send it to all my friends and ask if she had meant to make her posts public! We contemplated an intervention!"

"But you didn't intervene?"

"No, we decided it was kinder to just keep texting screenshots behind her back."

"Oh, right, right. Totally agree." Sasha nodded seriously. Her phone dinged and she looked down. "Oh, God, yikes."

"What?"

"My mom texted that there is a *bat* in the basement and my dad is trying to go catch it. The dog is freaking out."

"Can't bats have rabies?"

"I'm texting her back. 'MOM. DO NOT LET DAD IN THE BASEMENT. CALL SOMEONE.'"

A moment later Sasha's phone dinged again and she groaned. Her mother had texted a picture of someone wearing a hockey goalie's face mask and gloves, holding a fishing net.

"Is that your dad?"

"It's my brother, thank God."

Suddenly a raindrop landed on Darley's arm. Poppy and Hatcher ran over, dragging their slimy sticks behind them.

"Mom! It's raining!"

"Okay, put your helmets on," Darley sighed. Now they'd have to battle out the rest of the day confined to the apartment. The afternoon stretched before her as long as a cross-country car trip, or a jury-duty summons.

"Hey, come over to Pineapple!" Sasha offered.

"You guys want to go to the limestone?" Darley asked the kids, forgetting for a moment that they could say something socially horrendous like "No, Sasha's house smells weird," or "Only if they have better snacks than we do," but instead they surprised her, jumping up and down and beaming at Sasha. Her kids did love looking through her old stuff.

They followed Sasha out of the playground and up Willow Street to Pineapple. They parked their scooters in the foyer, shucked their muddy sneakers, and carefully laid down their gooey sticks, while Darley hung their swim bag on a hook before entering the apartment.

"Guys, I have a bunch of art stuff out in my room if you want to draw." Sasha ushered the kids up the stairs. "Is that okay with you? If they go?"

"Sure." Darley smiled. She was not going to object to her kids playing independently. Sasha tipped her chin to the kitchen and Darley followed. She pulled out a bottle of white from the fridge and poured some for each of them. The rain slapped the glass doors to the yard.

"I should text Malcolm." Darley pulled out her phone. "Let's see, his golf game should be over by now." Darley dashed off a quick note letting him know the kids got kicked out of the pool and they were at the Pineapple Street house. She then put her phone facedown on the table and apologized. "Sorry about that."

"Malcolm's playing golf?"

"Yeah, with some business school friends in Texas."

"Do you guys talk a lot while he travels?"

"Like four hundred times a day," Darley laughed. "Do you and Cord talk all day?"

"No, I think Cord goes into beast mode when he's at the office and basically forgets he is a human. He comes back all starving from skipping lunch and then eats a whole bag of chips before dinner."

"Does he actually like working with Dad?"

"He loves it. He and your dad are two peas in a pod." Sasha smiled. "Is it hard having Malcolm travel so much for work? Do you miss him?"

Darley paused. Even though Malcolm had been let go from Deutsche Bank weeks and weeks ago, nobody in the family knew. Darley had decided it was best this way. But the weekend had been so long, so lonely, and keeping the secret had started to weigh on her. "Don't tell Cord, but Malcolm was fired. He's interviewing for a new job."

"He was fired?" Sasha asked, putting her wineglass down on the counter with a clink.

"It wasn't his fault—an analyst killed a deal and Malcolm took the fall."

"Shit. He must be heartbroken. I know how much he loves his job."

Darley was surprised to feel tears spring to her eyes. It was like Sasha actually understood why it scared her so much. "He is heartbroken. And banking is brutal. You make one misstep and you're persona non grata."

"Is he interviewing with another bank?"

"No, he's looking at private equity. But he just doesn't have connections there." Darley took a deep drink of wine.

"Don't your parents know people who could help?"

"We're not telling them," Darley said firmly.

"Why not?"

"It's complicated." Darley didn't want to talk about her parents, how she was afraid that on some secret level, a level they could never even acknowledge to themselves, they might have welcomed Malcolm more readily to their family because he was financially secure. Once his money was gone, once the shine of success had tarnished, would they feel quite the same way? "Promise me you won't mention it to Cord. I'll tell him all about it once Malcolm has a new job. I just don't want to put that pressure on Malcolm right now."

"Of course." Sasha nodded. "No problem. And he'll be hired in no time. He's a genius." Her phone dinged and she looked down. "Christ on a cracker." She showed Darley the screen, her father and brother holding the small brown bat in a net, victorious.

"Unreal," Darley murmured, trying to picture Chip doing anything with a net other than skimming bugs off the swimming pool at Spyglass.

"Maybe Malcolm won't have to travel so much with his next job," Sasha mused.

"Do you know my friend Priya Singh? Both she and her husband work at Goldman, and I literally have no idea how they even got pregnant with their second. I don't think they *ever* see each other."

"That sounds so lonely."

"There's that mom at the Henry Street School who married the NBA star who got traded to Los Angeles. Those kids only see their dad on TV."

"I mean, that's still pretty cool, though," Sasha said. "I would not be sad to be married to a basketball star."

"True. They make a ton of money, then they retire in their thirties and you can just stop working and hang out together."

"I don't think Cord will ever retire. He loves his work."

"I feel like there are all these guys who go into finance, and they have grand plans to make it big and then retire at thirty, but then no matter how much money they make they see that if they keep going, they could just make more. Like, there's never a moment when they think, *Oh, I have ten million dollars and that's enough.*"

"No, because everyone they know is also making that kind of money and spending that kind of money, and even when they have more than they could realistically need in a lifetime, it doesn't feel like they have enough."

"Totally," Darley agreed, finishing her wine.

Sasha reached over and poured her more. She turned on the oven and pulled two pizzas out of the freezer. "Should I make pizza and salad?"

"That's all the kids eat."

When the pizza was done, she called the kids down and they sat at the granite island and devoured slice after slice while arguing animatedly about invisibility cloaks. Hatcher thought they were real, but Poppy was unsure. After dinner they moved to the sofas in the parlor and Sasha put on music. The kids shimmied around and piled cushions on the floor and played hot lava, while Darley and Sasha laughed and drank and occasionally tossed a rogue pillow at an exuberant child. Her mother would kill them if she saw what they were doing with the governor's furniture.

Somehow, it was suddenly eight thirty and Darley realized they had missed bath time and overshot bedtime, and the dreaded Sunday afternoon had passed in a happy blur. She snapped helmets on the kids and gathered their sticks, and as they set off into the warm evening she gripped Sasha's arm seriously. "This was the *most* fun."

"I'm so glad you all got kicked out of the pool so we could do this." Sasha grinned.

As they swept down the damp sidewalks back to their apartment, Darley pulled out her phone. She had a missed FaceTime from Malcolm and a text.

Hope you're surviving the Sunday scaries . . .

Darley was a little drunk and the letters swam, so she closed one eye and texted back.

So fun. Had wine. Baby carrots and regret tomrw.

THERE WERE THINGS you could do with family that you just couldn't do with friends: You could let them see you wearing the same outfit three days in a row. You could invite them over for lunch and then mostly ignore them as you finally got off hold with the internet provider. You could have an entire conversation while wearing Crest Whitestrips. Suddenly, with her new friendship with Sasha, Darley felt her guard drop. Sasha was funny and easygoing and genuinely enjoyed spending time with Poppy and Hatcher. She worked free-lancer hours and was often free to meet Darley in the park midday, joining her and the kids for bagels at second breakfast, rides on the carousel, ice cream from the truck. She was silly with the kids in the same way Cord was, pretending her sunglasses gave her X-ray vision, insisting she understood what the barking dogs were saying when they ran past, engaging in long and serious discussions about the relative merits of a pet Pegasus or unicorn.

Darley could tell it made Cord happy to see his wife and sister having fun together, and he invited Darley into their world of private jokes and goofy theories. They had a shared suspicion that the terri-ble butcher shop in the Hotel St. George was really a drug front and peppered Darley with evidence.

"They have like four cuts of meat and a bag of dried pasta. That literally cannot be their business model," Cord said.

"And the guy who works there seems annoyed whenever you try to buy anything, like you're messing up the stage," agreed Sasha.

"You guys," Darley interrupted, shaking her head. "This is New York City. Nobody needs a drug front. If you want drugs you just order them from the app on your phone."

"Which app is that?" Cord teased.

"I mean, I don't actually *know*!" Darley had to concede.

Sasha had never eaten Korean barbecue, so Darley decided they'd go to the new place that had opened in Gowanus—a sleek, wood-paneled restaurant nestled between a moving company and a mechanic—and served tiki bar cocktails and blood sausage. Malcolm was obsessed with their short ribs, and after six phone calls Darley managed to score a coveted Saturday night reservation for four. But it turned out that Cord had the Union Club cognac tasting that night. She called back, and after much begging and pleading got a reservation three weeks later, but then realized Malcolm had plans for his mother's birthday. "It's like they're Clark Kent and Bruce Wayne," Darley lamented to Sasha.

"Mom, they can't be both." Poppy rolled her eyes. They were sitting on the bench outside Joe Coffee waiting for their order.

"Right! Because they are secretly the same person! Like a superhero and his alter ego!"

"No, Mom, Clark Kent is Superman and Bruce Wayne is Batman. They're two different characters."

"Oh. Well, which one is Daddy?"

"Probably Bruce Wayne," Poppy said thoughtfully. "And you're Pennyworth."

"Who's Pennyworth? The cute girl reporter?"

"No, Pennyworth is his butler. He's old," Hatcher said.

"Oh, cool, cool." Darley nodded and made a horrified face at Sasha over Hatcher's head. "Because I'm old."

Darley hadn't realized how lonely she had been before. So many of her friends were stretched thin between their jobs and parenting, their weekends full of soccer and furtive emailing, never truly caught up on work. She had her brother and sister, she had her parents, she had Malcolm's parents and Malcolm when he was home, but they all had client dinners and tennis matches, they all had Venetian-themed anniversary parties, golf outings, a zillion things to do that were more fun that watching the kids ride their bikes in circles for hours in Squibb Park. Of course, Sasha had more interesting things to do too. Sasha had work, and she had her art school friends, but she was just down the street, and rather than eat lunch alone at her desk staring into her computer, now she chose to swing by Darley's with a salad on a random Wednesday afternoon.

On warm weekends Darley and Malcolm loaded the kids up in the Land Rover with Cord and Sasha crammed in the third row and drove out to the Spyglass house so that they could hit balls around the tennis court and grill hot dogs. They stayed up late drinking wine and playing cards after the kids went to bed. Chip and Tilda were usually there too, but always engaged with some dinner party or event at their country club, traipsing in close to midnight, tipsy and in high spirits, her mother making her father bring out the cognac so they could catch up and gossip. Somehow Tilda always had the best gossip after these parties—about minor New York celebrities, about board members at the various private schools, about which co-ops were gleefully refusing entry to the Hollywood actors and actresses who flocked to the leafy streets of Brooklyn Heights like parakeets, bright and noisy and utterly out of their element.

Now that Darley was on Team Sasha, she saw how awkward their family could be to an outsider, how tricky it might seem to make sense of their little clan. She knew about Sasha and Malcolm's little inside joke, whispering "NMF" when they felt left out, but Darley realized she could just extend a hand to include Sasha, and she could have done it ages ago. She reminded Sasha to pack tennis whites for Spyglass. She passed her a coaster when she saw her about to put a tumbler on her mother's coffee table. She made a frantic zipping motion by her mouth when Sasha mentioned a real estate reality show in front of her father.

They were eating family dinner at Cecconi's in Dumbo one night when the vegetable soup arrived in a bread bowl. As Sasha ripped off a chunk of the bowl to eat, Darley saw her mother look at her, goggle-eyed.

"You aren't going to eat the bowl, are you?" Tilda asked in surprise. To Darley's knowledge her mother hadn't eaten bread since the 1970s.

Sasha paused, the bread halfway to her mouth, dripping broth. "The soup soaked into it," she faltered, and the table came to a terrible standstill.

Darley had ordered the soup as well and, full with the knowledge that only she could make this moment right, she ripped off a big piece of her own bowl. "Oh, but it's kind of wonderful," she insisted. Then, pivoting with the grace of a Lincoln Center ballerina, she asked, "Have any of you been to the new Italian restaurant on Henry Street? I heard the food is terrible, but the new James Bond is an investor." Darley continued to enthusiastically dismantle her bread bowl as Tilda jumped at the bait, regaling them with the story of James Bond's wife's trouble with her brownstone renovation, and Cord gave his big sister a quick look, tweaking the corner of his lip in a private smile of thanks.

TEN

Sasha

When Sasha was ten she had such an intense crush on Harrison Ford that sometimes she would lie in bed and cry with deep sorrow that they would never be together. She knew it was weird. He was a grown man and a famous actor and she was a child with a dawning awareness that little hairs were growing up and down her legs, and it all compounded into a tragedy so devastating that she could barely stand to watch him in movies when anyone else was in the room. Her brothers obviously noticed her mooning after him and taunted her mercilessly. Later in life, when she saw in some celebrity magazine at the nail salon that Harrison got an earring, she felt embarrassed all over again that she had been obsessed with someone so old.

Sasha had been falling in love with Cord before he told her about his childhood crush, but the revelation was probably what sealed the deal. They were lying in bed one night, slightly drunk, and she told him about Harrison.

"Did you ever feel that way as a kid?" she asked. "So intense and confused?"

"Yeah, totally. I was in love with Little Debbie," he confessed.

"Who's that?" Sasha asked, running a finger along his bare chest. "A neighbor?"

"No, the little girl with a hat on the box of snack cakes."

Sasha sat up. "You were in love with the girl on the box of Swiss Rolls? Those little chocolate things that taste like wax?"

"I just thought she looked so nice. She had this wavy brown hair and a friendly smile . . ."

"Do you think maybe you were just really hungry?"

"Maybe," Cord considered. "I really loved those oatmeal cookies with the cream in the middle."

Sasha laughed and laughed. Together they made a list of cartoon mascots by fuckability. Sasha felt Tony the Tiger was the clear winner. He just exuded cis-male hotness with his big puffy chest and boundless enthusiasm. The Sun-Maid raisin lady was obviously also a babe, rosy-cheeked, wearing a peasant blouse and a bonnet. The Cheetos Cheetah would be a fun date, but they agreed he'd try to leave his sunglasses on during sex. The Jolly Green Giant was maybe even hotter than Tony the Tiger, but Sasha worried he would be a terrible boyfriend, spending all his time in the gym. He was ripped. "Oh, so you're more into the Pillsbury Doughboy?" Cord asked. "More to love?"

"No, the Pillsbury Doughboy is too white. Not sexy!"

"Colonel Sanders?"

"Ugh, no! Also too white, plus the goatee!"

"The Quaker Oats guy?"

"Stop! All the human mascots are old men! Why do guys get the hot ones?"

"Like who?"

"Miss Chiquita?" Sasha countered.

"Smokeshow," Cord agreed.

"Wendy?"

"No way." Cord wrinkled his nose.

"Wait, so you loved Little Debbie but not Wendy? They're the same thing."

"Shut your lying mouth." Cord shook her shoulder playfully. "Little Debbie is all kindness and cream-filled cakes. Wendy looks like Conan O'Brien with braids and smells like hamburger grease." That settled, they turned off the lights and cuddled up, and as they fell asleep Cord whispered in her ear, "You're grrrrrrrreat!" and Sasha knew he was the one.

Where Mullin was thunder and darkness, Cord was pure sunshine, always in a good mood, emotionally easy, a man of simple pleasures. He enjoyed so many things. When he took a first bite of food, whether it was a bacon sandwich or a seared scallop, he always paused and threw his head back in bliss as he chewed. "Oooh," he'd moan appreciatively. "That's nice. That's just really nice." When a server put a plate before him at a restaurant, he'd give a slight whimper that was nearly indecent, so full of lust and unself-conscious adulation. He rejoiced in the bounce of new sneakers, in the feel of sun on his face. He sang along to anything that he heard on the radio, even if he didn't really know the words, even if it was crappy pop for teenagers. He was equally indiscriminate about movies, willing to sit through absolutely anything Sasha wanted, so together they watched every single movie with Catherine Keener, then everything directed by Nancy Meyers, and they both cried during

Father of the Bride and had to rewind and watch the part again where Steve Martin plays basketball with his daughter.

"That's the kind of dad I want to be," Cord said, rubbing his wet cheeks with a blanket. "But probably tennis instead of basketball."

"You're the country club Steve Martin."

"But not as funny."

"But not as funny," Sasha agreed sadly, and Cord pouted.

Sasha knew he would be a wonderful father. His niece and nephew worshipped him. Cord was goofy and spoke to them in funny accents, he convinced them the Easter Bunny was a close personal friend, he pretended to think the spring in a gag can of nuts was a real snake and screamed upon opening it at least twelve times in a row.

While they were in agreement that they wanted children, they had only ever talked about it in the vaguest of terms, without a time line or any sense of urgency, but in June Cord's best friend, Tim, had a baby and Cord started getting broody. Sasha had only ever heard of the phenomenon in women, or maybe chickens, but there was no other word for it, really. Cord wanted babies. Walking down the street, Cord started checking out strollers the way some other men might ogle women or motorcycles, letting out a low whistle and turning to watch them roll away. "You know that one's the new YOYO that folds up smaller than a suitcase," he might remark. Or "That's the UPPAbaby Vista. You can add a rumble seat for a second child underneath." He dragged Sasha to Picnic in Cobble Hill so that he could buy Tim a baby present, spending a solid hour selecting tiny pajamas and a little rattle shaped like a taxicab. When they visited Tim at his apartment, he even followed Tim into the baby's room to watch a diaper change, announcing that he might as well start learning how to do it.

Tim's wife looked at Sasha wide-eyed, and she shook her head with amusement. "We're not pregnant. He's just excited."

"About diapers?" she asked.

"Cord is a very enthusiastic person," Sasha snickered in reply.

Sasha didn't know what would happen to her business when she had a baby; she was a one-woman design shop without a human resources department, so she supposed she would just have to take a pause on projects and hope her clients would come back to her on the other side. She had one client, a Brooklyn-based company that made bed linens, that she had been with since their launch. She'd designed their logo, their website, their packaging, and their subway ads. Another client, a luxury hotel in Baltimore, had hired her to design everything from their restaurant menus and matchbooks to the eight-foot sign above the entrance. She had a craft beer brewery, an organic baby food meal-delivery service, a 3D-printing vendor, and an (admittedly weird) Chinese Swedish restaurant. She could get them all through their holiday campaigns and then, she hoped, take her maternity leave in the spring when things calmed down. It was terrifying to contemplate, but she didn't see any other options.

"I just picture you as this badass mom," Cord told her later that night. "Doing your job with a baby strapped to your chest."

"And then teaching the baby how to use Photoshop?" Sasha asked.

"We'll teach the baby to do both our jobs so we can cuddle all day," Cord promised, snuggling his nose into her hair.

"You seem like you're ready, huh?"

"I am. Are you?"

"I'm getting there." Sasha nodded. Her friends were starting to have babies too. It no longer seemed crazy or irresponsible, and there was something incredibly cool about imagining a tiny human that was half Cord, half her. She could already picture him talking to the baby in weird voices, pretending the bathtub was a wild ocean, dancing around the living room with a child in his arms. He would pour all his natural silliness and joy into parenthood, and their home would be happy and full.

Sasha called her mom to talk it through. "Sasha, there's never a perfect time to have a baby," her mother said. "Your dad and I were flat broke when we had Nate, but it all worked out. You're healthy, you're in love, and you're under forty. In my day they would classify anyone over thirty-five as a 'geriatric mother' and make you wear a shameful paper bracelet at the hospital. Get on the stick."

They decided to start trying to get pregnant. Sasha had friends who had begun telling people as soon as they decided, saying, "We pulled the goalie," and it always made Sasha laugh because what were they really saying except that they were about to have a lot of sex? So instead of informing the entire Stockton family that they were embarking on a bonefest, they just made a note of the start of her last period and had sex five days in a row two weeks later. It didn't work the first time around, and Sasha was surprised at the disappointment she felt at the brown spot in her underwear, but when her period was a single day late the second month she ran out to the drugstore and bought four pregnancy tests.

"You can't tell right away," Cord said, squinting at the tiny print on the instructions.

"But I'm too antsy to wait!" Sasha peed on the stick anyway and there next to the control line was the ghostly pink of a second line.

"That's not a line." Cord shook his head.

"I think it is, it's just very pale."

"I don't know," he said, frowning. "Let's wait and see if it gets darker." They put the test on the bathroom counter and cooked dinner and returned to peek at it again an hour later.

"It's still pale, but I think it's there," said Sasha.

"Oh, but look." Cord read the instructions again. "It says the results are only valid for the first thirty minutes."

"Argh, fine, we'll do it again in the morning. It says your pee is less diluted in the mornings anyway."

The next morning the ghostly line was still there, the day after that it was a bit darker, and by the time Sasha took the fourth pregnancy test it was solid magenta. She was pregnant.

If Cord had been a hen who was broody, Sasha suddenly felt like a hen who was nesting. Looking around the limestone, what she had previously seen as clutter now looked like proper hazards: the vintage oyster-and-pearl glass-topped coffee table, the midcentury tasseled Italian bar cart with its array of expensive poisons, the bone-china lamps with frizzled old wires snaking the floor. There were hundreds and hundreds of opportunities for cuts or bumps or electrocution, and Sasha felt like she might break out in hives just thinking about it.

"Cord, I think we should set up Georgiana's room for the nursery," she suggested over breakfast one morning. Cord was drinking coffee and eating a bowl of cereal—he had mixed three kinds together and was using what seemed to be a serving spoon to deliver the sugary mush to his mouth.

"Let's use my old room." He chewed. The milk looked gray.

"But your room is on the fourth floor and I think we want the baby on the third with us."

"Won't we just have the bassinet in our room for the first few months anyway? My mom always says we slept in a little basket on the floor of their room."

Sasha tried to imagine Tilda putting the baby on the floor in a basket and then surrounding it with matching napkins and flowers. *Tonight's theme is Forty Winks!* "Okay." Sasha tried a different approach. "I also heard you can hire a consultant to come in and baby-proof the apartment. They show you all the things that might be dangerous to a baby."

"Oh my God," Cord laughed. "We don't need to pay someone to tell us that we live in a death trap. Let's just not worry about this now. The kid won't be able to get into trouble until he can crawl, so that's a full year away." Cord lifted the cereal bowl with both hands and drank the last of the syrupy milk, a small Cocoa Krispie clinging to his lip.

"A year?"

"At least. Let's just enjoy being pregnant."

Enjoy being pregnant. Men so often did enjoy their side of it. But Sasha let it go. She really was too tired to argue, the pregnancy already sapping all of her energy. She had once read that ants took two hundred short naps every day, and that seemed enormously appealing to her. She was just exhausted, and according to the internet she wasn't even allowed a sugar-free Red Bull.

The following Wednesday Sasha rode her bike down to Vara's loft for a Drink and Draw. Of course she could only participate in half the evening's activities, but honestly, missing out on Vara's wine was no great loss. She set up her easel next to her friend Trevor and listened as everyone gossiped: A classmate had started sleeping with a prominent interior designer and suddenly was selling paintings all around the Upper East Side. Another classmate had been named artist in residence at the Studio Museum in Harlem, and everyone made a point to say how great it was while privately seething with jealousy. Sasha didn't have much to add; she had been in her own world lately, but she was happy just to lose herself in the conversation.

When the nude model arrived a murmur of approval rippled through the room. The model was hugely pregnant, at least eight months if not nine. The other artists were thrilled—drawing a figure in such an extreme state was exciting—but Sasha felt herself studying her body in a different way. Instead of the perfect basketball she'd come to imagine, the woman's belly was low and egg-shaped, her belly button poking out like a thimble. The veins in her breasts were visible, weaving blue and purple beneath her skin. As Sasha drew, she felt more awake than she had all week. Somehow seeing this naked stranger made her own pregnancy real.

"You're so quiet," Vara whispered, coming up behind her.

"I'm just drawing," Sasha answered, using her thumb to smudge the pencil lines of the model's hair.

"You're not drinking," Vara continued.

"Oh my God, Vara," Sasha snorted.

"Do you think your tits will get that big? Probably not. But, ugh, maternity clothes are so gross. Are you going to be one of those annoying pregnant ladies who suddenly starts wearing polka dots? Promise me you won't start dressing like some adult baby."

"Vara, when I have a reason to discuss the sartorial choices of breeders I will do so. Now stop it," Sasha said. Vara smiled smugly and left her alone.

Once Sasha was eight weeks along and had confirmed the pregnancy with a doctor who let her listen to the little hummingbird heart on the scanner, she called her mother to share the news.

"Oh, Sasha! This is so exciting! Tell me everything! How did it happen?"

"Mom! God, yuck! I'm not going to talk about that."

"Lord, no! I didn't mean literally. Sorry, don't tell me how it happened. Just bravo! Bravo to you both! Are you nauseous? Are you sleeping?"

"I'm good, Mom, just tired. But really excited. How are you? How's Dad?"

"Oh, well, we're fine. Hold on, honey, I'm just going to run downstairs." Sasha heard the muffled sound of her mother stomping down the carpeted steps and swooshing down the hall. A door creaked open and closed, followed by another creak and slam. Their dog barked anxiously. "Okay, I just didn't want your father to hear me."

"Where are you?"

"I'm in the pantry."

Sasha laughed. Her parents' pantry was notoriously overflowing with jars of pickles and red sauce, so she must have been jammed up against the heaving shelves. "Why?"

"Your father is being very private about this, but he has been having some shortness of breath. He has that inhaler for his asthma, but it just isn't helping."

"Jesus, Mom! Is he okay?"

"The other night he scared me to death. He coughed for an hour and was just wheezing."

"Okay, what day was this? Why didn't you tell me?"

"Oh, well, you know there was no reason to worry you. We already have the boys breathing down our necks here, so the last thing we need is to have you worry."

"Of course I'm going to worry, Mom. Can you get him to the doctor?"

"I made him an appointment for tomorrow, I just have to get him to go."

"Can I come along?"

"No need, sweetheart. Your father wouldn't want us to make a big deal about it. He keeps saying he's just out of shape. He gets winded starting the motor on the boat. You know how that thing only catches with a big yank. I'm always afraid he's going to give one of us a black eye the way he rips at it," she chuckled. "Okay, I'm going to get out of the pantry now. Don't tell your dad I told you. And I'm so excited about your news, Sasha. I'm sorry to have changed the subject when this should have been a happy conversation all about you!"

"Oh, I know you're happy for me, Mom. I can't wait for you to come help me set up the nursery."

"I'll be there whenever you're ready, Sasha."

They said goodbye, and Sasha hung up and frowned at her phone. She suddenly felt so far away. In a fit of frustration, Sasha stalked into the sitting room and scooped up two dozen jewel cases of old CDs, dumping them into a bag. She opened the skinny drawer of a marble-topped side table and gathered up the assorted ballpoint pens, ancient Post-its, and paper clips and dropped them in as well. She moved through the room like a madwoman, tossing in old magazines, a dusty embroidered pillow, a remote control that paired with no discernable device, a ziplock baggie full of old batteries, and a small ship in a bottle that could have been worth a fortune but most likely was not. She didn't care. Before anyone could catch her in the act, she stomped the bag down to the basement, let herself into the alley, and buried it in the neighbor's trash can.

ELEVEN

Georgiana

fter the conference in D.C., Georgiana sent Brady one text. It said, "I know you are married." She then turned off her phone and spent three days in bed, not sleeping but not quite awake, hurting and broken. On Monday morning, unable to hide any longer, she woke up at seven, showered and dressed, and packed her lunch for work. When she walked out of her apartment building, Brady was standing by the stoop holding two paper cups of coffee. She accepted one, barely able to look at his face for the pain it caused. They walked to the Promenade and sat on a bench to talk. It was clear and warm, and runners zoomed past them, nannies with strollers fed their small charges croissants out of wax-paper bags. Down the bluff, beyond the piers, the ferries chugged along the river, and a big orange barge sounded a mournful horn, as though complaining about all this life carrying on when Georgiana's heart was broken.

She felt hollowed out, her temples throbbing, her stomach tight, and she held the coffee in her lap. She couldn't imagine finding the strength to lift the cup to her lips.

"I'm so sorry, George," Brady started. "I thought you knew. And then by the time I realized you didn't I had no idea how to tell you. It felt too late."

"How would I have known? You never said anything."

"I know, I know. But I thought everyone at work knew. Amina used to work here. She was a project manager, and then a few years ago she got a job at the Gates Foundation in Seattle and had to take it. The plan was that I would try to get hired there too, or find another job and move, but I didn't want to. I love New York. I love my job. So we've just left it this way. I live here, she lives in Seattle, some weekends she comes here, some weekends I go there."

"So your malaria conference in Seattle was a trip to see her?"

"Well, no, I had the conference, but I stayed with her."

"And everyone at work knows about her. That's why nobody knows about us."

"I'm so sorry, Georgiana. I can't explain why I lied to you. I just didn't want it to end."

"Do you love her?"

"I do. But I love you too." Brady was looking at her intently, his fingers white as he gripped the edge of the bench. Georgiana shook her head and stood, walking alone down Columbia Heights to the office. She stumbled up the mansion stairs, through the great hall, past the grant team, and into her tiny maid's room, where she turned on her computer and spent the next several hours staring at a leaf stuck to the window.

She didn't get up from her desk all day, not even risking a trip to the kitchen or bathroom, where she might see him in the hall. The next day was Tuesday, and instead of playing tennis with Brady in the park she left early, changing into her running clothes and heading down to the Navy Yard, through the never-ending construction of Dumbo, drowning out her thoughts as music pounded through her earbuds. She couldn't sleep, she was literally sick with despair, so she ran in the mornings before work, grinding out five miles before seven, then another three or four in the evenings, until she felt shin splints starting and a tightness developing in her hips.

Lena had been traveling with her boss all week, but on Friday night she came over with two bottles of wine and a pizza from Fascati's. They sat on her roof deck and watched the sun set over Staten Island, and Lena put her head on her shoulder.

"I'm so sorry, Georgiana. He's a fuckboy."

"The thing is, I can't make myself believe he is. I was so sure he fell in love with me."

"But he lied to you. That whole time he was hiding this huge thing. Have you seen him?"

"I saw him across the hall a few times today but just put my head down. I can't look at him. Not because I'm so angry, but because I still want him so much. It's humiliating. How could I be so pathetic?"

"You're not pathetic, Georgiana. You're heartbroken."

Of course, Amina had been there all along if Georgiana had just known where to look for her. In the tiny maid's room, Georgiana was surrounded by back issues of the company newsletter, years and years of stories about TB screenings in Solomon Islands, reproductive health in Haiti, an oral cholera vaccine program in the Democratic Republic of Congo. As Georgiana pored over the archive, she saw Amina's photo again and again, her name in the tiny captions. Amina teaching in a classroom, pointing at a colorful anatomy drawing. Amina with a clipboard, crouched over a cooler, counting doses of medication alongside a man in a khaki vest. Had Georgiana known about Amina on some level? Had Brady been fooling her, or had she been fooling herself?

The next Tuesday after work Brady caught up to her as she was walking home on Hicks Street. "Can we talk?"

Georgiana felt the blood rush to her face and a painful ache that shot from her throat to her groin. She nodded and took him back to her apartment. As soon as the door closed they began to kiss. She met his lips hungrily with her own, tears streamed down her face, but she didn't stop. She cried and kissed him and pulled off her shirt and her bra and her pants. He kissed her neck and her stomach and lay her across the bed and went down on her. She was overwhelmed by him, by getting to touch him when she was so sure she never would again. He entered her and she kissed him again, and then they finished and lay spent and silent in her bed as the sun set. They ate cheese and crackers for dinner like invalids and slept curled together in a knot, and Georgiana felt it was the first time she had truly rested in a week.

Soon it was as though nothing had changed, but something had. In a strange way there was a new intensity and seriousness between them. They stopped playing tennis together—it felt like a waste of time when they could be alone—and instead they spent hours and hours in bed. Brady was tender with her, combing her hair from her eyes, sometimes looking at her like he was afraid she was going to melt away beneath him. It was impossible to know how it might end. Would Brady leave Amina? Would Georgiana spend her entire youth desperately in love with a man whose heart resided thousands of miles away? They never spoke of it. When they were together Georgiana was too afraid of breaking the spell and watching him vanish like smoke.

BRADY'S APARTMENT didn't feel like another woman's apartment. The first time Georgiana went over she was nervous, sure there would be a dresser covered in perfume bottles, framed photos on a shelf, tampons and makeup in the bathroom. And while there were tampons under the sink, it was not the home of a woman. It was Brady's. Full of maps and thick rugs that he bought in Morocco, a brass Buddha from Cambodia, a neat row of basketball sneakers and running shoes by the door. His refrigerator was full of beer and hot sauce, a bicycle hung from the wall, his bed was made with a neat blue coverlet, and his bedside table was stacked with biographies. Georgiana wondered how it had looked before Amina moved out. Did they have wedding china she took to Seattle? A set of champagne flutes? A crystal cake stand that no single, takeout-eating man would ever think to buy for himself? She wondered if the apartment in Seattle bore traces of Brady, if there was a stick of Old Spice, a razor, a box of condoms.

She couldn't bring herself to think about that part. The fact that the person she loved was also having sex with someone else. They knew better than to discuss it, but it was a certainty she lived with. When Brady came home from a weekend in Seattle, she had to bite her tongue, had to pinch herself to keep from thinking about him lying on top of his wife, kissing her face and holding her hand, both of them slick with sweat.

Sometimes Georgiana felt she was trying to memorize Brady, preparing for him to disappear and leave her dreaming about the small freckles on his back. But other times it felt like their future together stretched out before them, and she saw Brady trying it out and flirting with that vision of life. They had discovered that they both liked to sleep the same way, with the big and second toe of one foot locked around the Achilles above the other foot's heel. "If we had babies I bet they'd like to sleep that way too," Brady said.

"If we had babies they would be pretty great athletes." Georgiana smiled.

"I'd want them to have your hair."

"I'd want them to have your face."

"I'd want them to have your breasts."

"That might be awkward if they were boys. Tiny little baby boys with a woman's breasts."

"I would love them anyway," Brady promised solemnly. "Our tiny little baby boys with beautiful breasts and long brown hair and man faces with five o'clock shadows."

When Amina came to visit, and Georgiana couldn't spend the weekend with Brady, her entire body thrummed with misery. She went to dinner with Kristin and Lena and tried to listen as they discussed Kristin's boss, who was always wearing AirPods in meetings; she played tennis with her mother at the Casino and they had lunch afterward at the apartment, sitting silently as her mother read Cord's Yale alumni magazine with a highlighter, looking for the offspring of social acquaintances. When Darley asked about Brady, Georgiana shrugged, mumbling something about things petering out. She couldn't tell her sister that Brady was married, couldn't tell her that she was knowingly sleeping with someone's husband.

ON MONDAY Georgiana awoke happy: Amina was leaving and Brady belonged to her again. When she passed him in the hall on the way to the library, he reached out and squeezed her arm and they grinned at each other like idiots before swiftly scurrying along in opposite directions.

Now that Georgiana was listening, Amina was everywhere. At lunch Brady's friends from the first floor mentioned Seattle all the time in conversation; they referred to him in the second person plural, asking, "Are you guys going back to Maine for Memorial Day?" or "Are you guys leasing that Prius?" Their colleagues knew Brady so well, while Georgiana felt they barely even knew her name.

Nobody at the office ever asked Georgiana's weekend plans or even commented on a new sweater. They were friendly, but they weren't her friends. It was mind-boggling in some ways. She had grown up in Brooklyn, in this very neighborhood, and yet the men and women in her office barely resembled those she knew in her real life. While her parents played golf, her coworkers did yoga. While her parents and their friends vacationed in Florida, her coworkers vacationed in Ecuador and Costa Rica. It was BMW versus Subaru, Whole Foods versus farmers market, shiny wingtips versus Birkenstocks with socks. There was one woman named Sharon, who worked on the first floor. Sharon had short gray hair—not fashionable icy gray but the yellowish gray of the unkempt; she wore linen that always seemed to be wrinkled and creased around her waist and armpits; and she was frequently coming up and giving people unsolicited back rubs. Georgiana knew she was a nice person, and yet she found herself waiting with vague horror for Sharon to finish rubbing her shoulders and move on to someone else. There was another woman, Mary, who had a glossy blond bob and always smelled of French perfume but exclusively wore clothing she had bought in Nepal—silk harem pants with a dropped crotch and embroidered tops. She wore a pin on her jacket that said FREE TIBET and had a small plastic Buddha with a cell phone on her desk. There were men with long, gray ponytails and small John Lennon glasses. There were women Georgiana's age with pierced septums and astrological tattoos. Georgiana would no sooner get a tattoo than shave her head.

While it would be easy to attribute her lack of work friends to cultural difference, it was also because of Brady. How could she entertain a real friendship when her entire work life was a charade, the exact place she needed to be most careful, the nexus of her and Brady's terrible secret? Ever since the conference in D.C. she felt that Meg on the grant-writing team was trying to befriend her. When Meg saw her at the lunch table, she sat next to her; they chatted amiably about Meg's deadlines, about Meg's schedule, about Meg's upcoming trip to Pakistan. Typically, only project managers were on-site, but they were competing for a massive new ten-year grant in women's health from USAID, so Meg was going along to get a leg up on the proposal. It would be her first time in-country, her first time in the Middle East, a huge step for her career. It did not go unnoticed by Georgiana that they only talked about Meg at these lunches, but in some ways that made the friendship easier. Georgiana didn't have to squirm when discussing her weekend plans ("Oh, I plan to have sex four times and eat Thai food naked with our colleague, Brady, remember him?"). Georgiana knew that her relationship with Brady was creating little barriers between her and her other friends too. Lena and Kristin thought she'd broken up with him when she found out about his wife. She lied when she was spending Saturday nights with him, claiming that she was helping babysit Poppy and Hatcher, that she was tired, that she was not in the mood to go out. They worried she was depressed and tried to talk her into joining them, but she closed them out and silenced her phone. Lying to Darley was logistically easier, since Darley was too busy with her kids to beg her to go to any parties on weekends, but the shame she felt knowing how much Darley would disapprove made her preemptively annoyed at her sister. Just because Darley was lucky enough to have met the love of her life in business school didn't mean it was that simple for the rest of the world. It was easy to feel high and mighty about the sanctity of marriage when you'd never fallen deeply and painfully in love with the wrong person.

When Georgiana found out Brady was going on the Pakistan trip, she was irritated. "Weren't you just gone?" she asked with a vague whine in her voice.

"I haven't been on a project in months. It's the best part of the job—getting out in the field."

"How long do you think you'll be there?"

"Probably a month?"

"This is the worst thing that's ever happened to me." Georgiana pouted.

"Then count yourself lucky." Brady kissed her on the nose. "Put WhatsApp on your phone and we can talk all the time."

The weekend before Brady left, they barely got out of bed. They laughed and joked that they were sex camels, storing up all the sex they could in their humps before Brady went off to the desert. On Sunday when Georgiana came out of the shower, Brady guiltily hid something behind his back.

"What are you doing?" she asked.

"I'm writing you notes," he admitted. "I'm going to hide them all around your apartment so that you find them while I'm away. Now either close your eyes or go back into the bathroom."

Georgiana grinned and retreated to the bathroom to comb her hair in front of the mirror, listening to Brady move around her living room, lifting pillows and opening and closing drawers. That night after he left, she found one in the pantry, taped to the bread, that said, "You have nice buns."

Four days after Georgiana kissed Brady goodbye, the company founder called an all hands meeting in the second-floor dining room. When Georgiana walked in, she could immediately tell something terrible had happened. People looked stricken, confused. Sharon, the receptionist, was clutching a tissue and wiping her nose as tears leaked down from behind her glasses. Somehow, Georgiana knew. It was about Brady. She could feel it whoosh through her, a cold pain that shot down her arms, shot through her stomach. The founder's voice cracked as he spoke, a sob caught in his throat. He told them that Meg from grant writing, a project manager named Divya, and Brady had boarded a flight from Lahore in the east of Pakistan, bound for Karachi. The pilot reported technical difficulties, and the plane turned to go back to Lahore. Thirty-five miles outside the city the plane crashed. There were no survivors.

When Georgiana heard the words "no survivors," she had to put her hand against the wall to steady herself. Her vision narrowed to a tiny pin of light, and the floor seemed to go sideways under her feet. She felt the old wallpaper against her palm and stood in the dark, unsure if she was standing or falling. When the pinprick opened back up and she could see again, all around her people held hands to their mouths in horror. Georgiana couldn't look at anyone. She couldn't go back to her desk. She quietly walked down the stairs and through the foyer and out onto the street. She didn't know where she was going.

Brady had died. His body, his freckled back, the toes he slept with latched to his ankle were all burned to ash somewhere Georgiana had never seen, would likely never go. She would never hold him again; she would never be able to see his face or kiss his mouth or even mourn over the body she had worshipped with such fervor. She stumbled up the stone steps of her childhood home and used her keys to get in. She was crying too hard to breathe or see, and she dropped her bag in the hall outside her room and crawled into her closet. She pulled her clothing from the hangers and buried her face in the musty fabric until she couldn't breathe. She kicked at the wooden beaver she had hidden. She had been a child, a stupid child, but Brady had seen her. Her love for him had filled her with shame, but also with a power that burned hot and bright. And now he was gone, and she would never feel that power again.

Georgiana cried until her stomach ached, until she could no longer see, until her face was swollen and her skin was mottled. She didn't know how many hours had passed when she heard a thump on the stairs and slowly the closet door opened. It was Sasha.

"Georgiana, what happened? Are you all right?"

"I did something terrible," said Georgiana. And she told her.

TWELVE

Darley

Before I was born I had a tail," Poppy said seriously, looking into Darley's eyes. They were eating dinner at the little restaurant called Tutt's on Hicks Street and Poppy had a large dollop of tomato sauce on her chin.

"You had a tail?" Darley asked, unsure if they were operating in the realm of fantasy or reality.

"I had a tail just like a tadpole."

"We both had tails like tadpoles," Hatcher agreed, carefully picking every olive and pepper out of his salad and placing them on the table.

"I could swim fast fast fast, and then I was an egg," Poppy said.

Darley looked quizzically at Malcolm.

"You know you didn't really have a tail, right? Humans don't have tails," Malcolm explained.

"I did! I had a tail like a tadpole and then I was an egg and then I grew in Mommy's belly!" Poppy replied indignantly.

Darley started laughing. "Malcolm," she whispered, "she means when she was a sperm."

The school had sent home a note saying that they would begin talking about health and human sexuality in science class. The section must have started. Darley didn't want to be an old lady about it, but back when she was a kid, they didn't take sex ed until the fifth grade. Kindergarten seemed so young. But she supposed it was better they learn it at school than on the internet. She just hoped Poppy wouldn't start talking about sperm at the racket club.

EVER SINCE DARLEY was a student thirty years ago, the Henry Street School had hosted an annual auction in the fall to raise money for their scholarship fund. The parents dressed in their finest and crowded into the school gym to bid tens of thousands of dollars on meals prepared by celebrity chefs, courtside seats to the Knicks, boxes at concerts, weeks on yachts, and even once the chance to have a child taught to swim by an Olympic medalist who'd appeared on boxes of Wheaties. In years past, the Stocktons had won a ski trip, a hot-air balloon ride, a family photo session with a *National Geographic* photographer, and a frankly hideous painting made by Cord's fifth-grade class that cost them four thousand dollars.

Families were encouraged to donate generously and bid competitively, and it was a chance to truly show off your best connections. If your son-in-law was in MLB management, you secured a meet-and-greet with the Yankees. If you were on the board of the Mark Morris Dance Group, you arranged a living-room performance with the premier dancers. Since most everyone had a second home either on Long Island or in Litchfield County, it wasn't special enough to offer that up as a trip, but if you had a third home in Aspen, Nantucket, or St. John, then you best make that your annual gift. Even better if you lent out your plane to get there.

The Stocktons had figured out their go-to gift when Darley was in middle school and the family had bought more property along the waterfront. They would offer up a themed party in one of the unoccupied buildings—an Oscars party in the vacant Brooklyn Heights movie theater, a masquerade ball in the former home of Jane's Carousel, a murder mystery evening in what was once part of the Navy Yard.

This year Tilda had outdone herself and arranged an Old Hollywood night at the former Hotel Bossert on Montague Street. The hotel had been one of the properties sold when the Jehovah's Witnesses began to divest themselves of Brooklyn Heights real estate in 2008, and the Stockton family had participated in the five-year bidding war to secure the property. (Rumor had it that the total cost of the place was barely shy of a hundred million.) It was a stunning building, with a marble lobby, massive chandeliers, and a two-level restaurant on the roof where players for the Dodgers had famously celebrated a World Series win in the 1950s. The hotel hadn't been open to the public in thirty years, and the neighborhood was quivering with curiosity about the place. It was clearly grand and smack in the middle of everything, and honestly Tilda probably could have donated an evening of eating peanut butter sandwiches on the floor of the lobby and people would have bid like crazy just to get in the door.

There were two parts to the school auction: the live auction and the silent auction. In recent years they had migrated the silent auction to an app so that people could mingle and drink and simultaneously bid on their phones. Darley had looked over the catalog with her mother ahead of time, and they strategized about what they might bid on to be polite and what they might actually hope to win. They agreed that in the live auction Tilda would bid on the ten-course dinner with celebrity chef Tom Stork because Tom's children were in Poppy's class, and they sometimes saw him at drop-off. In the silent auction she would bid on the vacation home on Nashaun, the private island near Martha's Vineyard, because they had friends in the Forbes family who also had a home there, and it would be fun to get together. (Nashaun had only thirty houses, and they all belonged to Forbes. Aside from marrying off one of her children to a Forbes, the auction was Tilda's only chance for a house there.) Of course, to be polite they would bid on the artworks made by both Poppy's and Hatcher's classes—a quilt with the children's faces silk-screened on the patches, and a canvas sling chair that the children had signed with their wobbly names. They hoped they wouldn't win either of them, but it would hurt the feelings of their teachers if they didn't sell for at least four figures.

Every year the auction opened with the sale of a small teddy bear wearing a Henry Street School shirt. Though it was worth about ten dollars, it was a show of good faith to bid it up and kick off the evening with a splash. The higher they could bid the bear the better the entire fundraiser might go. Chip and Tilda never jumped into that bidding war. The teddy bear was all about swagger, and they left that to the true heavy hitters at the school, the ones whose names were emblazoned on wings of the New York Public Library or athletic facilities at Harvard College.

The night of the auction Malcolm stayed home to watch the children, and Darley walked over to the school with her parents. Her mother looked gorgeous, her blond hair having been sprayed into a French twist and her makeup professionally applied. She was wearing a long green gown and carrying a purse so tiny Darley wondered if she'd even been able to squeeze her phone in there. Darley had bought an outfit for her cousin Archie's wedding in a few weeks, high-waisted silk pants with a matching top, and since there would be no guest crossover, she had decided she could wear it twice. As long as nobody posted pictures from the night on social media, she could get away with it.

When they checked in at the school gate, a team of young party planners showed them how to download the app onto their phones, how to enter a bid, and how to set it so that you could automatically top any bid made. "That way if you really want something you don't have to watch your phone all night to make sure nobody else gets it!" the woman explained.

"Should we do that for the house on Nashaun?" Tilda asked Darley.

"No, what if someone goes insane? We'll just watch it closely for the last twenty minutes of the night," Darley advised. It stressed her out to think of her parents spending all this money at an auction when there was a decent chance she'd be begging them to pay the kids' tuition at the end of the semester.

"Let's be reasonable about it." Chip frowned. "If I see either of you slinging back the pinot grigio and poking away at your phones, I'm going to confiscate them."

"Oh, Chip, don't be ridiculous," Tilda laughed. "You know I only drink chardonnay."

A handful of other parents from Poppy's and Hatcher's classes were already there, and Darley, Chip, and Tilda joined them at the bar for a cocktail. So many families at the Henry Street School had also gone to either Grace Church or Plymouth for nursery, so they all already knew one another and had spent the past few years arranging playdates and potlucks and different school fundraisers.

As they waited for drinks and chatted with the crowd, Chip scrolled through the silent auction items on his phone and spotted something Darley had somehow missed. "Hey, Darley, did you see this?" He pointed to a listing: "High Flying Adventure—Join an experienced pilot in a Cirrus SR22 for an afternoon excursion. From Montauk to Hot Springs, the world is your oyster, four hours in the air with a decadent picnic for two."

"I didn't see that," Darley said in surprise. "It must have been added today."

"Who donated the item?" Tilda squinted at Chip's phone.

"I don't know, I can't think of any lower-school parents with an SR22. I think most of the parents in Poppy's class use corporate planes or just do NetJets." Darley looked around the room curiously. "Okay if I go investigate?"

Chip nodded, and she headed off toward the cluster of women holding iPads near the stage. Sharon from the development office pointed her over to Cy Habib, a handsome man in an Hermès tie sitting at a high top with a group of upper school parents.

"Excuse me." Darley approached and tapped his elbow. "I'm Darley Stockton and my kids are in the lower school. Did you donate the ride on the SR22?"

"I did, are you bidding?" He stood to shake her hand and grinned, revealing a beautiful white smile.

"I might bid! I had to meet the owner."

"Guilty as charged. Insane I bought the thing. You know what they say: If it flies or floats, rent it."

That was, in fact, not the expression. Darley had heard it a million times: "If it flies, floats, or fucks, rent it." Paying for a plane, a boat, or a wife was a waste of money. She appreciated this stranger's sense of decorum.

"It's a beautiful plane. It's so luxurious on the inside, like a sports car—all that leather," Darley said.

"The first time I saw the gull wing doors I was a goner. And the avionics . . ." Cy shook his head.

"And the parachute. I love that the plane has its own parachute!"

"You know their slogan, 'Chute Happens.'" They both laughed.

"Do you work in the industry, or are you a weekend warrior?"

"I work in airlines. Then I leave the office and go fly. What can I say? I wish I were a more well-rounded person, but my golf game is terrible." Cy smiled and Darley grinned back. "What about you? Are you in the industry?"

"Oh, no," Darley demurred. "My husband is, but I'm just an avgeek."

"Half the people in this room have worse and more expensive habits. I think we're doing okay."

They chatted for a few more minutes before Cy gave her his card and invited her and Malcolm to join him on the plane anytime. Darley made her way back to her parents, glowing happily.

"So, who owns the plane?" Tilda asked conspiratorially. A Cirrus SR22 was worth at least a million dollars, and Tilda made it her business to know who had that kind of cash lying around for their hobbies.

"His name is Cy Habib. They live over on Gardner Place."

"What kind of name is Habib?" Chip frowned.

"It's Middle Eastern," Darley answered.

"Ah," Chip said, nodding, as if this confirmed a particularly clever suspicion.

Darley snorted in annoyance. But it wasn't surprising to her that one of the other parents who flew planes was a person of color. This was something she and Malcolm had reflected on, how diverse the world of American aviation was. Sometimes it started young, because children of immigrants just had more exposure to long international flights as kids, heading to India or Singapore or South Africa to visit their grandparents. While Darley had just walked three blocks to see Pip and Pop, Malcolm was flying to South Korea, poking his head into the cockpit to meet the pilots, affixing plastic wings to his carefully pressed shirt. There was also something glamorous about flying overseas, and once you got jet fuel in your veins it was impossible to shake. People who loved to fly were hooked for life.

When the live auction began, Darley's parents put down their cocktails and prepared their paddles. As the auctioneer introduced the Henry Street teddy bear and opened the bidding at a thousand, Darley felt a small thrill. Was it weird to get excited watching people spend money? She supposed it was no different from watching people who threw dollar bills in the air at a nightclub. Everyone liked watching cash splash about.

The NBA player and his wife raised their paddle over and over and ended up buying the teddy bear for eight thousand dollars, and the evening was off and running. They quickly sold a walk-on part on a soap opera, a guitar played by Bruce Springsteen, a 1959 Masters flag signed by Arnold Palmer, box seats to a Billie Eilish concert, and a kid's Spider-Man costume signed by Stan Lee.

"Damn it, we should have bid on that for Hatcher," Tilda whispered to Darley.

"You bought him one three years ago." Darley rolled her eyes. "We have it in a box so he won't try to wear it."

When the auctioneer announced the private dinner cooked by Tom Stork, Tilda grabbed her paddle and stood up straight. Tom himself was stationed at a nearby table, and Tilda smiled broadly in his direction. Darley cringed as Tom downed the rest of his drink and left the room, ostensibly to go to the bar but clearly to avoid the awkwardness of everyone staring at him.

"What's the point of bidding if he can't see it?" Tilda lamented. She raised her paddle up to five thousand dollars and then dropped out, letting it go to a couple on the other side of the room. "I do hope his wife tells him we bid." Tilda pouted and pulled her phone out of her handbag. "God, Darley, I can't see a thing on this app. How much is the Nashaun house up to on the silent auction?"

"Do you have your reading glasses?" Darley asked, looking over her mother's shoulder.

"No, they don't fit in my handbag." She held the phone as far away from her face as she could and lifted her chin, tapping away.

The rest of the party passed in a blur of cheek kisses and slightly sloppy conversations with the teachers and heads of school. Darley felt sorry for them, resigned to sipping single glasses of warm white wine so they could stay sober enough to remember all the parents' names. As the nine o'clock bell for the final auction bids approached, the Stocktons made their way over to the class donations to see the quilt and chair in person. A few familiar parents were hanging out by the kindergarten auction items, and an enormously pregnant woman was sitting in the canvas chair with the signatures on it.

"I've claimed this!" the woman laughed as they approached. "It is literally the only thing that has made my back stop hurting in nine months, so I have my husband obsessively bidding!"

"You deserve it!" Darley said, privately thrilled they wouldn't have to end up with it. She hoped someone would grow similarly attached to the quilt. As the minutes ticked ever closer to the bell, the guests became increasingly attuned to their phones, wanting to make sure nobody swooped in to steal their auction items at the buzzer.

"I think we're going to get Nashaun," Tilda whispered excitedly in Darley's ear.

"Someone is coming after me on this chair," the pregnant women's husband muttered.

"Who would do that when you're sitting right here?" Darley asked, looking around. She half expected to see another pregnant lady glowering at them.

The clock struck nine and the room erupted in cheers and groans. "We got Nashaun!" Tilda waved her phone happily in the air, teetering on her heels.

"Nooooo, I lost the chair!" the man lamented.

"What?" The pregnant woman looked like she was about to cry. "I have to get up?"

Chip helped her husband gently pull her from the soft canvas sling. She was wearing flats, and Darley could see that her pregnant ankles were swollen. Darley checked the app and clocked that her mother's party at the Hotel Bossert had sold for forty-four hundred dollars, a terrific price. Tilda went to collect her certificate for the Nashaun vacation from the desk but came back five minutes later biting her lip. "We should go," she whispered to Chip.

"Why? Did you get the certificate for the house? Did you give them the credit card?" Chip frowned.

"Yes, but we also won the chair."

"What? How?"

"I had ticked off the box to automatically outbid. We paid thirty-two hundred dollars."

"For a canvas chair with writing all over it?" Chip asked, turning red.

"We can give it to Cord and Sasha." Tilda shrugged. Darley looked at her dad sympathetically, but Tilda cut her off. "Don't be like that, Chip. It's all for a good cause." Done feeling remorseful, Tilda clicked ahead of them, out the door and home, followed by Darley and Chip carrying the flimsy, graffiti-covered chair.

WHEN DARLEY READ that Bill Gates was giving his children less than 1 percent of his fortune, a mere ten million dollars each, her first thought was *That's still too much*. Inheritance had a way of ruining people. Obviously being born into poverty was incomparably worse, but since both Darley's mother and father had come from great wealth, she had scads of first and second cousins who demonstrated just how badly money could fuck you up. She had cousins who had gone into law, politics, and medicine, sure, but she also had cousins who did absolutely nothing. Cousins who traveled and partied, cousins who pretended to work, masking their interest in shopping with careers as "collectors," day-trading their money nine to five while gambling it away at night playing online poker. One cousin married an artist and spent her days watching him work, referring to herself unironically as "his muse." Another cousin had used all his money to fund a start-up making trampolines for yachts.

Darley's nuclear family had dealt with their great privilege in mostly respectable ways, Cord joining her at Yale and then Stanford business school, Georgiana attending Brown and studying Russian literature at Columbia, for a master's. Darley hated to think of her own expensive education being squandered, hated to think she was using her exceptional advantages to while away days in the apartment arranging pediatric dentist appointments and looking after her husband's dry cleaning. But the problem was, having kids so close together was career killing.

The first pregnancy and return from maternity leave were brutal. Darley had debilitating morning sickness. She was an associate at Goldman Sachs and was expected to be at her desk by seven each morning. Like Malcolm, she was in the Investment Banking division. She was working like a dog in the associates pool, logging long hours, begging to be assigned as many projects as she could, desperate to differentiate herself from the pack and find her way into the Sector Coverage Group to focus on airlines. Her pregnancy with Poppy was a surprise and she was determined not to let it derail her. She got too carsick to ride in a taxi, so she took the subway to the office each morning, but the long stretch from High Street on the A train made her feel so woozy she had to get off at Canal Street and throw up in a platform trash can. She would arrive at work pale and sweaty, her mouth tasting of vomit and gum. The only way she could quell her nausea was to suck on little sour candies, which she carried in the leather pocket of her phone case, quietly slipping them into her mouth when none of the analysts or associates were looking. Once she started showing, her male colleagues seemed visibly alarmed and disgusted. "Are you sure you're not having twins?" Or worse, "Isn't stress bad for the baby? I would never let my wife pull all-nighters if she were pregnant." She was so afraid her water would break at work that she kept spare towels and underwear in a gym bag under her desk.

After Poppy was born, Darley returned to work six weeks later. Her colleagues asked her if she'd enjoyed her "vacation," they complained relentlessly about the extra work they'd picked up on her behalf, and when she tried to go to the nurse's office to use the breast pump they would all laugh and clench their fists, pretending to milk a cow while making squirting noises with their mouths.

Darley stuck it out for six months. She pumped in airplane bathrooms on cross-country flights. She left Poppy with Soon-ja and stored her expressed breast milk behind the valet desk at hotels and then FedExed it home. She missed bedtime and bath time and the first time Poppy crawled. She learned to keep cotton discs in her bra so that she wouldn't stain her silk blouses when meetings went long and she missed her scheduled pumping time. If she was honest with herself, she wanted to get pregnant again. She was falling apart at work. It wasn't a life. She couldn't do it anymore. She was just broken, and another baby gave her an off-ramp. Everyone would understand why she quit.

Malcolm was great about it when she revealed she was pregnant with Hatcher. She could stop working and raise the kids. This meant that for the foreseeable future they would be a one-income family. It occurred to Darley late in the game that when she gave up her trust fund, she didn't fully consider what that meant for her as a woman. While she had spent her childhood asking her parents for money to go on ski trips, to buy clothing, to pay for dinners and sunglasses and haircuts, she had begun to draw from her account in business school, leasing a car, buying a new laptop, joining the expensive gym that had a steam room. Once she got married, that access was gone, the money disappeared in a puff of cedar-scented steam, and her only bank account was the one she shared with Malcolm.

While she had read an article in *The New York Times* about how the happiest couples had "yours, mine, ours" accounts, that felt silly to Darley when Malcolm was the only one getting paychecks. So instead, they just had matching American Express cards linked to the same line of credit—Malcolm's. Now every time she charged eight hundred dollars at the dermatologist, a thousand dollars at Bergdorf's, four hundred at the SoHo hair salon, Malcolm saw it. She felt it was like peeing with the door open: something some couples did, but that was dangerously unsexy.

Still, it had worked. They had a beautiful apartment, they took nice vacations, the kids were being educated, and on the nights that Darley and Malcolm slept in the same bed they tucked themselves together like two silver spoons in a drawer. But with Malcolm unemployed, their life was too expensive. He needed a job. She needed a job. Or she needed to tell her parents she had been wrong all along.

THIRTEEN

Sasha

Sasha had hoped that being born a hundred and twenty years after the American Civil War might exonerate her from hearing cannon fire at close range, but alas, Cord's cousin Archie was getting married at a yacht club in Greenwich and the entire family was going. His father's assistant rented them a sprawling house on the water with six bedrooms, so that if Poppy and Hatcher shared a room, Berta could come along and babysit after the ceremony. Darley and Malcolm drove up in one car with the kids in the back plugged into an endless stream of Disney+. Cord's parents drove their car with Berta in the back seat, so Cord and Sasha invited Georgiana to ride with them. Sasha had been trying to talk to Georgiana ever since she found her in the closet, but it was clear Georgiana regretted having told her. Sasha had reached out to hug her in her bedroom that day, but Georgiana had pushed past her in a hurry. She called her the next morning to check in, but Georgiana didn't call back. She sent her a text inviting her to get a beer, but she didn't reply. Sasha felt totally stuck, unsure how she could possibly help someone who so clearly didn't want her to.

———

They met Georgiana at the parking garage on Henry Street, and she threw her duffle in the back, crushing Sasha's carefully arranged hanging bag with her dress in it. Sasha offered her the front seat, but Georgiana rolled her eyes and passed, choosing instead to sit in back wearing her headphones and looking out the window. On the ride Sasha caught Cord up on the latest gossip with her family. Her dad's breathing issues seemed better, so her parents had gone away for the night and asked her brother Nate to watch their neurotic dog. When Nate brought her back in the morning she ran into the house, tail wagging, so utterly thrilled to be home again that she promptly vomited in the kitchen, but instead of the usual puddle of regurgitated kibble, she vomited up a pair of black lace underwear, and thus Sasha's mother now suspected that Nate had a new girlfriend.

"Why do dogs love underwear so much?" Cord asked, laughing.

"Because they are perverts." Sasha wrinkled her nose.

"They are," Cord agreed. "But I kind of get it."

Sasha snorted and went to swat him playfully but then remembered Georgiana in the back, lost in her own sad world.

When they got to the house, Cord's parents had already taken the master suite on the first floor and set Berta up with the suite at the end of the hall. The kids needed to be either next to Darley or across the way, so Cord and Sasha took the smallest room, the one with a double bed under an eave; if Sasha lifted her legs too high she would hit the ceiling. She had bought a new dress—a long, silk, ice-blue sheath with spaghetti straps that would wrinkle easily—so she laid it flat on their bed and did her makeup in her underwear, waiting until the last moment to slither into it, her baby bump still too small to be noticeable. They made it to the ceremony just in time and sat in the back row, shielding their eyes with the programs as the afternoon sun sparkled on the water. Archie was apparently an avid sailor, and they fired off the dreaded cannon after their vows. Then some men in uniforms (probably just old members of the club) did a twenty-one-gun salute over the bay. Sasha giggled to herself, imagining them accidentally sinking a Sunfish, but she was pretty sure they were using blanks.

Archie was marrying a woman from Grosse Pointe, who the Stockton family all knew from their club on Jupiter Island. She was actually the younger sister of the girl Archie dated as a teenager, and Cord quietly wondered if they ever acknowledged that Archie used to give his fiancée's sister hickeys out by the gazebo at night or if that entire area of conversation was a complete no-fly zone. The sister was at the wedding with her husband and three little girls, all wearing massive hair bows, so it seemed like nobody was going to throw a punch over it.

More than half the guests at the party were members of the Jupiter club (the other half were probably all members of the same golf club), and as the wedding party processed back down the aisle and out to the dock for photos, Sasha suddenly realized how long the night was going to be. She was keeping her pregnancy a secret until their anatomy scan and hadn't told anyone aside from her mother. That meant she would have to spend the whole reception fake drinking and confused about which shellfish she could eat. *You're not in a coal mine*, she chastised herself. *Buck up.* It was a beautiful, clear evening, the boats rocked on the shimmering bay, cheerful music from a stringed quartet floated through the crowd, and the pop of champagne bottles filled the air.

Archie's mother came by with the wedding planner and asked the Stockton family to stay together—the photographer would be taking pictures of the groom's side shortly. Sasha and Cord were starving, so they made a beeline for the waitstaff, who were starting to circulate with appetizers. Cord had long ago perfected the art of eating like an absolute pig at weddings. He loved crispy coconut shrimp and tiny beef Wellington, skewers of chicken and little lattice chips topped with tuna tartare, so he quickly identified where the servers were emerging from the tent and stood nearby so that he could intercept each tray. He was shameless. He would stride right up to a group of strangers helping themselves to golden triangles of fluffy pastry exclaiming, "Oh! What do we have here?" even when he'd already sampled half a dozen. Georgiana was usually just as bad. They ate like wild animals together and delighted in chasing the waiters, while their mother was obviously horrified, but tonight Georgiana only stared glassily out at the water. Sasha wished desperately she could tell Cord his sister's secret, wished he could try to help her through this, but she knew better. Georgiana had trusted her.

Cord had just put a martini glass filled with crab legs in Georgiana's hand when a server rushed out of the tent holding a clattering rack of champagne flutes. Georgiana drew back to get out of the way and bumped her elbow into a tent pole, dumping the entire glass of crab and cocktail sauce down her front.

"Oh shit," she swore. Bright red tomato juice soaked her chest, her dress ruined. Cord grabbed a stack of white serviettes, but it was beyond help. No amount of blotting could save her.

"Oh, Georgiana, the photos are in five minutes," her mother said with dismay.

"I'll go see if they have Shout wipes or something in the ladies' room." Sasha excused herself and dashed inside. There were small baskets in the lounge filled with breath mints, bobby pins, hair spray, and tissues. Georgiana came up behind her.

"Anything?"

"No, only hair spray and mints."

"Here, I'll just wet a paper towel."

"You can't use water on silk. You'll completely destroy your dress."

"I don't think it can get any worse," Georgiana said despondently.

"If you bring it to the dry cleaner they can probably fix it. But if you put a wet paper towel on it you'll make a water ring that won't come out."

"Fuck." Georgiana looked glumly in the mirror.

"Here, trade dresses." Sasha reached behind her back and unbuttoned herself.

"Oh my God, no way."

"I have another dress at the house. You can put this on and do family photos and I'll just take an Uber back and change. I'll be here for dinner. I don't know anyone anyway. It's totally fine." Sasha stepped out of her blue silk dress and stood in her bra and underwear holding the dress expectantly.

"Are you sure?"

"Yes, now don't make me stand here naked!" Sasha laughed.

Georgiana worked her damp and tomato-scented dress up over her head. "You're so smart to pack two dresses, I never would have thought of that."

"Oh, I never know what to wear with your family, so I bring options."

Georgiana stepped into the blue sheath and turned so that Sasha could button her up. It was a little tight, but fine, and Sasha felt a rush of happiness and sisterly warmth. Sasha slipped the lavender dress over her own head and then cocked her hip in the mirror and grinned, the stain more disgusting than ever. "Okay, I'm going to wait in the driveway for my Uber. Tell Cord I'll be back in twenty minutes."

"Thanks, Sasha." Georgiana leaned forward and kissed her on the cheek before heading back out to the lawn for photos.

When Sasha got back to the rented house she flopped down on the bed, careful not to kick the low ceiling. How long could she get away with hiding from the wedding? She pulled out her phone and contemplated watching half an hour of something on Netflix. Surely nobody would miss her for that long. She put her hand on her flat belly. *Hello in there.* But then, guiltily, she got up and changed, calling a car to go back to the festivities.

By the time she found Cord, the family photos were over and cocktail hour was winding down. The seating chart had been arranged so that the Stockton siblings were separated, Darley and Malcolm across the room with the D.C. cousins, Georgiana seated with some younger siblings and her best friend, a cousin named Barbara who everyone called Bubbles, while Sasha and Cord were stuck with a table of bankers. Sasha shook hands and kissed cheeks with everyone at the table and then sat down next to Cord, carefully tucking her small handbag behind her back and draping her shawl across the chair.

"Finally," the man to her right grinned hugely, sticking out his hand, "I get to meet Cord's better half."

"Oh, hello." Sasha laughed uncertainly. It always struck her as sort of funny when a man described a woman as his "better half." It was said in a joking way, in the same way they might say, "My wife is the boss," and you knew they didn't really mean it. The phrase somehow inherently raised the prospect of status in a marriage: one half was better, one half was worse. Sasha knew that to most of Cord's family he was unequivocally the better half.

"I was so sorry to miss your wedding," the man continued. He was slightly older than Cord, but had his same exact nose, and Sasha found herself staring at it, hypnotized as he spoke. "I wanted to come, but my wife was nine months pregnant with our fourth and I was too afraid of missing the big moment."

"Oh, so you have a new baby! Congratulations." Sasha smiled.

"Thank you. It's a hole-punch thing like at the coffee shop— tenth one free, so I'm almost halfway there."

"Noah, stop flirting with my wife," Cord said, leaning over.

"Cord, stop interrupting me while I flirt." The man waved Cord away. "Sasha, I hear you're an entrepreneur and you started your own business. Tell me about it."

Sasha rarely thought of herself as an entrepreneur, but it was true that she worked for herself. After she graduated from art school she took a job as a designer at a boutique media agency. She designed book jackets and advertisements, corporate annual reports and catalogs. After moving up the ranks at the agency she set up her own design firm, realizing she could earn more money and focus on the kinds of projects she enjoyed, looking at a brand as a whole, coming up with an entire look and visual story. She leased a small office down in Dumbo where she kept a computer and where she could send and receive packages, and at thirty-five she was making more money than either of her parents ever had. She was, by her own definition, a success.

It wasn't the sort of success that meant much to other people. Her parents and her brothers knew she ran her own business, knew she did design work for brands they had heard of—the Transit Museum, Brooklinen, Sixpoint Brewery, the New York Philharmonic—but her work was abstract enough that nobody wanted to really spend time talking about it. Her in-laws were perhaps even less impressed, if that were possible. Sometimes it seemed that everyone in their orbit worked in finance, law, or real estate, and any field beyond that was irrelevant or possibly déclassé. Sure, Sasha wanted to be an artist. Yes, she would rather spend her days drawing and painting. But she had her drink and draw sessions and meanwhile had found a way to fold art into her life, to use her talents to make money.

It turned out that Cord's cousin was an avid art collector, that he knew one of her professors at Cooper Union, and that he was actually really fascinated to hear about the way she took her classical training and used it to create brand identities. They talked about their favorite photographers, their favorite Chelsea galleries, and he so completely charmed her that the entire dinner passed in a happy blur of easy conversation.

After dinner there was dancing, and Sasha found herself gamely following Cord out to the floor. It seemed to her that all the men in his family were so scarred by the ballroom dance classes they had been forced into as adolescents that none of them ever learned to dance like normal people, and just hid by the bar drinking at all the weddings. Cord was the exception to the rule: never one to miss the opportunity to look like a jackass, he dragged her around, dipping her theatrically and pretending to bury his face in her breasts while she laughed and acted like she was using his tie as a leash. Out of the corner of her eye Sasha saw Darley dancing with Malcolm and even Chip and Tilda making a brief appearance for a song by the Beatles.

When the cake was cut the older guests began to make their exits in a flurry of kisses and drunken embraces. The band finished and the younger cousins drifted out of the tent and into the club, where the bar was still open, and the caterers brought out trays of small hamburgers and cones of fries. Georgiana was curled up on a leather couch, her shoes long abandoned, with her cousin Bubbles splayed out inelegantly next to her. Darley and Malcolm joined them, looking flushed and happy. Malcolm had taken off his tie and stuffed it into the pocket of his suit jacket.

Archie and his new wife came in to cheers and hollers, and soon he started telling everyone his favorite story about the house on Spyglass Lane. Sasha had heard the story half a dozen times, but it never got old. Archie and his wife had been on vacation in Telluride and after a long day skiing they had some wine and decided to watch a porn in the hotel room. Five minutes into the thing, Archie realized why everything looked so familiar: the actors were having sex on the chaise longue on Spyglass Lane. It was unmistakably the Stockton home—you could see the hedge maze and the tennis courts in the background. Archie highly doubted Uncle Chip and Auntie Tilda had been so short on cash that they had started renting the place out to filmmakers, so he called up Cord to tell him. This put Cord in the wildly awkward position of having to tell his parents that their country house was featured in a porn and no, he hadn't seen it, but he knew someone who had, and they probably needed to call their lawyer.

It turned out the weekday landscapers had been using various vacation homes for years without getting caught, but you had to wonder how many people had seen the movies and been too embarrassed to ever try to solve the mystery. Tilda had the caretaker chuck the chaise longues at the transfer station, bought new ones with nicer cushions, had the place deep cleaned, and dumped enough chemicals in the pool to kill chlamydia and any neighboring wildlife.

As Archie and Cord fell all over each other laughing, Sasha excused herself to go to the ladies' room, peeing and then quickly fixing her makeup. When she emerged, she didn't see Cord anywhere, and Darley was caught up in conversation, so she let herself quietly collapse into an armchair, hidden from view so she could check her phone. As she scrolled through her emails, she half listened as Bubbles told them about a trip she was planning to the Caymans. Darley suddenly interrupted, confused. "George, weren't you wearing a purple dress before?"

"Oh, yeah," Georgiana said sleepily. "I've been wearing this dress since cocktail hour."

"Wait, you had a different dress?" Bubbles asked. She was drunk and talking more loudly than any sober person might.

"I was wearing a lavender dress, but I spilled crab and cocktail sauce all over it so Sasha traded dresses with me."

"Sasha gave you her dress?" Darley repeated, confused about what Sasha was then wearing.

"Wait, who?" Bubbles sounded genuinely lost.

"Sasha took off her own dress and gave it to me," Georgiana tried to explain.

"Oh, that's so funny! Sasha! I had no idea who you meant! You two always call her the Gold Digger!" Bubbles cackled. Georgiana laughed for what seemed like the first time all night and Sasha felt her skin grow cold. She quietly got up and walked out to the parking lot.

SASHA NEVER told Cord what happened at the Greenwich wedding, pleading a migraine and wearing sunglasses on the drive back to Brooklyn the next day. After that she decided that she was done trying with Cord's sisters. She was done inviting the family for dinner at the limestone, she was done bringing bagels to Orange Street for brunch, she was done joining for weekends at Spyglass or weekday lunch at Darley's apartment. Certain events would be unavoidable, like birthdays or holidays, but otherwise she would keep her distance. Yes, Georgiana was in pain. She had slept with a married man and he died. That was terrible. Yes, Darley was worried for Malcolm, scared his career had been permanently derailed. But it was now clear to Sasha that they had only confided their secrets in her because of how little it mattered to them what Sasha thought. She wasn't really their family; she wasn't someone who could pass any kind of meaningful judgment. She was a receptacle for an emotional outburst, the human equivalent of screaming into a pillow.

FOURTEEN

Georgiana

After Archie's wedding Georgiana didn't leave her apartment all week. She took personal days from work; when Cord called she sent it to voice mail and texted back the words "stomach virus." She sent the same text to Lena. She slept and slept, and her dreams were strange and alarming. She was in an airport and Brady was there, somewhere, and she ran down long hallways searching for him, stopped by security, stuck in throngs of people who wouldn't move and let her through in time. She woke covered in sweat, and it came to feel like she really did have a stomach virus. She ate dry cereal and tried to watch mindless television, but all around her house she kept finding Brady's love letters. With the teacups a note that read, "Your backhand is great—but your backside is even better." Under a pillow on the couch, "Let's make babies with breasts."

On Monday Georgiana went back to work, partially because she knew that if she continued to call in sick she would be fired, but also because she wanted to hear more about Brady, more about what happened. There was a pall cast over everything at the office. People wore dark colors, and from her chair in the maid's room Georgiana could see Meg's desk, and she watched as the others from grant writing packed her personal things in a box: a cardigan, a silver dish that held paper clips, a small stuffed bulldog wearing a shirt that said GEORGETOWN, the bottle of Advil. To think of all the ambition Meg had, to think of everything she would have done in her life made Georgiana ache with loss. Because they had lunch together on occasion, people in the office understood they were friends, and as she watched them pack Meg's desk, tears rolled down her face and the team in grant writing tutted sympathetically and handed her a Kleenex. They had been crying all week themselves.

Amina came to the office to pack up Brady's desk and see their friends. When Georgiana heard she was on the first floor she knew to stay in the maid's room. If she saw Amina she would break apart, her outrageous grief would expose her, and she would in turn double this woman's own heartbreak. She hated to think of Amina boxing up Brady's apartment, his bicycle, his blue bedspread, his maps, his stack of biographies. She would surely sell the place, and any evidence that Brady had ever even lived in Brooklyn would be gone.

Georgiana moved through the week like a zombie, taking half a Valium before work in the morning and letting it dull her out. She barely sent or responded to emails; she might miss a newsletter deadline, but nobody cared, the entire office dragging along as though through heavy drifts of snow. She ignored texts from Cord and Lena, Cord asking if she had his spare squash goggles, Lena trying to get Georgiana to come to a party on Saturday. Georgiana regretted confessing to Sasha, couldn't understand why she had confided in the GD of all people, but Cord hadn't said a word about Brady so she knew Sasha hadn't told him. On Friday after work,

Georgiana changed into her pajamas at six thirty, ordered tacos to be delivered to her apartment, and watched five hours of Netflix before falling asleep. The Valium made her drowsy, and she slept like the dead, waking ten hours later on Saturday morning with a headache and the sense that she would need to nap again in the afternoon. She was asleep at five when the buzzer woke her. She stumbled to the intercom and pressed the button before realizing that she could have ignored it. "Hello?"

"George, it's me, buzz me up." It was Lena.

"Hey, I'm sleeping."

"Buzz me up, dude," Lena insisted. Georgiana sighed and pressed the button, unlocking the front door and leaving it ajar before walking back to her bedroom and climbing into bed. Two minutes later Lena appeared looking impossibly tan and healthy.

"Honey, what's going on with you?" she asked, peering around in obvious distress. Georgiana searched her room for signs of alarm. It wasn't like she was living in total squalor; Berta had come and vacuumed while she was at work, but the blinds were drawn, there was an empty box of crackers in her bed, a glass of water had knocked over on the floor and she'd left it there, and the pile of love notes was scattered across her pillow. Georgiana snatched them up and put them in her nightstand.

"I had the stomach flu. It really fucked me up."

"The stomach flu lasts twenty-four hours. You've been MIA for two weeks. You look rough."

"I had my cousin's wedding."

"You had a wedding that lasted for two weeks?"

"Sorry. I just wasn't up for anything."

"You're becoming a hermit, and this is an intervention. Not only are you hurting yourself, but you're hurting me. Kristin and I are bored with each other and we need your dry wit and slight air of judgment. Now take a shower and get dressed because we're going to dinner and then Sam's birthday party."

"I'll come to dinner, but I don't feel like going to a party."

"We'll see about that."

In the shower Georgiana felt a wave of anxiety in her stomach. When she got out she took another half a Valium and then dried her hair and put on makeup.

At dinner Georgiana drank two margaritas and for the first time in weeks a lightness came over her body. She felt the sugar and alcohol thrum through her chest, and she laughed as Kristin told them about the girl from their high school who had fallen in love with an Argentinean polo player and spent all her family's money on horses. They talked about Lena's boss's wife, who had taken out the swimming pool in the bottom floor of their brownstone because she got so sick of lifeguarding playdates for her children seven days a week. Georgiana picked at a salad with slices of mango and licked the salt off the rim of her glass. Her friends asked so little of her. They didn't need to pry or have her fill the silences, they just made her laugh and told stories and ordered another round of sugary drinks.

They paid the bill and called an Uber and rode to Sam's apartment, where they fixed their makeup in the mirrored elevator. There were maybe fifty people crowded into the kitchen and living room, and music was blasting and the dining-room table was covered in bottles of wine and booze and mixers. Kristin poured them all tequila and soda—the ice bucket was empty and the bowl of limes had been knocked over—and they melted into the throng. When Georgiana saw Curtis McCoy standing in the doorway to the kitchen, it was like she had known he would be there. A puzzle piece had been missing ever since that night at the Russian dance hall, and now it clicked into place. She strode up to him and, smiling coldly, bumped her plastic cup against his, startling him and sloshing a small amount of his beer on the floor. "Curtis, I'm surprised you're here. I didn't realize your strict moral code allowed you to go to birthday parties."

"Georgiana, hi." Curtis winced and wiped some of his beer from his sleeve. "I was actually hoping to run into you one of these days."

"Oh, why? Are you having trouble finding people who will let you shit on them from a great height?"

"Actually, I wanted to apologize. I was in a weird mood and I was uncomfortable in the situation and I took it out on you, and that was wrong."

Georgiana paused. He looked genuinely distressed. "You were also very rude about my sunglasses," she said, frowning.

"I'm sorry. They were nice sunglasses," he said contritely. He looked so guilty and flustered. Georgiana relented.

"I'm just fucking with you. They're cheesy sunglasses. I borrowed them from my mom." She laughed.

"Oh, okay." Curtis smiled uncertainly. He had a lovely mouth, straight white teeth, pillowy lips, a dimple in his chin. People edged past them, moving from the kitchen to the dining room, and Georgiana bumped gently into Curtis's chest. She put her hand on his shoulder. The room was hot and spinning slightly, and Georgiana leaned forward and kissed Curtis on the lips. He held back at first, but she pushed her mouth into his until he gave and kissed her back.

"Hey, hey, hey, George, what the fuck?" Lena was suddenly at her shoulder. "We're in the middle of a party."

Georgiana stumbled back, and her face felt tingly and she realized with a jolt of shame how very drunk she was. She grabbed Lena's hand and pulled her through the dining room. "I need to go home."

The next morning she woke awash in self-loathing. Her head ached, her stomach was tender, her memories of the night were patchy and incomplete. She looked down and saw she was still wearing her jeans and blouse. Her hair was in a braid. In the kitchen, the microwave yawned open, the light on, a frozen pizza sitting on its cardboard sleeve, thawed but uncooked.

"Fuck," she whispered. She went into the bathroom and looked in the mirror and brushed her teeth. She didn't think she had thrown up, but her tongue felt strange and her throat hurt. She had a bruise on her forearm that she didn't remember getting. She threw her jeans and blouse into the hamper and pulled on an old soccer jersey. She had three texts from Cord about tennis. He had reserved them a court at noon. It was already eleven. She texted Lena.

Did I kiss Curtis McCoy?

Lena texted back immediately. I am so glad you are not dead. You only had three drinks but you were WHITE GIRL WASTED. Maybe stomach virus?

LENA, DID I KISS CURTIS MCCOY???

Um yes that happened

But I hate him, Georgiana texted back, and threw herself onto the couch. Why the hell would she kiss Curtis McCoy? She had a vision of herself pressing her face against his, him pulling back. It was too horrible to contemplate. She ate four pieces of toast and drank two Vitaminwaters before putting on her tennis clothes. Cord had been essentially stalking her—he still hadn't said a word about Brady, so he clearly had no idea why she'd been ghosting him—but if she canceled tennis he would show up at her place and make her talk. She wasn't in any kind of shape to have a conversation, never mind one that required obfuscation or careful lies.

She met him on the ground floor of the Casino, and they hit for an hour, Georgiana screwing up her footwork and missing easy shots and serving like a complete asshole. When they finished Cord teased her gently. "You a little hungover, George? Big night last night?"

"What makes you think that?" she replied icily as she changed out of her tennis shoes.

"Um, maybe the fact that you stink of booze or that you sweat a line of eye makeup down your cheek? Did you even wash your face last night?"

"I did not," she admitted.

"Did you sleep at a dude's?" Cord asked. "Did you hook up with someone?"

"No, God." Georgiana's face prickled with heat.

"Oh you did. You had sex with someone. You got a maaaaaan," he started singing.

"Stop, Cord," Georgiana said, annoyed. Cord grinned and zipped his racket into his case. They walked down the stone steps and onto Montague Street. Georgiana felt wretched. Her face was red, her hair was dirty, and, apparently, she had mascara all over her cheek.

As they walked, Cord linked his elbow through hers like they were a courting couple promenading in Elizabethan times. He knew he had pushed too far and was trying to make up for it. As they rounded the corner of Montague and Hicks they nearly smacked into another couple, a man and woman walking a big greyhound. Georgiana locked eyes with the man. It was Curtis McCoy. There was a moment when they both stopped and time froze. Georgiana felt lightheaded, woozy with humiliation. And then Cord said, "Whoops, hey big dog," and led her on by the elbow and Curtis quickly looked away. He and the woman continued down Hicks with their dog, and Georgiana let her brother chatter, carrying on a one-sided conversation all the way to her apartment, where she would lie on the couch and stew in a fetid swamp of anger and self-recriminations for the rest of the day.

Georgiana had her first panic attack the summer before college. At the time she thought she had just smoked too much weed, but in retrospect the dizziness, the closing in of her vision, and the sense that her heart was no longer working were a product of a life she felt was spinning out of control: moving away, leaving her friends behind, the knowledge that outside of her neighborhood and school nobody cared who her parents were, and the bit of glitter and fairy dust that came with being Darley and Cord's sister couldn't help her anymore. In the weeks following Brady's death, she felt that old panic nipping at her heels. She would be in meetings at work and feel certain she was sliding out of her chair, unable to remain upright. She would speak and her face would go numb and her mouth would go dry. She would hang up in the middle of calls as the words stuck in her throat. She had a bottle of Valium her mother had left in a handbag, and by breaking them in half she managed to ration them out, but when she shook the bottle and heard the sound of distinct pills hitting the plastic cap, she called her GP.

Her physician was away for the week, and Georgiana wept on the phone to her receptionist until she made her a same-day appointment with a doctor who had agreed to fill in. He was old and kind, and when Georgiana described her symptoms, he pulled a large drug manual from his bookshelf and read her descriptions of the different choices aloud. Regular antianxiety medications could take two weeks to begin working. He wrote her a prescription for sixty Klonopin and told her to take them morning and night.

The day of Brady's memorial she swallowed one and a half pills before putting on a black dress and taking the subway to the Upper East Side. She sat with a group of her colleagues in the back and watched Brady's parents, both broken with grief, greeting family at the front. They both worked for Oxfam; he was following in their footsteps. Brady so closely resembled his mother that it pained Georgiana to look at her. At the service his best friend spoke, his older brother spoke, and Amina spoke. Amina was small and elegant, in her early thirties, and Georgiana felt herself staring. This was the woman who held half of Brady's heart. His friend, his brother, his wife—one by one they stood and laid claim to Brady's memory. But he had loved Georgiana too. She knew it, and yet she suffered alone, groggy and dizzy from the medicine, listening quietly in her pew as Brady's wife cried and wrapped her arms around his family.

Without Brady at work, Brady on Tuesday nights, Brady on weekends, she had nothing to look forward to, and she measured her days only in miles run and hours slept. Darley noticed an article in the paper about the plane crash, but when she asked about it, Georgiana deflected. "They were project managers in Pakistan, I didn't know them," she lied, sure that even saying Brady's name aloud would break the dam of her emotions. Cord continued to drag Georgiana out to play tennis on weekends, unable to ask about her clearly visible pain but convinced, as all WASPs are, that exercise would cure whatever ails you. Lena was the only one to ask directly about the anxiety pills, noticing that when they drank Georgiana slipped quickly from buzzed to blackout. "Babe, whatever you're taking isn't working with alcohol. You have to pick your poison," she advised. Georgiana was still humiliated that she had kissed Curtis at the party in front of so many people, but somehow his snubbing of her on the street made it strangely better. She pictured his frozen expression, his girlfriend and his dog, and though she still felt a measure of embarrassment, she also, in some ways, felt a surge of power.

She was eating lunch at her parents' apartment, picking at a plate of smoked salmon and dark pumpernickel and reading the sports section of the paper, when her mother held up *The New York Times* Sunday Style section. "Do you know someone named Curtis McCoy? He was your class at the Henry Street School."

"What?" Georgiana startled. How did her mother know about Curtis?

"There's a piece about young billionaires giving away their inheritance, and he is interviewed. His father is Jim McCoy. I remember he was quite unpleasant at the winter fundraiser." She sniffed and handed Georgiana the section.

It is August and much of Curtis McCoy's cohort has absconded to Martha's Vineyard, where the McCoy clan has their notable array of properties, a private section of the island that has been known to host rock stars and presidents, where it is not uncommon to see motorcades quietly swooshing past the stone gates. The McCoy family has, for three generations, owned the second-largest defense company in America, Taconic, manufacturers of cruise- and guided-missile systems, sold to both the U.S. government and, controversially, Saudi Arabia. Curtis McCoy, at the age of 26, is ready to wash his hands of the family business—but divesting himself of his great fortune is a more complicated matter than one might guess.

"Giving away my inheritance isn't something I can legally do in one day—nor is it something I would want to do in one day. I am still learning a lot about the best ways to shed myself of this blood money." Curtis McCoy is part of a growing movement of millennials who have grown up as one-percenters but are unwilling to perpetuate the systems that have put them there. "People like me shouldn't exist," McCoy says from his Brooklyn apartment. "I'm twenty-six years old. There is no logical reason for me to have hundreds of millions of dollars." McCoy and his contemporaries reject the very concept of inherited wealth and are working to dismantle the regulations that allowed for their situations in the first place. Despite the fact that the title suits him, McCoy doesn't define himself as a philanthropist ("There is something gross and elitist about claiming the mantle of 'philanthropist.'") but is working with family lawyers to try to gain access to more of his inheritance sooner, doing all he can to distribute his wealth among a variety of nonprofit organizations. "This money came from warmongering, and it's my goal to use it to promote peace. I hope that by speaking out I can encourage

others in my position—or people with any sort of inherited wealth—to search their souls and decide what that
money means and how they might use it to undo wrongs
of the past."

Alongside the article was a photo of Curtis in his apartment, sitting in a wooden chair looking seriously at the camera, the dimple in
his chin just visible.

"Uggggh." Georgiana made a strangled noise.

"What? I thought he came off well. You should reach out to him.
You would probably have a lot to talk about," her mother said.

"Not happening," Georgiana croaked, and picked up her phone
to text the article to Lena and Kristin before angrily shoving fourteen dollars' worth of lox in her mouth. Her father came and joined
them at the table, carrying with him a pink copy of Saturday's *Financial Times*. He poured himself a tomato juice and poked at Georgiana's newspaper.

"Real men read pink papers," he joked.

"Georgiana's school friend is on the front page of the Style section," her mother chimed in.

"He's not my friend," Georgiana said grumpily.

"What's the story?"

"His family owns Taconic and now that he has access to his inheritance, he's giving it away to amend for all the people his family's
company has killed."

"That's probably a pretty substantial fortune." Her dad wrinkled
his brow.

"He doesn't have access to all of it."

"I wouldn't imagine so. It's typically parceled out over time.

Nobody would give a kid in his twenties hundreds of millions all at once."

"Is my account parceled or could I take it all out?"

"Well, you'd never want to take it all out." Her father looked at her, alarmed.

"But can I legally get access to it?"

"Sure, but it's nothing like the Taconic kid's."

"How much is in my account?" Georgiana pressed.

"Don't you open your statements? You get statements like all investment clients."

"I haven't looked lately," Georgiana admitted. The truth was, ever since the firm went paperless, she hadn't checked the balance of her trust. That had been about five years ago.

"And you have two trust accounts. One from Geegee and Deedee and one from Pip and Pop."

Georgiana knew this. The trust from her mother's parents, set up at her birth, was the more substantial of the two. The mortgage payments for her apartment were drawn from the interest income earned in that trust account. While she could have purchased her one-bedroom outright, the mortgage rates were so low that her father's assistant explained that it was cheaper to get a mortgage and pay it off, leaving the principal of her trust in the stock market to grow. The trust from Pip and Pop was also set up when she was born and then multiplied exponentially when they died, but since they were a real estate family most of their fortune was tied up in property that her father now controlled, so that trust was only in the seven figures. The trust from Geegee and Deedee was comfortably eight.

It was embarrassing to admit, but Georgiana never paid any

attention to money. Her job paid her about forty-five thousand dollars, then her mortgage payment was made automatically from her trust account, and then her father's assistant transferred another chunk into her checking each quarter to cover things like trips and clothes. She hadn't ever thought about seeking access to the trust to pay for college or graduate school—it was more efficient in terms of taxes for her grandparents to cover that separately.

"How much could I take out today, though, if I wanted to, Dad?" she pressed.

"Today is Sunday, so probably about two thousand bucks or whatever the ATM at Chase Bank will give you," he laughed.

"Dad," she whined.

"It would be problematic for them to suddenly make any significant cash distributions to you. The way they have your trusts invested in so many small companies, it would move the market on those guys to suddenly cash out. It would cause pretty big problems for the other accounts the team manages. But what would you even want to do that for? Are you thinking about a bigger apartment? I expect you'll want to upgrade once you get married and start a family, but until then . . ."

"No, I love my apartment. I'm not moving." Georgiana did love her apartment. It was plenty big for one person, it was sunny and new, and more than that, Brady had slept there. "Are Cord and Darley invested in the same small companies I am? Do our accounts look the same?"

"Well, Cord's trust investments are almost identical to yours, but Darley doesn't have any trust investments since she got married."

"She doesn't?" Georgiana asked, surprised.

"No, she chose not to ask Malcolm to sign a prenuptial agreement, so she forfeited her benefit from her trusts."

"So she doesn't have any money?" Georgiana had known this on some level, but it still felt shocking to hear the details.

"She has plenty of money. Malcolm does very well for himself."

"But what happened to her money?"

"It's held for her kids. When a beneficiary marries without a pre-nup it is treated as though they are deceased. Things will just go to the next generation."

"Huh. Were you mad she didn't have Malcolm sign the prenup?"

"Darley is a romantic," her father sighed. "She kept talking about how signing a prenup was 'arranging for certain divorce.'"

"But Sasha didn't sign the prenup, did she?"

"Of course she did. That's why Cord still benefits from his trusts."

Georgiana paused, surprised. Why did Cord say Sasha hadn't? Or maybe he never actually said that. All she knew is that he had been upset and that Sasha had briefly moved out. "Did Cord take a big chunk of his trust to buy the limestone?"

"No, he doesn't own the limestone. He and Sasha are living there, but your mother and I still own it."

"So Sasha won't get half our house if they divorce?"

"Georgiana!" her mother interrupted. "That is a horrible thing to say about your brother and his wife. Nobody is getting a divorce. And, frankly, none of this is your business. I don't know why we are talking about money. This is certainly not lunchtime conversation. My goodness. Now, pass me the real estate section. I heard Fannie Keaton is selling her apartment for ten million and put it in the paper today."

Georgiana pulled out the section and handed it to her mother, and they spent the rest of the meal in relative silence, pausing only to peer at Fannie's colossal brownstone and lament the horrible layout.

("You'd think for ten million you'd get a proper laundry room," her mother said, and shook her head sadly.)

As soon as Cord sent the email inviting the family to dinner Georgiana knew: Sasha was pregnant. "Please join us for a celebratory dinner." What else could they be celebrating?

"I'm not going," Georgiana emailed Darley.

"You have to! I think they have baby news!" Darley replied.

"Do you think she's going to do a gender reveal with blue and pink smoke bombs and set the limestone aflame?"

"Don't be a brat," Darley fired back.

When Georgiana got to Pineapple Street, her family was already assembled and drinking champagne. "What are we celebrating?" Georgiana asked, ready to act surprised.

"We waited for you to make the big announcement," Cord said happily, ushering her into the parlor, where Sasha sat, looking stiff and cranky. He gently clinked a spoon against his glass even though everyone was already waiting for him to speak. "So . . ." He paused dramatically, his eyes twinkling. "We're having a baby!"

"Congratulations!" they cheered and Georgiana realized her parents were far and away the worst actors she had ever seen in her life.

"Did you guys already know?" Cord asked, crestfallen.

"Well, Berta told me," Tilda acknowledged.

"How did Berta know?"

"She said she just had a premonition. Women can sense these things," Tilda said wisely.

"Oh, I think she also saw me throwing up," Sasha said.

"Have you been throwing up a lot?" Darley asked.

"Yeah, every day."

"Oh, no. Do you know what I did? I put little packs of oyster crackers in my bedside table and ate them whenever I woke up in the night so that my stomach wasn't so empty in the mornings. That's the thing—you don't want your stomach to get empty."

"There were so many crumbs in the bed," Malcolm said, "it was like my body got exfoliated every night with all these little shards of cracker and salt in the sheets."

"I also found the best sour pregnancy candies to help with nausea." Darley started scrolling on her phone and texted Sasha the link. Sasha barely seemed to register Darley's enthusiasm. She looked bored by the entire thing, and Georgiana felt herself grow annoyed. Here they all were celebrating Sasha and she looked like she could barely be bothered to hang out with them.

"Oh! We have the bassinet from when you all were babies!" Tilda jumped up and strode out of the parlor. She came back three minutes later carrying a wicker Moses basket. The canework looked sharp and it smelled slightly weird. "All three of you slept in this," she said fondly.

"That's amazing," Cord said, his eyes glistening.

"Do you think that's mold?" Sasha asked, inspecting a slightly green crust on the bottom. Everyone ignored her.

Berta had made roast chicken and squash and then plain pasta for the children. She poked her head into the parlor to let them know dinner was on the table, and Georgiana grabbed the bottle of champagne and tipped the rest in her glass before following them out. They had wine with dinner, except for Sasha, who drank a LaCroix out of the can, which earned her a horrified look from Tilda. ("A can is fine on the beach, but bubbles deserve stemware!") The more they discussed the baby the more Georgiana felt a tightness in her throat. When she and Brady had talked about having a baby they had only been joking, but some tiny bit of hope had lodged within her. There had to be a reason he hadn't had a baby with Amina but had talked about it with her. She knew he loved them both, but part of her wondered if over time his love for Amina would have faded, and his love for her would have eclipsed it. Seeing Cord and Sasha's joy made her ache freshly for the baby she wouldn't ever have with Brady.

After they finished eating, Malcolm led the children to the family room to watch a movie, and Sasha stood to help Berta clear the table. Georgiana pretended she had to use the bathroom and made her way up to her bedroom. She felt groggy and tired from the wine and couldn't keep making normal faces as they discussed the pros and cons of a live-in baby nurse. Darley had used the same baby nurse that all her friends had used, and while the woman was wildly eccentric— she wore a starched, white nurse's uniform every single day in the house despite Darley's urgings to wear jeans, she exclusively read celebrity gossip magazines, she had gotten married in Las Vegas in a Celine Dion–themed wedding, and she talked to the baby nonstop in a ceaseless stream of animal voices—she and Mrs. Kim saved Darley's life for the first few weeks after Poppy and Hatcher were born.

Georgiana closed her door. She felt slightly dizzy and closed one eye so that she could focus better. On the bookshelf she spied her high school yearbook. On a whim she grabbed it and flopped down on her bed, leafing through it looking for a specific page. Halfway, in the *M* section, she found it: Curtis McCoy. She hated that he occupied so much of her brain, but she was having an impossible time reconciling the guy she saw in the Style section with the brooding and slightly frightening teenager she remembered. But, as though it were proof, there he was at seventeen: hair in his eyes, wearing a button-down shirt and sweater, looking vaguely annoyed at the camera. Next to it, a blurry photo of him with three friends standing by a bonfire on the beach, an action shot of him on the soccer field, and then a quote: "The question isn't who is going to let me; it's who is going to stop me."

"Asshole," Georgiana whispered to herself. She must have passed out, because the next thing she knew Darley was shaking her awake from a dream. She had been following Curtis down a grassy path. Gross. Bleary and annoyed, she sat up in bed, knocking the yearbook to the floor.

"Why are you asleep in here?" Darley hissed. "How much did you drink?"

"Not that much, I'm just tired," Georgiana said defensively.

"Even Mom noticed you were wasted, and that says a lot."

"Shit, she did?"

"She also said you look thin, but I think that was a compliment. What's going on with you?"

For a moment she contemplated telling her sister. Or telling her part of the story. She could tell her that she'd broken it off with Brady when she found out that he was still married, but that he'd died. But the half-truth would kill her. Having Darley think she understood the loss when it was so much greater. She couldn't. "It's nothing, Dar. I'm just anxious about work and I took a pill and it messed me up with the wine."

"Don't mix pills and alcohol!" Darley scolded. "What are you, a teenager? Do I need to explain to you the dangers of drinking and drugs?"

"No, I was just so happy for Cord I got carried away. It's fine."

"Okay. Don't be an idiot. Now go tell Mom you took a water pill for bloating and say good night. We have to take the kids home for bed anyway. Hatcher got gum in his hair and Poppy tried to pick it out and pulled out a clump and now Hatcher is crying about having a little bald spot."

"Christ." Georgiana tucked her yearbook under her arm, and they headed off into the night.

GEORGIANA HAD never spoken to the founder of her company. He was her boss's boss, and she always figured she would have to mess something up in a pretty epic fashion to find herself in conversation with him, so it surprised her when he poked his head into the maid's room on a Wednesday morning. She was crouched on the floor of her office sorting through the boxes of newsletters fresh from the printer when he knocked on the doorframe and startled her.

"Peter! Hi!" She quickly wondered if it was okay she had called him Peter. Should she have called him Mr. Perthman? No. That was weird. He was her boss, not her headmaster.

"Georgiana. How are you doing?"

"I'm great!" She rose to her feet with a surfeit of nervous enthusiasm.

"I had a question for you. You know, we have the benefit next month, and we're looking to increase our pool of individual donors and family foundations."

"Absolutely. I have already been in touch with the venue and I'm working closely with Gabrielle to arrange our guest list for the event."

"If I recall from your résumé, you went to the Henry Street School here in Brooklyn, right?"

"Yes, I did." Why was the founder looking at her résumé? Obviously, someone had mentioned it to him.

"I was reading the *Times* recently, and I saw that an alumnus of Henry Street named Curtis McCoy was doing lots of charitable giving. It seems his goals align with our work here, and so I was wondering if you could reach out to him about the benefit."

It was the Baader-Meinhof phenomenon, whereby once you noticed something new you saw it all over the place. Had Curtis McCoy always been bumping around the periphery of her life and she'd just never noticed? Because he was suddenly impossible to avoid. When Georgiana was in middle school a friend had pointed out the castle in *The Little Mermaid* that looked exactly like a penis, drawn in by some bored illustrator. Once she saw the thing she could never stop seeing it. It had been there the whole time, right under her nose, and she'd been completely oblivious. She felt the same way about Curtis.

"I do know Curtis," Georgiana admitted. "Not well, but we were classmates."

"Oh, terrific," Peter Perthman smiled. "I'll send you a letter to forward him. And I hope you'll introduce me next month! You're such an asset, Georgiana. You've really distinguished yourself in your short time here." And with that he bowed his head and swept out of the maid's room, leaving Georgiana to sink back to the floor with her boxes.

She forwarded the invitation to Curtis with the absolute minimum amount of eagerness. Peter (or his assistant) had crafted an elegant letter of introduction, framing the work of the organization and highlighting the recent loss of three colleagues in Pakistan. Of course, this was a country where civilians had a great deal of mistrust of America. While the letter didn't expressly say "the drones your family made were used to kill people in thousands of strikes on northwest Pakistan so you should give us money to teach the survivors to care for themselves," it basically did. Georgiana pulled Curtis's personal email address off the invitation to the Russian dance hall birthday party and wrote only the briefest note at the top: "My boss asked me to send this along. Hope you are well." An hour later Curtis replied.

If I come to this fundraiser are you going to try to kiss me?

Georgiana reeled back from her computer monitor as if splashed by cold water. She quickly shot back a reply. "This is my work email."

An answer appeared right away. "Oh, okay. Is there a theme for this party? Is it Third World Chic?"

Georgiana snorted. What an asshole. "You don't have to come. I'll just tell my boss you're too busy being a philanthropist."

"Are you stalking me? Reading all my press?"

"It was the Style section. It's like you placed the article purely to appeal to women. Truly there must be easier ways to get a date. Did the photographer ask you to glower at the camera, or did he say you should just smolder?"

"It sounds like you spent a lot of time looking at it."

"Apparently it's my job to liaise with the anticapitalist youth."

"Well, I'm happy to liaise. I'll be there next month. Do let me know if I can borrow your mom's sunglasses."

"WHOA, CURTIS MCCOY with the witty email banter," Lena laughed. They were at an Italian restaurant on Atlantic and Lena and Kristin huddled over Georgiana's phone.

"Does he have a girlfriend?" Georgiana asked.

"I have no idea. Are you interested?"

"No! I'm just trying to figure out if everyone thinks he's a dirtbag or if someone sees a human in there."

"A dirtbag who is giving away a hundred million dollars in the name of peace. What an a-hole."

"I mean, it *is* a mindfuck, right?" Georgiana asked. "It's like he's either a total jerk or a saint, and I just can't figure out which it is."

"Terrible people can do good things," Kristin mused. "Like, even Bin Laden loved his grandchildren."

"Super helpful insight. Thank you."

"Look at the guys I work with," Kristin continued. "You have all these men in tech who have big dreams about creating a utopian society but instead have enabled more hate than previously imagined, mostly for money."

"It can also work the other way, right? Like Angelina Jolie? Wears Billy Bob Thornton's blood in a necklace and does lots of drugs but then grows up and becomes a Goodwill Ambassador? That's what Curtis is doing, right? Trying to grow up?" asked Lena.

"So Curtis is Angelina Jolie. Cool, cool. I get it now." Georgiana laughed. It wasn't the same thing, but there was a nugget of truth there. He wasn't responsible for his family's sins. He wasn't even necessarily responsible for what he had believed in high school. People could change. People could evolve. Who was she to hold him to some strict moral standard? Everything she had believed about herself had gone out the window when she fell in love with Brady. Good people did fucked-up things.

WHEN SHE TOLD HER SISTER, Darley, that she had invited Curtis McCoy to the benefit, Darley grabbed Georgiana's arm and howled laughing. "Who's the Gold Digger now?" she cackled. They were playing tennis at the Casino and Georgiana died a little inside that everyone at the club would think she was a social climber.

"Shut up." She glared at her sister.

"What are you two fighting about?" Cord and their mother let themselves onto the court and handed Georgiana a can of balls to pop.

"Georgiana's going on a date with Curtis McCoy!" Darley squealed.

"Oh, I set them up," her mother said, pleased, and smoothed her hands over her hips. She had terrific legs and it sometimes seemed like she played tennis purely for the skirts.

"What? No, you didn't, Mom!"

"Well, I gave you the article about him and told you to be in touch."

"Who is Curtis McCoy?" Cord asked.

"He's that billionaire kid giving away all his money, the one whose dad owns Taconic," Darley said.

"He's not a billionaire," Georgiana muttered.

"Not if he gives it all away," trilled Tilda.

"Oh, I read about him." Cord cocked his head. "Seemed like kind of a Bernie Bro."

"He's not a Bernie Bro." Georgiana peeled back the lid of the balls and stuffed three under her skirt. "He inherited millions of dollars made from selling Tomahawk missiles that killed Syrians and rather than spend his days on a yacht he decided to try to make the world better. It hardly makes him a ridiculous person."

"But he does still have a yacht, right?" Tilda asked. "I can check in the Social Register summer edition."

"That is not the point, Mom." Georgiana rolled her eyes. "Can we please play tennis?"

They always played doubles the same way, Georgiana and Darley against Cord and their mother. It was annoying, but Cord was stronger and faster than either of his sisters and so he made up for the fact that Tilda was not quite as nimble as she once was. Darley was strong if slightly erratic, and alongside Georgiana the teams worked out evenly. Although their father was a decent player himself, he and Tilda never played together—they always ended up fighting and so had decided at some point in the nineties to preserve their marriage and keep their tennis lives separate.

Georgiana was often amazed by the variety of experiences the word "marriage" encompassed. Her parents lived together, they slept in the same room, but for all their physical proximity they seemed to live separate existences. They had completely different interests, different friends, they read different books and watched different movies. While they went on vacation together, they spent their days apart, Tilda shopping, getting manicures, and exercising, Chip reading the paper, golfing, and drinking with his friends. Darley and Malcolm were the exact opposite. They were apart more than they were together, but they talked all day, they agreed on nearly everything, they sometimes sat in bed on entirely different continents and ate identical takeout and watched movies together. It almost irked Georgiana how loyal Darley was to Malcolm. She sometimes wished that Darley would just find fault with her husband, would hate the way he brushed his teeth, the way he pursed his lips when he read. But their marriage was an egg, a yolk and a white, all surrounded by shell. Darley may have played family tennis as a Stockton, but Georgiana was beginning to suspect that in her heart of hearts Darley was becoming a Kim, leaving Georgiana all alone.

THE BENEFIT was held on the first floor of the Brooklyn Museum. A stage was erected where the tickets were usually sold, and a DJ set up for after-dinner dancing. Georgiana had helped work on the table arrangements, so she knew that Curtis had bought an entire ten-top for twenty thousand dollars. The hope, of course, was that he would be so moved by the evening's proceedings that he would leave a pledge in the small envelope set under his dinner plate. Georgiana hadn't recognized any of the names he had submitted as his guests, but she shouldn't have been surprised. It wasn't like she expected him to bring a crew of high school friends to a presentation on international health care masquerading as a fancy dinner.

The night of the benefit, Georgiana considered wearing her mother's Chanel earrings with two giant Cs hanging to her shoulders, but she wasn't convinced Curtis would get the joke, and it was probably in poor taste to wear something like that when talking about children without access to clean drinking water. She opted instead to wear her mother's Missoni dress and a pair of heels that made her absurdly tall.

She got there early and set herself up by the door to greet guests but was helping one of their big donors find the coat check when Curtis arrived. He was with a beautiful woman who was clearly his mother, which made Georgiana feel strangely happy. She had somehow assumed that his public statements about Taconic would have put him at odds with his parents. She spent the entire cocktail hour watching him out of the corner of her eye, unable to make her way over as various crises emerged and resolved—a last-minute addition was required for table 3, the photographer needed to know who to shoot, the iPad that Gabrielle was using for registration had frozen.

As cocktail hour ended and servers encouraged guests to find their tables, Georgiana dashed back behind the stage to make sure Peter was mic'd for his remarks. When ten minutes later Georgiana took her seat close to the edge of the stage, she saw that the rest of Curtis's guests had arrived, and the woman she had seen with him outside the Casino, the one walking her dog, was seated to his left. Curtis caught her looking and smiled, nodding his head briefly in greeting. Georgiana felt her cheeks warm, and she waved back then promptly felt like an idiot.

She hadn't seen the video about their recent work, and once it started she realized what a terrible mistake that had been. There, before the entire room, was Brady's face. He stood alongside Meg and Divya at a small airport, a backpack slung over his shoulder, sunglasses on his head. The photo must have been taken the day before he died. There were pictures of him leading a meeting in a hospital boardroom, wearing a blue lanyard and holding three vaccine boxes with orange stickers, pictures of him alongside the rest of the team in Pakistan leaning over a laptop. Georgiana felt tears spilling down her cheeks. Someone should have told her there would be pictures of Brady in the video. She pulled her eyes from the screen and tried to gather herself, tried to slow her breathing, and when she looked out across the crowd she saw Curtis's eyes on her. She quietly slipped away from her seat and stumbled to the bathroom, unspooling a sheaf of toilet paper to press against her face. Once she regained her breath, she wet her hands and patted her fingers under her eyes to try to blend the stain from her mascara. She smoothed her dress and tucked her hair behind her ears, broke a Klonopin in half, and let it dissolve under her tongue. She was fine. She could hold herself together.

She busied herself along the periphery of the party through the salads, the main speaker, and the entrées. When coffee was served, she emerged from backstage to see people starting to drift from the tables, a line forming at the coat check for those not interested in dancing. When Curtis tapped her shoulder, she jumped.

"Hey, great event, congrats," he said.

"Thanks so much for coming. I'm sure your calendar is full of these things." The old nervous blush tickled her cheeks, and she felt strangely aware of the space he had touched on her shoulder.

"It is, but these evenings are my job right now. I want to learn as much as I can about different organizations." He was wearing a slim navy suit that made his eyes look bluer than usual, his blond hair was combed neatly, his face freshly shaven, and he smelled slightly of coffee.

"Who were the other people at your table?" Georgiana peeked over and saw empty chairs, dessert plates untouched.

"I'm working with a team now. A group of people with experience in corporate giving."

"That makes sense." Georgiana smiled, the blush finally cooling from her face. "How'd we do?"

"Really well. I love the focus on teaching health-care providers in-country. You have to create a meaningful structure that will work after the money is gone."

She nodded. "I think that's part of why the work in Pakistan is so important. So many women are hesitant about seeing male doctors. Their husbands or mothers-in-law won't allow it. So we train the female health volunteers to work in their communities with family planning and immunizations."

"That makes so much sense." Curtis took a breath uncertainly. "You looked really upset during the video. Were you friends with the people who died in the plane crash?" He looked at her intently, and his eyes were so full of light she suddenly felt flustered. He was uncomfortably handsome.

"Yes," Georgiana stammered. "My friend Meg was one of the three people who died." She couldn't talk to Curtis McCoy about Brady. She'd start crying all over again.

"I'm so sorry. Was she our age?"

"A few years older, but yeah, really young. It was her first time going along to see a project, and she was so excited. She was really smart, she worked all the time, and she was just going to *be somebody*, you know?"

"I do. It's terrible." Curtis paused and in the silence he looked around. "I heard they opened the first floor of the museum to guests. Do you want to take a walk?"

"That would be great," Georgiana said. The DJ was playing, and her coworkers were dancing with their spouses in the colorful lights. They walked along the glass corridor where murals from the 1980s stretched to the ceiling. "Was that your mom at your table?"

"It was. She was in town, so I convinced her to come along."

"I wondered if you got along with your parents or if they were upset with you."

"My mother is more understanding than my father," Curtis admitted sheepishly.

"I'm sorry." They stopped in front of a twenty-foot red mural, the paint thick and bumpy.

"He's really proud of what he's done at Taconic. He doesn't see it the way I do. He sees defense as patriotic. He feels like our family has made an important contribution, like we're a military family, almost."

"Is he more angry about you giving away your money or about you undermining Taconic?"

"He thinks I'm virtue-signaling. He keeps calling me A.O.C. and Comrade Stalin and insisting I'll regret this when I have kids one day."

"He thinks you'll wish you could give your kids a bigger inheritance?" Georgiana asked.

"Yeah, he's part of that generation that thinks financial stability is the greatest gift you can give your family." He tipped his head, indicating that he was ready to move on to the next mural.

"I think there's a difference between stability and obscene wealth," Georgiana ventured.

"There's a big difference. Income inequality is the most shameful issue of our time. I'm worried that my kids will look back and see a country that completely abandoned morality, that let people die of hunger while the wealthy took tax breaks."

"Warren Buffett says he doesn't believe in dynastic wealth, doesn't believe your life should be determined by your membership in 'the lucky sperm club.'" Georgiana blushed slightly at the word "sperm."

Curtis laughed. "Did you know that between Warren Buffett, Bill Gates, and Jeff Bezos, those three individuals hold more wealth than the entire bottom half of the population?"

"Is that true?" she asked.

They stopped in front of a mural of two enormous breasts, and they both pretended to study it briefly before moving on to the next. Art was so awkward.

"Have you always disagreed with your father's politics?"

"No." Curtis shook his head. "I sort of started to read beyond *The Wall Street Journal* in high school, but I didn't fully engage with my own complicity until college. I think we were sort of raised in a bubble." He looked at her questioningly.

"It's sometimes hard to get out of that bubble," she agreed, thinking about her tiny corner of Brooklyn Heights. If she sneezed loudly enough in her living room, her parents could probably bless her from their bedroom on Orange Street.

"Seems like you're pushing out of your bubble," Curtis said, and Georgiana felt flattered and then embarrassed at how much she seemed to want his approval. They wandered back to the dance area and Georgiana saw her team starting to collect the envelopes from the tables.

"I should get back to work."

"Hey." Curtis caught her arm. "Are you seeing anyone?"

"No, are you?" She smiled.

"No, but I thought maybe that guy? When I ran into you? After that party?" Georgiana appreciated the great pains he was taking to avoid saying, "That morning I saw you staggering down the street looking like you'd been huffing glue after you tried to lick my molars."

"That was my brother, Cord."

Curtis said he'd write her to set up a night for dinner and she felt a glittery happiness that carried her through the cleanup from the party, but when she got home and opened her medicine cabinet, she found a note from Brady behind her mouthwash that read "Free nose jobs for debutantes!"

Holding the folded slip of paper, Georgiana remembered the photos of Brady and Meg. She saw him standing by the plane with his backpack, hours away from the crash. He had died and his body had turned to ash, and yet Georgiana was still here, alive and dressing in stupid designer clothing, flirting at a museum gala, pretending to be a good person when she knew that she was a liar.

FIFTEEN

Darley

Tilda was throwing Cord and Sasha a gender reveal luncheon and the theme was "Mad Hatter's Tea Party." She had transformed the Orange Street apartment into a psychedelic wonderland, with teacups stacked in alarming towers, a candelabra with pocket watches hanging from the arms, playing cards fanned around the base, and porcelain rabbits peeking out from the floral arrangements. Frankly, the whole thing made Darley feel like the time she took too many mushrooms in Amsterdam and threw up in a canal. But she dragged Malcolm along to be a good sport and even wore a feathered fascinator she had from an old Kentucky Derby party.

"Welcome to Wonderland!" Tilda said dramatically as she threw open the door. She was wearing a hat so big it was touching the hallway on either side, and she applauded appreciatively at Darley's outfit before handing Malcolm a black top hat with playing cards sewn in the brim. "Everyone's wearing a mad hat! Now pick a drink. If you think the baby is going to be a girl have a Pink Lady, if you think it's a boy have a Blue Arrow."

"What's a Blue Arrow?" Malcolm whispered to Darley.

"Blue curaçao and gin. Avoid," Darley whispered back.

Cord and Sasha were already there, Cord wolfing down heart- and spade-shaped tea sandwiches and Sasha looking flushed and pretty in a flower crown.

"I love your headpiece," Darley complimented her, kissing Sasha hello.

"Oh, your mother had it made for me. She came over yesterday to see what outfit I was planning to make sure it would go."

"Of course she did," Darley said and laughed.

The table was teeming with food: cucumber and cream cheese on pillowy white bread, chicken salad with grapes, egg and water- cress, each plate with a little tag that read "EAT ME." The cocktail table had similar tags reading "DRINK ME."

"Oh my God, 'Eat me'?" Darley scrunched her nose.

"Really classy, Dar," Cord grinned. "This is a family party."

"So, is it a boy or a girl? You can tell me, I won't tell anyone," Darley wheedled.

"We don't actually know," Sasha said. "We had the doctor write it on a piece of paper, and your mother gave it to her caterer. When we cut the cake it'll be either pink or blue inside."

"Wow, that's cheesy," interrupted Georgiana, walking up and popping a cherry tomato in her mouth.

Sasha laughed tightly. "It wasn't our idea."

"NMF," said Malcolm, winking at Sasha. Darley pretended she didn't know what their little private code meant.

Georgiana had brought her best friend, Lena, and Darley was happy to see her. She had known Lena since she was a little kid, and Darley had fond memories of babysitting them when she was home from college, painting their nails and letting them eat entire tubs of cookie dough while watching Zac Efron movies. Georgiana had been so erratic lately—it seemed like she was already tipsy—and it made Darley glad to think Lena was also watching out for her.

"Let me taste that." Malcolm gestured to Georgiana's cocktail, which looked like antifreeze in a martini glass. He took a sip and winced. "That's like naked-wasted stuff."

"Well, it is a gender reveal party," Cord joked, clearly slightly hyper. "We didn't say whose gender we would be revealing."

Sasha had invited a handful of her friends, some from work and some from art school, including Vara, and Darley made a point of introducing herself to everyone, steering them away from the blue drinks when possible. Sasha's parents had canceled at the last minute—her dad wasn't feeling well—and Darley's heart broke a little they wouldn't get to be a part of this, drinking Pink Ladies and seeing Sasha in her flower crown. But Tilda was relishing her role as the matriarch, swanning about in her hat, breaking her own edict and sipping a glass of champagne, unwilling to stain her teeth either boy or girl colored.

After an hour of eating and mingling, the party gathered around the cake, a gargantuan, wedding-style tower with three tiers covered in white and yellow roses. Sasha's friends pulled out their iPhones to document the reveal, and she and Cord used a Tiffany knife to make the cut. Cord held the first slice aloft—but the inside of the cake was white.

"What does white mean?" Cord asked the room.

"Cut farther into it! Maybe there's a filling!"

They cut again, this time all the way to the center. White. Cord

dramatically started spearing each layer as though he were a magi-
cian attempting the woman-in-a-box trick. It was white all the way
through.

"Oh raspberries, I'll call the bakery," Tilda announced, batting
her hat brim out of her eyes and punching their number into her
phone. It turned out the bakery had also filled an order for a fiftieth
wedding anniversary that day, so somewhere across town a couple of
old people were eating bright blue or pink lemon curd. The party
gathered around the iPhone so that the baker could read aloud the
note from Sasha's obstetrician.

"It's a boy!" the baker cried from the tiny screen, and Tilda
screamed merrily and hung up on her. "What fabulous news!"

Cord and Sasha laughed and kissed, and everyone who had pun-
ished their livers with the Blue Arrow cocktails raised their glasses
in victory. A boy! Darley was happy. The baby would be six years
younger than Hatcher, but her kids would have their first cousin.
And Cord would be an unbelievable father. As she looked around
the room at their friends and family eating and laughing over the
cake debacle, she noticed Georgiana wasn't smiling.

"This is such a fucked-up thing to be celebrating, you guys," she
said loudly, and the party quieted as though someone had called for
a toast. She was swaying lightly, her cheeks aflame as she spoke. "It
shouldn't matter if it's a boy or a girl. Gender is a spectrum."

"Georgiana, dear, nobody knows what on earth you're talking
about," Tilda admonished her from beneath her enormous hat. "We
would be just as happy if it was a girl."

"That's not the fucking point, Mom," Georgiana said dismissively.

"Georgiana, do you want to come talk in the kitchen?" Sasha
intervened. She was suddenly at her elbow and steering her out of
the room.

"No, I'm fine, *Sasha*." She said her name as though it were a swear.

"You've been through a lot," Sasha said quietly. "It's okay for you to be angry."

"Don't act like you know everything," Georgiana hissed. "You don't!"

"Okay, I don't," Sasha backpedaled. "I just think you're ruining a family party when you're actually hurting about something else."

What the hell are they talking about? Darley wondered.

"I'm not ruining anything. This whole party is so out of touch. Gender isn't binary. Gender isn't about genitals!"

"Jesus, keep your clothes on, George." Cord tried to reel his sister in, but she was only escalating, and Darley suddenly saw that tears were running down her face.

"Georgiana, let me walk you home." Sasha reached for Georgiana's elbow.

"Don't!" Georgia jerked her arm out of Sasha's grasp.

"I think you'll feel better—" Sasha pressed.

"Sasha, back *off*. This isn't even your house." Sasha looked as though she'd been slapped, but Georgiana kept going. "Is this all you care about, Sasha? Your big house and your heir? It's fucking embarrassing. You're all embarrassing." She looked around, glaring as if daring anyone to speak, and when nobody did, she stormed out, down the hall, into her parents' bedroom, and slammed the door.

"What the hell was that?" Darley asked nobody in particular.

"Well, who knew we'd be in for a bit of dinner theater?" Tilda announced with a laugh. "Now everyone please have a slice of cake! Well, the slices Cord hasn't defeated in a fencing match!"

Darley was often amazed at her mother's ability to gloss over awkward situations. It was either incredibly sophisticated or completely psychotic, but in these moments, she supposed she was grateful for it.

People quickly shoveled down slices of cake and then made their excuses to leave. Lena had been standing at the bedroom door, trying to talk to Georgiana, but the door remained locked.

"What's up with her?" asked Darley.

"I don't know." Lena shook her head. "She's been kind of chaotic."

"What kind of chaotic?"

"Getting drunk really easily. Obviously mixing with anxiety meds. Kissing some guy she hates at a party then beating herself up about it and wallowing in self-loathing."

"Yikes." Darley felt her eyes go round. How has she missed so much? She rapped on the door. "George? It's me. What's going on, babe? Open up."

Tilda joined them. "Sweetheart, everyone's gone home now. Come on out and let's talk about what upset you. I apologize if my theme missed the mark," she tried.

There was a thump, a click, and the door swung open. Georgiana stood before them, her hair wild, her lips stained blue from curaçao, radiant with fury.

"George, what's going on?" Darley begged, her eyes filling with tears seeing her sister in such pain.

"Ask the Gold Digger," Georgiana said, glaring at Sasha, who stood frozen at the end of the hall. "Ask the fucking Gold Digger." And with that she swept out of the apartment and left her family gaping in her wake.

SIXTEEN

Sasha

Sasha told them. They sat in the living room and Sasha explained what Georgiana had confessed the day she found her sobbing in the closet. She had fallen in love; she didn't know Brady was married. After she had found out, she did the unthinkable and kept sleeping with him. They were having an affair. Then the plane crashed, Brady died, and Georgiana couldn't stop the grief.

"The secret has been tearing her apart," whispered Lena. "She told me she broke it off with him."

"The plane crash was more than two months ago." Darley winced. "She said she didn't know the people who died."

"Brady died. And her friend Meg," Sasha said quietly.

"You've known this the whole time?" Cord asked, and the look on his face was one of such betrayal Sasha could barely stand it.

"I'm sorry," Sasha whispered. "She told me in confidence."

"She's twenty-six," Darley spat. "She's a baby. She was dealing with something incredibly traumatic. She needed help."

"I tried to help her, but guess what? She shut me out, just like everyone in your family!" Sasha shot back defensively. "I called her and called her, but she didn't want help from a gold digger."

"Why do people keep saying that?" Tilda interrupted.

"Because that's Georgiana and Darley's nickname for me: the Gold Digger. They think I married up. They think I give two shits about what clubs you belong to or how to set a fucking table. They think I actually wanted to move into your family museum of antique crap."

"Hey, Sasha, simmer down," Cord said and frowned.

"No, I won't simmer down. Georgiana is spoiled and selfish and has been rude and snide to me since the moment I met her. And you," Sasha turned to Darley. "It's almost worse because you pretended to be my friend while joking about me behind my back."

"This isn't about you, Sasha," Darley snapped.

"It never is, is it? I'm over all of you. I am sick and tired of everyone acting like I should be kissing the flea-bitten Oriental rugs in gratitude just so I can keep living in a janky Grey Gardens full of old toothbrushes and moldy baskets. And guess what?" She glared right at Tilda. "The governor's couch gave me a *rash*!" Cord looked at her and shook his head, *too far*, but Sasha was done anyway, spent. Her face was sweaty and with her wilting flower crown she looked like some kind of demented Medusa. She turned and, with as much dignity as one can muster while surrounded by a family in weird hats, stomped out the door.

In the wake of the party the Stockton family closed ranks. Cord would take phone calls from Darley and walk into the bedroom, shutting the door firmly behind him. He went to Orange Street so that he could huddle with his mother and discuss the Georgiana problem, presumably while rubbing her feet pornographically.

Cord thought Sasha had overreacted. So they called her a name, so what? Georgiana had loved someone who died. Sasha's problems paled in comparison. He couldn't see that it was about so much more than that, couldn't see she'd been ostracized all along. With each passing day after the party she felt the curtain being drawn between them, making it clear as day that she was not and would never be a Stockton.

To Sasha's surprise, Darley didn't text or call. Sasha knew she and Cord were mad about her house comments, they were mad she had kept Georgiana's secret, but didn't Darley feel any shame for calling her a gold digger? Maybe Sasha should have told them about Georgiana, but at the same time she couldn't fathom how they would have reacted if she had sounded the alarm two months ago. Georgiana already treated her with such disdain, what if she'd broken her trust? She felt she had seen something the Stocktons wouldn't have liked her to see. They were all so private. They were secretive. They were desperate to keep up appearances and make sure no cracks showed in their facade. Well, Sasha had seen the cracks and now they hated her for it.

The more Sasha thought about it, the angrier she felt. She was stuck in a lose-lose situation, a member of a family in which she had no voice, she had no vote, where doors were closed and envelopes remained sealed and money was a string that tied them all together and kept them bound and gagged. To Sasha it suddenly made sense that the Stockton family had settled in the fruit street neighborhood of Brooklyn Heights all those years ago, that they wanted to live in homes protected by a historical preservation society: they didn't actually want to change, they wanted to stay exactly as they were.

IT WAS A MONDAY afternoon and Sasha was working, trying to choose which shade of cream to use in an advertisement for bed linens. She had narrowed it down to coconut cream, double cream, and cannoli cream—the whole thing was making her hungry—when her mother called her from her pantry.

"They are going to keep your father overnight for observation," she said, her voice muffled by bags of rice and pasta.

"Why? Did they find something at his appointment?" This was his third doctor's visit in six weeks and he was still short of breath, his inhaler doing nothing to help. Sasha stood and closed her book of printer samples so she could think clearly.

"No, they didn't find anything. I'm sure it's just the last of a chest cold. Your father is pretty cranky about it. He wanted to come home tonight, but I convinced him that he should stay until they release him."

"How did you do that?" Sasha asked incredulously.

"I told him that if he dared step outside the hospital before he had express permission from a physician, I would sink his boat."

Sasha laughed in spite of herself. Her mother had once thrown a pair of paddles off the dock when her brothers were three hours late coming back from fishing, so they all took her threats seriously. "I'm going to come up," Sasha said.

"Oh, don't. There's nothing to do here. You'd keep me up tonight worrying about you on the road after dark and then he'll be home tomorrow."

"Why are you in the pantry if Dad's not even home?"

"The boys said I shouldn't worry you," her mother said guiltily.

Annoying. Another family trying to keep her out of their business. "Okay," Sasha sighed, and they hung up, her mother promising to call her from the hospital in the morning. But he wasn't released the next day either, or the day after that. Sasha felt stupid. If only she'd just left on Monday, she could have been with her parents all week. On Friday she was dithering about whether to drive up when Olly texted her. Hey, they found blood clots in Dad's lungs.

She threw a change of clothes, a bottle of prenatal vitamins, and her laptop in a bag and got in the car. She berated herself the entire drive up to Providence. She hadn't seen her parents in months—she had been too busy with work, with her house, with Cord and Darley and all the stupid Stockton family celebrations and housewarmings and bewilderingly themed dinners. She had been trying so hard to fit in with a family that didn't want her that she'd forgotten all about her own.

Driving into town, Sasha experienced the funny sensation of seeing her old home as an outsider might. It had started happening her freshman year of college, when after living in New York, a place of towering glass and endless discovery, everything at home looked smaller and somehow shabbier. The Dollar Store, the empty building that used to be a Blockbuster but had never filled back in, the paint store that somehow always needed a fresh coat—she could barely remember the time when this town represented the entirety of her world.

Her father was only allowed three visitors at a time and her mother and brothers were there, so Sasha drove to her parents' house, and when she pulled up she saw Mullin's truck in the driveway. The front door was locked and the lights were off, so she fished the spare key from beneath the rock and let herself in. She dropped her bag on the floor, walked to the refrigerator, and got a can of Coke. She was tilting her head back to drink when she saw Mullin in the backyard. He was the last person she felt like talking to, so she ignored him, leafing through the unopened mail on the counter, unloading the clean dishwasher, and helping herself to a box of Girl Scout cookies in the cupboard.

When Mullin tapped on the sliding-glass door she startled.

"Hey, I didn't mean to scare you." He looked tired. He had grown a beard and his jeans were covered in dirt.

She eyed him warily across the kitchen. "What's going on?"

"Just trying to keep busy until we hear about the blood clots." Mullin shrugged. He walked over to the refrigerator, pulled out a can of Narragansett, and popped the beer open.

"Help yourself," Sasha said sarcastically.

"I bought them."

"Then keep them in your own house."

"Why do you have to be like that?" Mullin asked, scowling.

"Like what?"

"Like such a bitch all the time."

"Because I don't want you here. And yet," she paused, "you're always here."

"And you're not. So why do you care?"

"Because it just seems like you should have moved on by now. We broke up more than fifteen years ago, but I still have to see you all the time. I just don't understand why."

"Well, it's certainly not to try and win you back, charming as you are," he said bitterly.

"Obviously." Sasha scowled. It enraged her that he was here at the house, playing the doting son when he wasn't even part of her family. When he had elbowed her out of the way. She stalked out the sliding-glass door, down the steps of the deck, and into the yard. There was a new Japanese maple planted in the back corner of the lot, about five feet tall, with dark red, shiny leaves. All around it were bluestars, the leaves a brilliant yellow, a swath of plumelike astilbes, and a row of small boxwoods. "Wow," Sasha murmured. It looked like a spread from *Cottages & Gardens*, a far cry from the cinderblock beds where they had dug for worms and made mudpies when she was a kid. She walked over to the maple tree and looked at it more closely. She peered at the careful strings someone had tied around the base to keep animals away. She looked at the neat grass now covering what had once been a bald and lumpy pitch. She closed her eyes and listened for a while, the noises of her childhood so different from the noises on Pineapple Street. Here she heard the distant sound of a dog barking, the creak of a neighbor's screen door opening, the rattle of the leaves in the breeze. In Brooklyn Heights she was surrounded by the rhythmic purr of a refrigerated truck parked outside her window as groceries were delivered, the sirens of police cars and fire trucks along Henry Street, and sometimes, on Sunday mornings, the clang of the knife truck, a charming neighborhood feature, a guy who drove around Cobble Hill, Carroll Gardens, and the Heights ringing a bell so that you could run down your kitchen knives and have them sharpened for twenty bucks. Sasha let her mind wander. Was it possible she'd never live here again? Would she spend the rest of her life in Brooklyn, raising her baby hours away from her parents? She wanted so desperately for her father to be okay, for him to be able to teach her son to fish and flip a pancake, to wade around in the river looking for the mooring, to whistle with a blade of grass, to spend hours picking through the hand-tied flies they sold behind the bar at Morgan's.

Why was she so mad at Mullin? Why did it make her so angry to
see him in her home? Yes, he'd been a horrible boyfriend, but that
was ages ago. She was still punishing him. Was she just as bad as the
Stocktons? Desperate to keep her family of origin sheltered from
outsiders? The irony crashed down on her. She was such a hypocrite.
She'd moved into Pineapple Street and felt furious at Georgiana for
the very thing she had been doing to Mullin for the past decade and
a half. Fuck.

"Hey, Mullin?" she called, and he ambled to the door. "Did you
help with these plantings?"

"Yep," he said, taking a swig from the can.

"They look really good."

"I know. People pay me a lotta money for it."

"Well, it's worth it," Sasha said contritely. "I'm sure Mom and
Dad appreciate it."

Mullin sauntered down the steps and surveyed the garden.
"Penny for your thoughts?"

"They cost more these days," Sasha deadpanned, and Mullin
smiled. "I feel guilty I didn't realize things were so bad with my dad."

"I think it surprised everyone," he offered.

"I know. But I've had my head up my ass. I've been a terrible
daughter. I hope my mom will forgive me," she confessed quietly.

Mullin thought for a minute. "Do you remember the dances we'd
have in middle school? The ones in the gym?"

Of course Sasha did. They were her favorite thing. She and her
friends would pick out their outfits weeks in advance, they would get
together ahead of time and spray themselves with drugstore perfume, would wear dangly earrings they bought at Claire's Boutique,
would spend ages with curling irons and hair spray getting their
bangs just right.

"There was one dance in seventh grade where you danced with Andrew Bowalski, do you remember that?" Mullin asked and Sasha shook her head. Sure, she remembered Andrew Bowalski. He was in her classes from kindergarten through high school. He was in their gifted and talented program. He had a dark buzz cut, wire-rimmed glasses, he was lanky and nerdy and had just the biggest crush on Sasha for years. She found it mildly embarrassing, but he was a nice enough guy. She never went out with him, and sometime in high school he moved on. He was in the chess club and got into Rutgers and ended up dating a girl from Boston. Sasha thought they were married now.

"Andrew liked you so much, and he told everyone that night that he was going to ask you to slow dance to 'Stairway to Heaven' because it was the longest song." Mullin laughed remembering it. "And you did. Everyone knew you didn't like him that way, but I remember you being so nice about it and letting him put his hands on your waist and rock back and forth for all seven minutes. That was when I fell in love with you."

"Mullin—" Sasha tried to interrupt him. Whatever he was about to say, she didn't want to hear it. She didn't love Mullin and wasn't going to change her mind.

"But here's the thing," Mullin pressed on. "I loved you, but what I really saw was how loved you were. How you had this amazing family, parents who would do anything for you, a mom who took you to buy the clothes you wanted for a dance, a dad who coached your softball team. You had friends, you had so much love surrounding you that it was easy for you to share it. You could dance with Andrew Bowalski and make his night. You were just so open and light, and I saw how closed and dark I was. I was like twelve years old and I knew I didn't want to live like that. I wanted to have that kind of love. So I fell for you. And no, it didn't work out between us, and that was my fault. I acted like an idiot. And who knows? Maybe even if I hadn't it wouldn't have worked out anyway, we were kids. But being with you and being with your family saved me. I know that. I knew it then too. Your mom will forgive you because that's how she is."

Mullin was staring intently across the yard, and Sasha saw how much it cost him to say this, to say it to someone who had hurt him so badly. She could stop hurting him now. She could be kinder to Mullin than the Stocktons were to her. She could be open even if the Stocktons were closed.

"Did you know that the pineapple symbolizes welcome and hospitality?"

"Yeah." Mullin gave her an amused frown. "Sailors would bring them home and put them in front of their houses back in the day."

"Exactly. But it's actually kind of messed up. Columbus first saw them in Brazil and brought one back to Europe for the king of Spain. They were a prestige fruit for the uberelites. A status symbol that only the wealthy could have. We think of pineapples as this whimsical fruit, but they're actually a symbol of colonialism and imperialism."

"Good to know." Mullin nodded, smiling.

"I'll take a penny for that one."

"Come here." Mullin reached out. Sasha stepped in and let him hug her. She wasn't sure she'd felt his arms around her since she was nineteen; it was strange. The way he smelled was both familiar and not, the way his beard scratched her cheek, the broadness of his chest. Mullin pulled away and together they sat down on the bottom step of the deck, facing the maple tree and listening to the neighborhood.

Sasha's mother and brothers came home an hour later. The

treatment had gone well. His lungs had been filling with blood clots, so the doctors injected him with a medicine they use for stroke patients. It had restored blood flow and then after a few hours they put him on heparin. He'd be on blood thinners for six months, but he was already breathing better. It was a reprieve, but a reprieve from a fate Sasha hadn't even known to fear, as abstract as the truck that barrels through an intersection an hour after you're safely home making a sandwich, scaffolding that collapses onto an empty sidewalk while you're snug in bed. How could Sasha know what to even worry about when the world was so random? It left her further unnerved, imagining how easy it would have been for her to be working, poring over three different shades of cream, eating tea sandwiches in a flowered crown, eavesdropping on her husband outside her own bedroom door while hours away her family was on the brink of sorrow and loss. She composed a text to Cord, telling him the good news, and let her finger hover over the button before sending it, wondering for a moment why he wasn't there by her side.

SEVENTEEN

Georgiana

When Georgiana woke on Monday morning, her head aching with a potent mix of Klonopin, Blue Arrows, and remorse, she couldn't remember anything from the night before. She knew she had embarrassed herself, she was awash in shame, but she wasn't sure why.

She showered and dressed and went to work, sat in the maid's room where she tried to focus on writing an article, but she couldn't. Georgiana was tired of herself. She was tired of being drunk and hungover. She was tired of dressing up for parties. She was tired of tennis at private clubs. She was tired of waitstaff asking still or sparkling. She was tired of Berta cooking her meals and mopping her floors. She was tired of clicking away in the smallest room of an enormous mansion pretending to be doing something—anything—that mattered when, in her entire life outside her job, she was yet another cog in the machine that kept everything moving away from fairness and justice and humanity. She couldn't do it anymore. She couldn't be this person. She needed to change. But she had no idea how, and it made her so sad she could barely stop herself from crying into her hands.

She had an email on her work account from Curtis McCoy.

Hi Georgiana, It was great seeing you at the event. Would you like to get together this weekend? I hear the Whitney has an exhibit of nudes we can go and feel awkward in front of? You can wear your sunglasses?

Georgiana wouldn't let herself drag anyone else down with her. She tapped out a quick reply.

Hi Curtis, I have a lot on my plate at the moment so it's not a great time. Thanks.

She pressed Send and heard the electronic whoosh of her note flying off into cyberspace. She stared out the window, trying to make sense of the night before. Why did she have such a bad feeling? What had happened at the party? When her phone buzzed with a text from Lena, the penny dropped.

Hey George why didn't you tell me Brady had DIED? I am so sorry. I love you so much and I am here for you. Tell me how I can help.

Fuck. Lena knew about Brady? Georgiana didn't reply. An hour later Darley sent a text.

Hey, Sasha told us about Brady. Why didn't you say anything? We need to talk.

Sasha told them? She told everyone? Georgiana's stomach roiled and she felt she might be sick. Her phone buzzed with a text from her mother.

I've booked us for tennis on Wednesday at 6. We can order from Jack the Horse Tavern after.

Humiliation coursed through Georgiana's body. She had made a scene, something about the stupid binary theme. Her friends and family knew about Brady, they knew what she had done. Suddenly her stomach lurched. She was going to throw up. She stood from her desk and stumbled down the hall into the bathroom with the big map of Cambodia, locking the door behind her. She was spinning, and a darkness was spreading in from the sides, making it so that she could barely see the pinpricks of light before her. It was panic. She was falling, falling, falling, but the floor wasn't rising up to meet her.

She leaned her body against the door and slid to the bathroom floor, the panic attack taking over. It was like she had been thrown by a powerful wave and her body was being tossed, forced further and further under. As she pressed her eyes closed, she remembered a time when she was in high school and the Henry Street School was scrimmaging a basketball team from the Bronx. As Henry Street scored, her classmates taunted the other team chanting, "Flip our bur-gers! Flip our bur-gers!" She was nine, and Berta took her to drop off a classmate who had missed the bus, and when Georgiana saw the girl's peeling yellow house she said, "When are you going to get your house painted?" and the girl shrugged and got out. She was twelve at summer camp, and when a counselor told her to clear her dinner plate she sneered and told the older teenager that was someone else's job. Georgiana had been horrible. She had been so horrible for so long, and she was trying so hard to stop and she couldn't. Because it hadn't just started with Brady. Sleeping with Brady wasn't what made her a bad person—she had always been one, and she couldn't even be good when she tried. She sat in the dark bathroom, shivering, Brady's name pounding through her head.

It was the money that made her so horrible. It had made her coddled and spoiled and ruined, and she had no idea what to do about it. Then, with a jolt, she remembered something from the night before. She had taken off her shoes and crawled into her parents' bed. She had been so upset. So mad at everyone. So frustrated and lost, and she felt there was just nothing she could do to stop being herself and start being someone else. But there, on the nightstand, she saw a newspaper clipping. It was the profile of Curtis, of course.

Georgiana opened her eyes and saw the map of Cambodia. The floor wasn't moving, she wasn't slipping sideways anymore. She stood, still slightly dizzy, and looked in the mirror. She was red and hot and she felt like she'd run up twelve flights of stairs, but she was okay.

She used a paper towel to blot her face and walked quietly back to her desk, unnoticed by anyone. She went into her Gmail and found the latest trust statement from the asset manager. She hadn't opened an email, never mind looked at a statement, in years. She wasn't sure she had a password, but she went ahead and tried the password she used for everything, from Neiman Marcus to Amazon: SerenaWilliams40-0. It worked. The page was confusing, there wasn't just one account with a total. It was broken up into different sections, maybe two dozen separate blocks. She pulled a piece of scrap paper from her notebook and added the totals, sure she was missing something, but she just needed a rough idea. She added it together. It looked like she had about thirty-seven million dollars. And so she decided: She would rid herself of the entire inheritance. She would give all her money away just like Curtis, and it would be like ripping off a Band-Aid. She would change. She would change all at once and leave no room to ever go back.

SHE MADE an appointment with Bill Wallis, the investment manager. She knew Bill, he'd been a friend of the family since she was a small child. She'd seen him at Darley's and Cord's weddings, she remembered once joining him and his wife for lunch at a seaside restaurant in Ogunquit, Maine, when they were all there on vacation. He was soft-spoken and wore small round glasses; he gave the impression of someone who played bridge or studied architecture in his free time.

The morning of her appointment she dressed carefully, tucking a silk blouse into trousers as though she were a professional adult and not someone who routinely ate peanut butter out of the jar for dinner. She took the subway to Grand Central Station and walked up Park Avenue to the offices of Brotherton Asset Management, nestled in a tower so reflective it was nearly invisible against the sky. A secretary welcomed her and offered her a bottled water, which Georgiana politely refused—single-use plastic—and led her to Bill's office, leaving her in a leather guest chair facing the window.

The office was massive, the size of the Pineapple Street dining room. Bill had a large mahogany desk, a tawny leather sofa, a tall orchid on a pedestal, and a coffee table showcasing a series of white ceramic vases. The walls were glass, and from where she sat Georgiana could see the arches of Grand Central and the stone pillars of the Park Avenue Viaduct. Georgiana's underarms prickled with sweat, and then Bill came in and she stood, letting him kiss her hello on both cheeks. He smiled warmly. "Georgiana! I haven't had the pleasure of seeing you in the office in several years now."

It was true, Georgiana hadn't come in since her grandfather passed and the family gathered to sign paperwork for his trust. "Thanks for making time today, Bill," Georgiana said stiffly. "I'd like to close the account."

"What do you mean?" Bill smiled uncertainly.

Georgiana hadn't rehearsed this part, but she pressed on. "I understand that much of my trust is currently tied up in investments. I'd like to sell off my stakes in everything, as soon as it's feasible, and then I want to take all the money and give it away to a charity."

"Have you spoken to your family about this?" Bill asked, concern creasing his brow.

"No, I don't want to. This is entirely my decision."

"Well, it's not your decision, and it's quite a bit more complicated than that, I am afraid. While you're the beneficiary of the trust, you are not the trustee. There are two trustees, and you would need to compel both of them to make any significant moves with your investments."

"My father told me that the fund was mine," Georgiana stammered. "He told me he didn't oversee it."

"He doesn't. He's not a trustee."

"Well, who is?" Georgiana felt blood rushing to her neck and cheeks.

"I am one, and your mother is the other."

"My mother?"

"Yes, when your grandparents set up your account it was with the provision that both your mother and an investment manager from Brotherton would help manage the trust for you."

"To stop me from doing something like this?"

"Well, there are lots of reasons that people assign trustees. It's really there to protect the beneficiary."

"Like if I were to develop a massive drug addiction or gambling problem."

"Well, sure." Bill nodded his head sympathetically.

"I don't have a drug addiction or a gambling problem. I just need access to the money my grandparents left me." Georgiana was horrified to realize she was starting to cry. She wiped her eyes and yet more tears spilled down her cheeks. She was so frustrated.

"I think you need to talk to your mother."

"But I can't!" Georgiana said, and her voice cracked.

"Georgiana," Bill said softly. "Tell me what's going on. I can help you."

Georgiana told him she had fallen in love with a man who was married, that he died in Pakistan, that he had been trying to help people, and now the only way she knew how to make it better was to get rid of the money. Georgiana spoke in a rush, and when she finished she took a tissue from Bill and wiped her face, which was covered in tears, and her nose, which was running.

"I'm sorry," Georgiana whispered, exhausted.

"Don't be," the kind man replied. "I think what you want to do is incredible and I have some ideas."

GEORGIANA'S SENIOR YEAR of high school, her mother had surgery for her tennis elbow and couldn't play for eight months. That marked the lowest point in their mother-daughter relationship, including the time Georgiana got bangs at fifteen and her mother made her wear a hat in her presence until they grew out. Without tennis they were like two strangers who both happened to have the exact same ears.

Georgiana accepted Tilda's invitation to play at the Casino and decided ahead of time that she would let her mother win, partially to make up for the Mad Hatter's party and partially in preparation for the trustee conversation, but once they got on the court Georgiana couldn't help herself and beat her with a nasty drop shot that would have made Andy Roddick break a racket. Tilda took it entirely graciously and even applauded before changing her shoes and leading Georgiana back to Orange Street.

Happily, Chip was out at a business dinner so Georgiana could talk to her mother alone. They ordered supper over the phone— Tilda didn't trust online ordering and insisted on talking to her favorite bartender, Michael, to place the order. It made Georgiana cringe to watch her mother demand a different level of service from everyone else, but at least she was a good tipper. They had agreed that they were having hamburgers, but they bastardized them in two wildly different directions, Tilda ordering a burger, rare, with no bun, and substituting a salad, Georgiana ordering a meatless burger with avocado and cheese and a side of ranch for the fries. Tilda poured them each a glass of white wine and they curled up in the living room to wait for the food.

"So, Mom," Georgiana started.

"Yes, dear," Tilda replied a bit too eagerly.

"Have you ever done something you were really ashamed of?" Tilda nodded in concentration, so Georgiana continued. "Have you ever paused and wondered 'Am I actually a good person? Or am I moving through this world making things a little worse instead of better?'" Tilda continued to bob her head. "Have you ever felt like you just couldn't keep going down the same path, and that you needed to stop and really evaluate what it meant to be a part of this planet? What it meant to be a good human?"

"Of course, my dear," Tilda agreed.

"So, what did you do when you felt that way?"

"Well, lots of things, dear," Tilda reflected. "When I'm really blue, I like to buy myself a bouquet of flowers. Not the ones at the deli on Clark Street, though those are certainly better than you'd expect, but I go down to that florist on Montague, the one that sometimes has the table of succulents out front, and I have the little woman who works there put together something fresh from the re- frigerated case—not the ones they already have premade, they al- ways put too much green in there—but I have her put together something really bright and fresh, and just smelling that bouquet and looking at the flowers can work wonders for the soul."

"That's not at all what I am talking about, Mom."

"Oh, well, some people like to look at the ocean," Tilda consid- ered, nodding her head wisely.

"Mom, let me try something else. Were you ever in love before Daddy? Did you have anyone you really fell for before him?"

"Well, I was engaged, you know."

"Um, *no*, Mom, I did *not* know that," said Georgiana, shocked.

"Oh, well, yes, I was. His name was Trip."

"How did you never tell me this?"

"Well, you never asked!" Tilda replied indignantly.

"What? I never said, 'Hey Mom, were you previously engaged to a man named Trip?'"

"Right! You never asked that."

"Well, I didn't realize how specific I had to be in my inquiries about your past, Mom!" said Georgiana sarcastically.

"You know I am an open book to you children," Tilda said mag- nanimously. "You all just never think to ask about me!"

"Oh, okay. Got it. I need to ask better questions."

"Maybe you do," Tilda sniffed.

"Okay, so do I have any secret siblings or half siblings I don't know about?"

"No! Don't be ridiculous."

"Um, have you ever been arrested for possession of illegal drugs?"

"No! God, no!"

"Was it you who secretly farted that time we were in the elevator at the Carlisle with Martha Stewart?"

"GEORGIANA!"

Georgiana started laughing in spite of herself. Their food arrived, and they set it up in the dining room and as they ate Georgiana started over and, in the way she had opened up to Bill Wallis, a man she barely knew, in his office in a glass tower, she tried again, this time to the woman she'd known her whole life, the woman who made her the angriest, the woman she couldn't always understand, who had nursed her and grown her in her belly and yet often felt so very far away. Tilda listened.

EIGHTEEN

Darley

Darley knew she was an orange. Growing up, her group of friends amused themselves by deciding who was the "Charlotte," the "Samantha," or the "Carrie" (nobody was Miranda). They decided who was the "Blanche," the "Dorothy," or the "Rose." But Darley had a different game she privately played with her siblings, where they were the fruits of their neighborhood. Cord was the pineapple, obviously. He was joyful bordering on goofy, he was thrilled to be the center of attention, he made every gathering more festive. Georgiana, meanwhile, was the cranberry. She was the baby of the family, she was bright and beautiful, but she was not entirely sweet. That left Darley to be the orange—boring, dependable, always around, rarely celebrated. Also, she knew, protected by a thick layer of rind, only truly accessible to those willing to put in the time to peel it away.

Darley had awakened midlife to the knowledge that she was entirely impotent, and she blamed it entirely on that blue-blooded twit Chuck Vanderbeer. If Chuck Vanderbeer hadn't leaked to CNBC and gotten Malcolm fired, then Malcolm would still have his job, and they would still be able to afford their co-op fees, and Darley would never have to face the realization that she had given up her fortune, given up her career, and no longer had any agency in her own life. But no, that little idiot had gone and forced a reckoning, and she had half a mind to go burn down his house. When Malcolm told her that he hadn't gotten the private equity job, she tried to act like it didn't matter. She told him she couldn't have moved to Texas. She told him it was better for the kids to stay at the Henry Street School. She told him he had nothing at all to worry about. For the first time in their marriage, she was lying to him.

It made her mad all over again that her parents had given the limestone on Pineapple to Cord. Sure, Cord and Sasha were expecting a baby, but what if they only had one? She had two. (Not three. Never three.) She wanted so badly to raise her children in her childhood home. Why hadn't anyone ever asked her if she wanted to live there? She wanted to feed them scrambled eggs in the kitchen breakfast nook, she wanted to read them bedtime stories in the mahogany four-poster bed, she wanted to host the class potluck in the parlor with the Capodimonte porcelain chandelier, she wanted to see Poppy walking down the stairs to meet her date for her deb ball. She loved that home, and she knew, thanks to the hideous gender reveal party, that Sasha didn't. Why did she take a home she didn't even like? Why did she hide Georgiana's breakdown? To Darley it was unfathomable. Georgiana was a child. She was an innocent, a shy kid who hid behind tennis and schoolwork and her parents. She'd been seduced, she'd fallen in love, she'd suffered a terrible loss, and when she reached out for help, when she confessed to her brother's wife, she was met with silence. It killed Darley that

Georgiana hadn't confided in her when she asked about the crash. It killed her that Sasha buried the secret while pretending to be her friend.

If she could go back in time, she would do so many things differently. She would have had Malcolm sign the prenup. She would have told her parents she wanted the house. She would have watched her sister more closely. And she would have made herself keep working when she got pregnant with Hatcher. She would have thrown up every morning in the trash can at the Canal Street subway station. She would have carried her cooler of breast milk past the bullpen of associates mooing like cows. She would be deep into a career, she would have her own income, and she would hold all the cards, no longer entirely at the mercy of a racist, nepotistic system blackballing her husband for a foolish boy's mistake.

DARLEY WAS awake after midnight, lying on the sofa in the living room scrolling endlessly on her phone, when an email from Cy Habib popped up on her screen. Darley scrambled into a seated position and swiped it open.

Darley,

I found your email in the Henry Street School directory. I hope you don't mind me writing out of the blue. It was lovely talking to you at the auction. It's not often I meet people as smitten with SR22 avionics as I am. Any chance you and your husband are free for a drink next week?

Cy

Darley had, of course, Googled Cy after the auction. She had studied his LinkedIn profile, the mentions of him in *The Wall Street Journal*, the photos of him smiling at a charity gala at Lincoln Center. She contemplated waiting until the morning, but instead she quickly, impulsively replied.

> Cy,
>
> *How wonderful to hear from you. We'd love to meet up next week.*
> *Just let me know where and when.*
>
> Darley

THE NEXT MORNING Darley dropped off Poppy and Hatcher with her parents at Orange Street. Malcolm had driven to Princeton to go to church with his parents, and Darley had foolishly signed on to chair the Henry Street School Holiday Book and Toy Fair and had to attend the first of about seven hundred meetings.

At half past noon, Darley jogged over to her parents' to pick up the kids, and her mother fairly shoved them out the door before waving her off. They had agreed to babysit with even less enthusiasm than usual, and it made Darley wish all over again that the Kims lived in the neighborhood.

Poppy and Hatcher each wore a giant backpack with a water bottle tucked in a mesh outer pocket, keychains with stuffed animals and beaded lanyards dangling from the zippers. They moved along the street like little bouncing turtles, homes on their backs, Hatcher dragging his feet so that yet another pair of shoes would be scuffed across the toes.

"Did you have fun?" Darley asked Poppy as they galumphed the three blocks home.

"It was the worst day of my life," Poppy said.

"Why?" Darley laughed.

"Glammy doesn't know how to turn on the TV and for snack they only had olives and machine cherries."

"Maraschino," Darley corrected. Her parents had fed the kids from the bar cart. "What did you play with?"

"Glammy let us watch YouTube on her phone so she and Gramps could have an argument."

"What were they arguing about?"

"Auntie George."

"Oh," Darley sighed. Her parents really needed to watch what they said in front of Poppy and Hatcher. The kids had turned into expert eavesdroppers, and they gossiped with the fervor of middle schoolers.

"Auntie George wants to give away all her money and Gramps says over his dead body. Is Gramps almost one hundred?"

"No, honey, Gramps is sixty-nine," murmured Darley. What had her parents been talking about? When she got home, she called her father's cell phone.

"Daddy, Poppy told me Georgiana is trying to give away her money."

"Hold on a moment," he said, and she heard her father walk down the hall and close a door. "Georgiana has gotten this idea in her head that having financial advantages is somehow an abomination and that the only way to move forward is for her to give it all away like some kind of millennial communist saint. This is why I didn't want to send her to Brown."

"She wants to give her whole trust away? When? And to who?"

"As soon as possible. She went and made an appointment with Bill Wallis behind our backs. She's planning to set up a foundation."

"Dad, you know she's having a mental health crisis, right? This is all related to that married guy. You can't let her do this." Darley was pacing the hall and possibly yelling.

"The problem is, it's beyond my control. She's over twenty-five and I'm not a trustee. Your mother is. Talk to her."

"Mom won't talk to me! I tried to tell her Georgiana needed therapy and she said, 'What happened with that friend of Georgiana's is her business,' as though I'm a complete stranger!"

Darley hung up the phone and felt adrenaline coursing through her body. Georgiana was barely an adult. She had no idea what money even meant. She'd never worried about it, she'd never been without. But who knew what the future might hold? What if she fell in love with an artist? What if she one day had a child with disabilities? What if Georgiana needed some medical treatment herself? What if there was a nuclear war and she needed to escape to another country? What if her husband was fired? What if, what if, what if? There were countless things that could go awry, and money was the best way to shore yourself up against tragedy. Darley couldn't stand by and watch her baby sister throw it all away.

She called Georgiana but it went to voice mail, so she sent her a text: George, please call me. I'm v worried about you. I know you're having a hard time, but this is a huge mistake.

She then texted Cord: Georgiana went to Bill Wallis to take all her money out of her trust. Did you know about this?

Cord replied: What? No. But Dad was being a nightmare at work yesterday and tried to pump the brakes on the new Vinegar Hill acquisition because "we are going to be poor" so that tracks.

Darley texted, I'm coming over and when Cord wrote back, I'm tied up right now, she didn't see it—she was already on the way.

The Pineapple Street house was swarming with people when Darley arrived, kids in tow. She sent Poppy and Hatcher into the backyard and found her brother in the parlor talking to a woman wearing big wire-rimmed glasses and holding a tablet.

"Hey, Cord," she said uncertainly. "What's going on?"

"Oh, Darley, hi." Cord looked embarrassed, which was maybe a first for him. "I'm just getting an estimate. We'll be done in about half an hour."

"An estimate on what?"

"We're going to have all the furniture and art and stuff taken out and put into storage. We have to make room for the baby."

"The baby?" Darley asked in disbelief. "The baby that's going to be the size of a loaf of bread needs you to move out the mahogany organ clock? The baby needs you to put Geegee's Napoleon the third hall chair in storage?"

"I'm just going to check in with my team upstairs." The woman in glasses excused herself awkwardly and scurried out of the room.

"Yeah, Darley," Cord scowled at her. "Sasha doesn't need to live in a Stockton family museum."

"It's not a museum, Cord. It's a home." Darley sat down on the sofa, then remembering the rash, stood up and moved to the velvet chaise.

"I don't know what else to do," Cord said and sat down next to her. "Sasha is so unhappy here. She says she feels like we exclude her from the family, like she isn't comfortable around us. And so I thought that maybe if I took all the stuff out of Pineapple Street she could make it her own."

"But she pretty much told us all she hates the house. That was really vicious."

"And you and Georgiana called her a gold digger. That's not vicious?"

Darley winced. "That was bad. I'm really sorry."

"You should probably say that to her." Cord rubbed his eyes, looking tired.

"Aren't you mad she didn't tell us about George, though? She kept that whole thing a secret."

"Yeah, I'm really mad." Cord washed the nap of the velvet back and forth with a sweep of his hand.

Darley sighed. "Where is Sasha, anyway? Is she working?"

"No, she's with her parents for a few days. Her dad is in the hospital."

"Her dad is in the hospital?" Darley asked, shocked.

"Yeah, he had blood clots in his lungs, but he's going to be okay."

"Jesus Christ, Cord, you need to tell me these things!" Darley jumped to her feet, as though she could run somewhere to help.

"But you were so angry at each other. I figured—"

"So what? We're still her family!" Darley interrupted, and she meant it. She had made a mistake and Sasha had made a mistake, but she loved her, and Sasha loved her brother, and it was within her power to make it right. With that, she scooped up her phone and placed an order with a Rhode Island florist that was so extravagant that her credit card company had to call her and make sure it wasn't fraudulent.

NINETEEN

Sasha

Sasha couldn't sleep. Her father was home from the hospital, his breathing was improved, he was in good spirits, but still, she tossed and turned in her childhood bed, flipping her pillow over and over, searching for a cool side to calm her scurrying mind. She had been the Georgiana of her family the whole time, throwing elbows at Mullin because he didn't belong. But there was one crucial difference: Her brothers had let her know she was wrong. Her brothers made it clear that if they had to choose sides, they chose Mullin's. Had Cord done the same? No. He had somehow managed to play both sides, never calling out his sisters, never truly promising to pick Sasha and put his wife first. It hurt. Sasha knew that when she had fallen in love with Cord she had said she wanted someone who loved her but didn't need her. But maybe she had been wrong. Maybe, when it came to marriage, she actually needed Cord to need her too.

She fell asleep sometime at dawn, and when she woke, she could hear the neighborhood sounds through the window she'd left cracked open. Birds in the trees, the cars driving to the wharf, the growl of a leaf blower down the street, but she heard voices in the kitchen as well, so she pulled on a pair of sweatpants, raked her hair out of her eyes, and stumbled downstairs, where she stopped and felt her face light up in a smile. Behind the spray of Peruvian lilies and magenta snapdragons Darley had sent, Cord was sitting at the table, drinking coffee with her parents, a spread of bagels and cream cheese on the cutting board before him.

"Morning, sleepyhead." Cord jumped up and kissed her hello, then bent down to kiss the bump of her belly. "I brought breakfast from Hot Bagel on Montague."

"Did you bring me a rainbow bagel?" Sasha pretended to inspect the bag.

"You know I did." He held one out with a flourish, the strange red and green swirls looking more like plastic than bread.

"The food coloring just makes it taste better," Sasha insisted happily, and set about cutting it in half and spreading the perfect amount of cream cheese on each side. Cord had already eaten three bagels and was eyeing a fourth, to everyone's horror.

"After you two are done eating, can you please bail the boat?" Sasha's mother asked. "It rained last night and your father is trying to go do it himself and he's going to end up in an ambulance."

"Dad, you're ridiculous," Sasha grumbled with her mouth full. "You just started breathing again, you're not bailing the damn boat."

"You're pregnant. You can't do it. I've felt worse from eating a bad taco, I'm fine," her dad said belligerently, but Cord insisted he would do it, and so after they finished breakfast they bundled up in jackets, grabbed the oars and two empty milk jugs, and walked down to the river. Sasha still knew the combination for the lock on the dinghy, and she climbed aboard while Cord shoved them off the dock and jumped in after her. Together they rowed out to the boat, which did, indeed, have about three inches of water in the bottom.

Cord used the milk jugs to bail, and after he finished he sat back, stretching his arms and rolling his shoulders. It was a fall weekday and the landing was calm. The serious fishermen had gone out hours ago, the summer people were long departed, and the fussy weekend boats floated idly on their moorings.

"Hey, I missed you." Sasha leaned over and kissed Cord on the cheek. "Why'd you come?"

"I was worried about you. And your dad. I've been feeling so stupid the past week. I should have gotten in the car with you as soon as I heard."

"Well, I didn't really give you the chance," Sasha admitted.

"No—" Cord started.

"But I was also sort of mad at everyone," she continued.

"I know you were. I'm sorry about Georgiana. And Darley."

"I'm mad at you too, Cord."

"Yeah, I know. But I wasn't thrilled with the way you yelled at everyone. You were pretty out of bounds."

"It was three against one! Your whole family was ganging up on me! You were taking their side—you always take their side," Sasha cried.

"I don't think that's true." He frowned.

"You know why your sisters didn't like me, right?" Sasha pushed. "They didn't like me because I'm not your class. Because I'm not old money."

"No, that's not it." Cord shook his head, wrinkling his brow. "It's nothing like that."

"Cord, it *is*," Sasha insisted. "It's uncomfortable to talk about class, I know you get all awkward and WASPy whenever it comes up. And it's most uncomfortable for the really rich and the really poor. But you and I are from two different classes. And that's weird. When

you marry outside your class it's somehow too difficult to even discuss. We just ignored it."

"We ignored it because neither of us cared about it," Cord said.

"God, you know what sucks to think about?" Sasha stopped and
pressed her lips together, unsure if she could keep going.

"What?"

"I probably did like it that you were rich. I feel like a terrible
person saying that. Obviously, it's not why I love you. I love you because you are funny and kind and sexy and you make everything
exciting. I didn't even know anything about you when we met. But
probably on some level it was attractive. I feel disgusting saying that.
I'm not a gold digger. I'm just being honest."

Cord was watching Sasha carefully, and she kept going. "But I
didn't know what it would actually mean for our lives. I didn't know
that I'd always feel like an intruder."

"You're not an intruder. You're my wife."

"But I feel like one. And you aren't doing enough to help say that
I belong."

"What can I do?"

Sasha leaned over and put her forehead against his. "You can
choose me," she whispered.

"I do choose you."

"I want you to take my side. I want to be your family now. I want
you to put me first." She never thought she would ask for this. She
never thought she would have to. But she needed Cord to say it.

"I can do that. I'll put you first."

She looked at him. He was so serious, wearing an expression she
rarely saw, his eyebrows pinched and his eyes bright. She knew he
meant it. The pregnancy was changing things between them. She felt
her anger and frustration draining away. "You know, I think that

flower arrangement Darley sent cost more than the flowers for our wedding."

"I saw your mom taking a Claritin this morning."

"But Darley also wrote me an apology note. About the whole 'GD' thing."

"Can I see it?"

"Yeah, here." Sasha pulled her phone out of her pocket and opened the text chain.

> Sasha, I've been thinking of you so much, hoping your father is feeling better. But I have also been thinking about what I said and feeling like the biggest idiot. Do you remember that time Hatcher scooped a stranger's hair off the floor of Choo Choo Cuts and put it in my purse and I was finding strands in my wallet for weeks? Or do you remember the time I picked up the wrong beer at Fornino's on the pier and when I sipped it a cigarette butt went in my mouth? Or when the dry cleaner accidentally dropped off my neighbor's Pucci dress at my apartment and I figured it was my mom's so I wore it and the neighbor saw me in the lobby and yelled at me? This is so much worse than any of that. Please forgive me.

Cord laughed in spite of himself. "Are you still mad at her?" He passed Sasha her phone.

"Nah, we're good." She smiled.

"Thank God. I mean, I'm still on your side! But thank God you're friends again."

Sasha leaned forward and kissed him and Cord kissed her back then slipped a hand under her jacket. When she pulled away he grinned. "Do you think we'd capsize the boat if we . . ."

"If we capsize the boat that would definitely put my dad back in

the hospital." Sasha laughed. She straightened her jacket where Cord
had pulled it up and then together they climbed into the dinghy,
rowing past the big fiberglass cruisers, past the tiny aluminum ca-
noes, back to the shore.

SASHA AND CORD ate an early dinner with her parents, pasta and
meatballs with paper towel napkins in the kitchen, not a tablescape
in sight, and then went to meet her brothers at the marina. Nate had
a new girlfriend with a boat, and he had apparently been living on-
board with her ever since they met in a bar months earlier. Sasha
parked the car in the lot, and they made their way down the board-
walk, Cord carrying a six-pack of IPAs. While Sasha's father kept his
small aluminum boat moored in the river, the marina was home to
the vessels that were too big to make it past the wharf at low tide—
cabin cruisers, sailboats, bowriders, and deck boats. The marina had
hookups to electricity and wi-fi, and it wasn't unusual for folks in
town to take up residence at the marina when they got tired of staring at the same four walls. Sasha knew most of the boats by sight,
and as they walked along she pointed out their names to Cord. There
was the big, thirty-four-foot Chris-Craft that belonged to her middle
school soccer coach, a floating RV with a sleeping area, a dining
table, and a bathroom down below. It was named *Sweet Samantha*
after his daughter, a girl Sasha knew had gone on to marry a Croa-
tian kickboxer with sleeves of tattoos. There was the 1985 Tollycraft
Sundeck motor yacht named *Wifey* that belonged to a gay couple
who lived out on Marsh Road. There was the pretty little Bayliner

with red and blue stripes named *Fishin' Impossible*, the Axopar 37 Sun Top named *Liquid Assets*. Sasha's brother Olly had often fantasized about buying a yacht and naming it the *Wet Dream*, but luckily he was too broke to buy even a kayak. Sasha waved hello to each boat as they passed, owners relaxing on the aft deck with red Solo cups or serving dinner on the fly bridge, and she briefly felt like they were walking through a series of living rooms.

"Where are Nate and Olly?" Cord wondered.

"He didn't say where her slip was, but I'm sure we'll hear them," Sasha said dryly.

They rounded a bend in the dock and Olly's voice boomed out over the water. "Sashimi! Umbilical Cord!"

"Yep, there they are." Sasha rolled her eyes.

Her brothers were sprawled out on the aft deck of a sixty-foot Carver motor yacht, the name of the boat, *The Searcher*, stenciled on the transom, with the hailing port, Newport, RI, below. It was a huge vessel, old but gleaming white, with stairs that led up to a glassed-in deck, a flybridge and cockpit, and through the sliding-glass doors Sasha could spy a bedroom.

"Wow, nice digs," Cord whistled.

"Shelby got it like ten years ago." Nate stood to hug them both hello as Olly reached into the cooler to fish out a can of beer. "She bought it when she was still living in California."

A woman appeared on the staircase, barefoot in jeans and a light-blue hoodie. "Hey! You're here!" She was tall and skinny, maybe early forties, with her hair pulled back into a stubby ponytail. "I'm so excited to meet you!" She gave both Sasha and Cord huge, tight hugs and bumped Nate over on the cushioned bench to make room for them to sit. "How's your dad doing today? I've been worried."

"Oh, he seems like himself," Sasha answered. "He was making my mother crazy refusing to sit still and rest. He bought four boxes of nightcrawlers to take fishing, but she won't let him go, so now half the fridge in the kitchen is full of sea worms." Sasha had seen guests at their house recoil in horror when they realized that the shiny white pastry boxes were filled with writhing piles of bait rather than cookies or chocolates.

"We'll come take them off his hands, right, Nate?" Shelby grinned. "We've been going out fishing most mornings before work."

"What do you do for work?" Cord asked.

"Oh, I work in app development." Shelby waved her hand vaguely. "Hey, Sasha, congratulations on the baby! You must be so excited! And I haven't offered you anything to eat or drink! I got these seltzers." Shelby reached into the cooler and pulled out two White Claw spiked seltzers, one lemon and one blackberry.

"Oh." Sasha smiled politely, "I'm not drinking while I'm pregnant. I mean, I'm sure a few drinks here and there would be fine, but I just lost the taste for alcohol."

"These are seltzers, though." Shelby frowned.

"They're hard seltzers," Sasha explained. "They're like beers."

"Oh, oops," she laughed. "I've been drinking them all afternoon! I wondered why I was in such a good mood! I think I've had four."

Sasha tried to catch Nate's eye—his girlfriend was kind of funny—but he was just smiling and shaking his head.

"How long have you guys been seeing each other?" Cord asked Nate.

"Couple of months, I think."

"I picked him up at the Cap Club."

"No, I picked her up." Nate nuzzled Shelby's neck.

"Gross." Olly frowned.

"You guys should come fishing with us tomorrow. Nate and I have been getting really lucky with stripers."

"Any keepers?" Cord asked.

"A few." She pulled her phone out of her pocket and tapped a little icon. "This is one of my projects. It's an app where you can take a picture of your catch and it will identify the fish for you. Then you scan the length, and it tells you if it's a keeper or if you need to throw it back."

"Oh, I'll download that." Cord pulled his own phone out of his pocket, leaning over so that Shelby could help him find it in the store.

"Cord," Olly said, "when, in Brooklyn Heights, do you plan to catch a keeper?"

"I mean, it wouldn't be a daily thing," Cord muttered.

"It's okay, Cord." Shelby laughed. "I'm always working on a million ideas. What should my next project be?"

"I actually do have an app idea," Cord said, brightening. "I can't stand those people who honk all the time. I want an app that tracks how much people honk, and then at the end of the day, when they are trying to fall asleep, their phone just blares a honking noise at them for the exact amount of time they honked."

"Cord, I love you man, but who the fuck would put that on their own phone?" Nate asked.

"Okay, I have one," Olly jumped in. "You put in the contact info for any girl you're hooking up with and every Thursday night it automatically texts, 'Hey beautiful, I was just thinking about you!'"

"Yeah, I'm not making that app." Shelby poked Olly on his shoulder.

"I know," said Sasha. "An app where you point your phone at an avocado and it tells you if it's stringy or brown inside."

"I want one called Richup," said Nate. "It goes through all your photos and adds in a Rolex and a horse."

They all laughed and spent the next hour coming up with terrible ideas as Shelby gamely pretended to consider them. After a while Sasha needed to use the bathroom and Shelby led her inside, showing her the two staterooms, the galley, the dining room, the salon, and then finally the head. While the boat was at least fifteen years old, it was neat and well maintained, with shiny chrome and cherrywood details. It was truly a floating apartment.

Shelby made up snacks in the galley, Ritz Crackers with cubes of Vermont cheddar, a pile of grapes, and a plastic tray of Oreo cookies. She carried them out to the deck with a stack of paper napkins all bearing the name of the boat, *The Searcher*, in fancy gold foil. Around midnight Sasha yawned, and so she, Cord, and Olly said their goodbyes and left the lovebirds alone in their floating nest.

Olly gallantly offered to carry their trash and recycling to the bins by the parking lot, and together they made their way along the pier, talking quietly so as not to rouse anyone who might be sleeping in the neighboring boats.

"She's a sweet girl," Sasha murmured. "She seems to really like Nate."

"Shocking, right?" Olly replied.

"I hope one of her projects works," Sasha mused.

"She'll be fine."

"I mean, there are millions of apps published every year. It's a long-shot career path."

"Oh, these are just for fun. She's basically been retired since she was thirty." Olly chucked the trash into the bin.

"What do you mean, retired?" asked Sasha, confused.

"Shelby was employee seventy-three at Google. That's millions in stocks."

Sasha felt her jaw drop. Shelby was loaded, super-super-superrich. She started to laugh. "Oh, Nate," she said, shaking her head. "He can just buy himself a Rolex and horse."

TWENTY

Georgiana

When Georgiana was a teenager Truman Capote's house was sold for a record-breaking $12.5 million to the founder of Rockstar Games. The house, a four-bay, five-story townhome on Willow Street between Pineapple and Orange, was sacred ground in the neighborhood. Capote had famously written both *Breakfast at Tiffany's* and *In Cold Blood* while living there, he had lounged on the porch, he had published an autobiographical essay about the neighborhood, and given his friends tours of his place. Capote belonged to the fruit streets. When the maker of *Grand Theft Auto* slapped down his checkbook and took the keys to 70 Willow, the sound of collective pearl-clutching could be heard from the Promenade to Montague Street. The new owner applied for some permits: to put in a swimming pool, to strip the yellow paint, and to demolish the porch. It was a nightmare. Who, in Brooklyn Heights of all places, would trade Audrey Hepburn for that?

In the weeks following the terrible gender reveal party, Georgiana kept thinking about Capote's house. The Landmarks Preservation Commission met with the new owner and together they came up with a plan. He could have his pool, but then he would return the home to its Greek Revival heritage, restoring the original facade, matching the historic brick, and using those deep *Grand Theft Auto* coffers to rejuvenate it to nineteenth-century glory. The owner would get to live there comfortably, but he could still honor the history and culture he inherited. In fact, he would make it better. Maybe that's what Sasha was doing at Pineapple Street. Maybe Georgiana was just a pearl-clutching neighbor being a giant snob.

Kristin had a therapist on Remsen Street and Georgiana made a weekly appointment. She spent the first hour telling the story of Brady and used up half a box of tissues, but in the following weeks they talked more about family, about money, about Sasha and the prenup. Georgiana was starting to see that her relationship with money was all intertwined in how she thought about friends and marriage. Unbeknownst to her, she had been trained her entire life to protect her wealth. They had tax advisers and investment advisers, they made careful end-of-year adjustments to offset losses, and while they could enjoy the fruits of their labor (or the fruits of their ancestors' labor) they were raised with the holy understanding that they must *never, ever* touch the principal. Intertwined with this doctrine was the fact that marrying outside their class would dilute their wealth. It was best for the rich to marry the rich. Georgiana hadn't ever realized how deeply ingrained this belief was in her psyche.

The fact that Georgiana had called Sasha "the Gold Digger" made her burn with shame. Georgiana had been wrong about Sasha not signing the prenup, but that wasn't even the point. It was classist, it was snobbish, and it was exactly the kind of attitude that she needed to work against. You couldn't seek to fight inequality in the world while preserving it in your own family.

"It's like the Truman Capote house," Georgiana explained to her therapist, twisting a tissue between her hands as she sat on the tweed sofa of her tiny office. Her therapist was a trim woman in her sixties, carefully dressed in neutral colors, a local in the neighborhood who shared an office with a child psychologist, which meant the bookshelves displayed not only Freud and Klein but also tiny plastic figurines, miniature moms and dads and babies. Georgiana was sometimes tempted to play with them as she talked. "Everyone in the neighborhood was outraged when Truman's house sold to someone with new money," Georgiana explained with dismay.

"You know what's funny about that?" the woman asked, her eyes twinkling merrily. "Capote didn't even own Seventy Willow Street. He rented the basement apartment from his friend. He just gave tours of the house when his friend was on vacation." Georgiana had to laugh.

When she got home that night she called Sasha, biting her lip as the phone rang. She really hated talking on the phone—everyone her age texted—but when Sasha answered, Georgiana cleared her throat and pressed past her awkwardness. "Sasha? It's George," she said. "I was wondering, would you like to play tennis sometime?"

SINCE GEORGIANA had been confronting a lot of uncomfortable truths about herself lately, she lay on Lena's pullout couch on a Sunday morning and decided she felt ready to admit to one more: she really actually liked onion rings. There was no excuse for her to order them that Sunday. She wasn't hungover, she wasn't on her deathbed, and she hadn't even gone for a run that morning, but, she acknowledged, they were wonderfully crispy and sweet and so, together with Lena and Kristin, she paid ten dollars for a large order from Westville.

As they lounged and watched rich ladies fight on TV, they waited for their food and dissected the night before. They had been out in Cobble Hill, and Kristin had ended up kissing the bartender at Clover Club. It was regrettable because now they couldn't go back there, and they had such nice cocktails.

"There must be some night he's off," complained Lena.

"I think he's the manager. It's ruined." She sighed, full of remorse. "So what are you going to do about Curtis, George?" Kristin was drinking her second Gatorade of the morning, wearing a matching sweatsuit that made her look like either Hailey Bieber or a very stylish Teletubby.

"I don't know what to do. If I were him, I'd probably block my number. I've been so hot and cold," Georgiana admitted, pulling Lena's dog onto her lap for support.

"How did you last leave it?" asked Lena.

"I told him I was too busy to hang out."

"So, could you just tell him you got less busy?"

"No, I think that would be fake. I lied to him about Brady, and if I want to move forward with him, I should probably try to be honest from now on."

"Ugh, honesty is the worst," Kristin groaned.

"The worst," Georgiana agreed and got up to meet their onion rings at the door.

A few days later, Georgiana stayed late after work, watching her colleagues shut down their computers in their various bedrooms and parlors and butler pantries. She took a deep breath and opened up the Scribus layout designer she used to make the company newsletter, changed the font to Times New Roman, and crafted her version of a mea culpa, her attempt at a boom box held aloft outside a suburban window, a dispatch that would lay her heart bare in a way Curtis might understand.

It is November and much of Georgiana Stockton's cohort has absconded to the far reaches of Brooklyn where her clan dresses in sequined gowns to dance to nineties pop music while chugging vodka and eating pickles. Georgiana has, for more than two and a half decades, blithely joined in these costumed celebrations, her greatest concerns chiefly centered upon finding good outfits for theme parties and maintaining a 5.5 tennis ranking. But now, at the age of twenty-six, Georgiana Stockton is ready to grow up.

Georgiana is part of a growing movement of millennials who have been raised as one-percenters but are now realizing they are assholes. "People like me shouldn't exist," Stockton says from her Brooklyn apartment. "I'm twenty-six years old. There is no logical reason for me to have Chanel sunglasses." Further to that, Stockton has been untruthful with someone she would like to get to know better. When he attended a

presentation on her company's work in Pakistan, she led
him to believe that only her friend Meg had perished in
the plane crash. The truth is that she had also been
sleeping with a married man who died that day. Her
grief and guilt were real, but she deeply regrets having
obfuscated the truth from someone who had shown her
great kindness. Stockton knows that it will be hard for
people to believe she has turned over a new leaf, but
she hopes that by finally acknowledging her mistakes
in this article, Curtis McCoy, local heartthrob and
excellent kisser, might give her a second chance.

Georgiana dragged in a photo of herself smoldering at the camera and saved the article as a PDF. She composed an email to Curtis,
attaching the file and simply writing, "In case you missed this week's
Style section." She pressed Send and listened to the whoosh as her
missive made its way across the air, chopped into little data packets,
hopped between hubs, carried by the airlines of cyberspace to reas-
semble before Curtis's eyes.

She hoped he would read it. She hoped he might understand how
a good person would have done something so stupid. She hoped he
might help her be better.

Georgiana wanted so badly to be better, but she still had so much
work to do. Bill Wallis had come up with a plan for her to set up a
foundation and fund the first million from her own account. He had
consented to sit on her board, and so had Tilda. Together the three
of them would agree on grants to nonprofits, and Georgiana hoped
that over time they would move more and more money from her account to the foundation until her trust was gone.

She still thought about Brady, still thought about Amina. Sometimes she sort of wondered if she would always regard Brady in the same way. Or if over time she might consider the fact that he was older than her, more powerful than her, as evidence that he might not have treated her fairly. She wasn't sure. For now, she just hoped that Amina was okay, she hoped that she had found peace. Georgiana knew that their paths might cross again someday, working side by side toward the same common good, and she liked to think that would make Brady happy. That his legacy on this earth, however complicated, had doubled in his absence, the two halves of his heart joined in the same pursuit, that all the love he had shown Georgiana might radiate out into something truly good.

TWENTY-ONE

Darley

As Darley and Malcolm got ready to meet Cy Habib for drinks, she dabbed perfume on her wrist, she swept mascara through her eyelashes, she brushed her hair until it shined, and she slipped her Saint Christopher necklace over her head.

Malcolm's mother had worn a gold Saint Christopher necklace for as long as Darley had known her. Etched in the center of the medallion was a man holding a staff and carrying a child on his shoulder. The story of Saint Christopher, Soon-ja had told her, was that of a giant man who ferried passengers across the river to safety. He was the patron saint of travelers.

When Malcolm was twelve years old, he had a soccer tournament three hours away, so Soon-ja and Young-ho had packed up the car, a forest-green Ford Explorer, and driven him. An hour into the trip, flying along at sixty miles an hour on the New Jersey Turnpike, a tractor trailer lost control of the breaks and slammed into the side of their car. The Ford Explorer flipped, tumbled, landed upright again, and skidded to a terrible screeching stop against the guardrail. The way Soon-ja told the story, she opened her eyes and it was as though she had imagined the entire thing. She turned to look at Malcolm, who was sitting in the back seat, still buckled in, still holding his Game Boy in two hands. Young-ho was in the driver's seat, gripping the steering wheel, completely unharmed. The three of them opened their doors, shaking, and huddled and clutched one another on the side of the highway. None of them had a single injury, not a bruise or a scratch or a sprain. The paramedics came to examine them, the police came to file a report, a fire truck arrived as a precaution. As an EMT checked the vehicle he found one thing: Soon-ja's Saint Christopher medal, the one she had been wearing around her neck, hanging from the rearview mirror.

On the day of Darley's wedding Soon-ja presented her with the necklace, and Darley wore it whenever she flew, whenever she took a long drive, whenever she needed that extra bit of luck. As she and Malcolm walked along the leafy sidewalks of Willow Street to meet Cy, the necklace warming against her chest, she felt good. Her breath made little white puffs in the cool air, her long coat swirled prettily as she moved, and the neighborhood smelled lightly of woodsmoke. Darley felt lucky. She reached down and took Malcolm's hand.

Darley and Malcolm had spent the week cramming as though for an exam, learning everything they could about Cy Habib. Cy was a divisional senior vice president of Aeropolitical and Industry Affairs for Emirates Airline. He had started out in the graduate training program of British Airways before he was recruited by Cathay Pacific. He was so talented and his reputation was so good that Emirates had brought him over and created a position for him. Cy was the perfect example of why the aviation industry was so appealing—his success wasn't based on pedigree, it wasn't predicated on the banking hierarchy, it was a meritocracy that rewarded sheer intelligence and passion.

When they arrived at Colonie on Atlantic Avenue, Cy was already seated at a small table in the front. Darley made the introductions, Cy ordered a bottle of wine, and the three of them talked flying: they compared adventures they had taken by Cessna and Cirrus, swapping stories of their favorite spots to land. Malcolm's was the runway at Ingalls Field Airport in Hot Springs, Virginia, one of the highest airports east of the Mississippi, with a runway cut into the top of a mountain. Cy was sentimental and he liked the First Flight Airport in North Carolina, where the Wright Brothers practiced gliding. They liked Block Island despite the short runway, they were both desperate to make a Grand Canyon trip, and Cy showed them a video on his phone of landing on Dauphin Island, Alabama, where the runway started an inch off the water.

Darley bragged about Malcolm, about the blog he had made when he was just a kid, about his meteoric rise from analyst to managing director, about his work ethic and the year he was on the road so much he managed the hat trick of achieving secret status on all three major U.S. airlines. Then Malcolm talked about Emirates, about his market observations, about their long-anticipated IPO and how he thought it could unfold.

They were having so much fun they ended up ordering dinner and more wine and then even dessert and only stood to leave when the waitstaff began subtly flipping the chairs onto the tables in the back.

Unlike Darley, who came to be fascinated with planes because of her interest in the financial side of the industry, Malcolm had wanted to be a pilot when he was a little boy. He went to business school instead, but as soon as he had a little money, he started taking flying lessons. He would get up at the crack of dawn and catch a New Jersey Transit train to the general aviation airport in Linden, just five miles south of Newark Airport. He'd fly for an hour or two and then change into his suit and tie and join the commuters heading into the city, at his desk on Wall Street by eight forty-five.

There were days when Darley could resent Malcolm, could feel like she'd sacrificed her career for their family, left a big, interesting life to have babies, but then she remembered all Malcolm had sacrificed as well: a career flying the planes he studied, early mornings on the airstrip in New Jersey, the smell of carbon and jet fuel filling him with an excitement he could rarely feel for life on the ground.

That was good, right, love?" she asked as they walked home along the Promenade, their fingers interlaced.

"So good," Malcolm answered. "It felt amazing just to have a real conversation with someone after being on eggshells for months."

"What do you mean, eggshells?" Darley asked. Did he mean with her?

"It's been so hard pretending everything is normal, keeping your family in the dark and not telling them I was fired."

"Oh, yeah, sure." Darley nodded and rolled her eyes.

"We need to come clean soon, though," Malcolm pressed. "It's been a long time."

"I know, I know. I'm just dreading talking to them about money after everything with George."

"I have to be honest with you, Darley, the more you try to keep my firing a secret, the more humiliated you're making me feel about it," Malcolm said quietly.

"Oh no." Darley stopped and turned to him. "I'm not trying to make you feel humiliated! I'm just protecting you! You know how my parents are."

"I mean, I do know how they are." Malcolm dropped her hand. "They like that we met at business school, they like that I'm in banking, but Darley, we have two kids, I've spent every Christmas and Easter and birthday with them for a decade. I think they know me by now, and they'll still accept me even if I'm briefly unemployed."

"Oh, gosh, I know they will, of course." Darley's face crumpled. She hadn't realized how much it had been hurting him, how with every day of this lie she was telling her husband, over and over, that he was only welcome to be a Stockton as long as his paychecks were flowing in.

Malcolm pulled Darley in for a hug, and she pressed her cheek against his crisp blue shirt. "Give your folks a chance, Dar. I think they might surprise you."

THAT NIGHT, as Darley lay in bed next to Malcolm, listening to his even breathing, comforting as the sound of rain or a kitten's purr, she tried to figure out why she wanted to keep Malcolm's story such a secret. Why was she so worried he would be exiled from her world?

Darley had noticed something about people with money: they stuck together. Not because they were intrinsically shallow or materialistic or snobbish, though of course those things could very well be true, but it was because when they were together, they didn't have to worry about the differences their money meant in their lives. They didn't have to worry about inviting a friend to Bermuda for the weekend, they didn't have to worry about flights to Montreal, they didn't have to worry about car rentals and overpriced restaurants and jackets and ties at the clubs. Their friends could all keep up, they could all pay their way, there was no awkwardness about offering to cover shares or lend a tux or waiting until a paycheck cleared on a Friday. There was just a built-in assumption that if a trip, a party, an occasion seemed fun, their friends would be along for the ride, and they would know how to act when they got there.

The other thing, the thing that sucked to talk about, was the secret lurking worry that other people were using them. Using them for their weekend homes, their good alcohol, their big apartments, their parties, their internships, their closets, their, well, their money. Darley saw it all the time to varying degrees—guys who bought their girlfriends jewelry and laptops and paid for expensive vacations, only for them to realize the guys were essentially bribing their way into a relationship; guys who amassed crowds of hangers-on when they paid for bottle service or houses in the Hamptons. There was a difference between sharing your good fortune and being taken advantage of, and sometimes discerning the difference could break your heart. It was just easier, in some ways, to stay close to those who liked you but didn't need your AmEx to have fun.

There was a clique of girls at her high school, a clique Darley occasionally joined for lunch when her own friends were out sick or traveling. They were called the Rice Girls because, everyone said laughingly, "They were all white and they stuck together." Darley's own group was exempt from such derision because Eleanor was Chinese, but deep down she knew it was the same thing—she hung out with a group of rich girls who all had nearly identical upbringings. They all had wealthy parents and grandparents, they all had maids and nannies, they all had tropical vacations and restaurant birthdays and closets full of skis and rackets, and, in Eleanor's case, a three-thousand-dollar set of golf clubs.

Since the Stocktons were old money, they were more or less discreet with their filthy lucre. They flew coach unless the flight was really long, they drove their cars until the clanking noise became untenable, and they never, ever redecorated. But upon closer examination, the daily cost of life was eye-watering. The maintenance and taxes on the limestone on Pineapple, the maisonette on Orange, the country house on Spyglass, the memberships at the Casino, the Knickerbocker Club, and Jupiter Island, the kids' Henry Street School tuition (kindergarten and first grade were fifty grand apiece), and Berta's salary all added up. Sometimes Darley wondered if her father even knew how much was flowing from the taps, or if his assistant wrote the checks and he signed them without bothering to take his eyes off his blueprints.

Whenever a bill or an expense surprised Darley—the closing costs when she bought her apartment, an assessment from the Jupiter club when a hurricane ripped off the deck—her father would shrug and say, "It's a rounding error." And it was true. He could make or lose more in one deal than any of them could realistically spend in five years, including years when they bought property. It was a life of great privilege and ease, and Darley was grateful. But she also knew it made it harder for her to make friends. There were only so many people to whom her world made sense.

When Darley told this to Cord once, he squinted and looked perplexed. He didn't seem to feel this way at all. "You need to loosen up, Dar. This is a city full of interesting people." To Darley this was the central difference between them, and the reason she ended up with Malcolm and he ended up with Sasha. She needed someone she had known and trusted for years, while he could fall in love with a girl at a bar. For Darley, deep connections were made over time, through years of friendship, a slow unveiling of the many layers we build up around ourselves. She had been burned too many times by supposed friends: The college roommate who dropped out of school and begged her for a two-thousand-dollar loan to help her sick mother. It was only months later that Darley discovered there was no sick mother, only a cocaine habit, that the money was gone. The camp friends who stole her phone card and used it to call their boyfriends from the pay phone by the dining hall, racking up a hundred dollars in six weeks. The girls her first year at Yale who came over to watch movies on her projector and borrowed her car to get pizza but talked about her as a spoiled rich girl behind her back. The time one of those girls put a dent in her car and never even offered to help have it fixed. Darley knew that her family money made her vulnerable to these sorts of leeches, so she had long ago built up walls to protect herself. She had worried Cord never built those walls, that he let himself follow women and friends like a pilot flying through fog. That's why she had been so resistant to Sasha, why it had taken so long for her to let her sister-in-law in.

She thought about her own prenup for the millionth time. Maybe she had made a stupid mistake when she gave up her trust, sure. But her biggest mistake had been giving money so much power over her life. By keeping Malcolm's secret she was buying into the idea that her world was a club only available to those with a seven-figure income. And she didn't want to live that way. She wanted, for the first time in her life, to peel back her bitter rind and open up to the sweetness within.

EVERYONE ALWAYS said that it was the moment you stopped trying to get pregnant that you finally conceived. That you found love when you'd stopped looking. That your silk midi-length La DoubleJ dress went on sale the day after you bought it full price. (Okay, maybe that one was different, but it annoyed Darley nonetheless.) So it was, by that same law, that Malcolm got a new job the week after they confessed his Deutsche Bank firing to the Stocktons.

Tilda and Chip were outraged on Malcolm's behalf about the Azul debacle. They understood right away that the CNBC leak wasn't his fault, they were unequivocally compassionate about his ordeal, and, even better, Tilda took revenge into her own hands and served it in the most fabulously snooty way possible: She made sure that Chuck Vanderbeer and Brice MacDougal were blacklisted from every private club in New York City and disinvited from every society gala from the Junior League Winter Ball to the MoMA Armory Party. They wouldn't be able to get a squash court in this town ever again, and Darley had to laugh knowing that Tilda had actually hit them where it hurt.

After their epic dinner at Colonie, Cy Habib had introduced Malcolm to Sheikh Ahmed bin Saeed Al Maktoum, the chairman of Emirates, and the sheikh had created a position for Malcolm: president and chief strategy officer. Malcolm would be based in New York and, among his many responsibilities, he would oversee the IPO of Emirates on the New York Stock Exchange. It was Malcolm's dream. He was out of banking, he was poised to rise at the most impressive airline in the world, and while he was unlikely to achieve the hat trick of triple secret status on the three big American airlines anytime soon, he'd be home a lot more to watch his kids grow up and obsess about pigeon death. An unforeseen bonus of overseeing the massively lucrative IPO was that Malcolm got to decide which investment banks would be invited to pitch for the business. He invited everyone—except Deutsche Bank. Tilda said it best: the wrong guests could ruin even the best parties.

TWENTY-TWO

Sasha

Chip was turning seventy and everyone was too busy to plan a proper celebration, but if Sasha had learned one thing, it was that you couldn't take fathers for granted and also, she really needed to make up for calling the limestone "janky." She told Tilda she would host a dinner party for him at Pineapple Street and the theme would be Sailor's Delight, a tribute to Chip's childhood love of sailing. It was her penance. Vara's girlfriend, Tammie, ran the props department on big film sets, so Sasha brought her in and together they turned the Pineapple Street dining room into a seafaring phantasmagory. They hung fishermen's nets from the chandelier, creating a canopy over the table that they strung with fairy lights and tiny glittering lures and feathered flies, using the hooks to dangle them from the netting. They melted red candles into wine bottles, wrapped heavy rope in coils on the table, and set a clamshell at each place so that guests might open them up to find their name card. She put Chip and Tilda at the heads of the table. Sasha might have technically been the hostess, but she couldn't fathom sitting at the head on Pineapple Street.

When Tilda arrived, wearing sailor pants with gold buttons, a white blouse, and a jaunty red scarf, she saw the room and her eyes filled with tears. "Oh, it's beautiful, darling," she said and hugged her daughter-in-law close, and Sasha was pretty sure Tilda was more emotional over the tablescape than she had been over their pregnancy announcement. The Stocktons all turned up, more or less on time, more or less dressed for the theme, and took in Sasha's creation. Cord was jittery, wearing a pirate's hat and button-down, and he kept coming up behind her and patting her bum and whispering, "Good job." She mixed Dark 'n' Stormys, though she noticed Georgiana wasn't drinking. She brought out a silver tray of cold shrimp with cocktail sauce and passed it around, but despite all her efforts at festivity she couldn't help but feel the tension in the air. There was still so much uncertainty around Georgiana's decision to give away her inheritance. Chip and Tilda were treading lightly, looking at Georgiana as one might regard a newly housebroken pet. Darley seemed preoccupied, and Sasha felt even more grateful than usual that Poppy and Hatcher had come along. Children had a way of diffusing social discomfort. You could ask them anything and count on their answers being amusing. You could leave the room to cater to any one of their needs. Or, worst-case scenario, you could at least rest assured nobody would scream much profanity in their presence.

When they sat down to eat—miso black cod with seaweed salad—Sasha tried to play the part of a hostess and spark some kind of festive conversation. "So!" she said brightly. "Maybe we could all go around and say something nice that happened this week?" Cord gave her a sort of panicked-looking smile and she realized how deranged she sounded.

"I'll start," said Tilda gamely. "I found out they are going to have a Tory Sport trunk show at the Jupiter Island tennis shop! I absolutely love her running skirts!"

"Great!" Sasha said enthusiastically. "Chip?"

"The Knickerbocker changed their lunch buffet and now they have white asparagus," he said thoughtfully. "But it doesn't taste all that different from green asparagus."

"Okay, Georgiana?" Sasha directed, hoping she wasn't opening the floodgates for a diatribe on the offensive history of sailing culture.

"I had a really amazing morning, actually." Georgiana smiled. "I met with a woman who provides feminine hygiene products to schools in northwest Pakistan. She told me that less than twenty percent of women in Pakistan have access to pads. Otherwise, they just use a piece of cloth. And women are told not to bathe during their periods because they have been taught that it will make them infertile. I donated ten thousand dollars and that will pay for almost five hundred school-age girls to have pads for a year."

"That's amazing," Sasha said. It *was* amazing. What an incredible thing to do.

"I'm really not sure that is dinnertime conversation, Georgiana," Tilda interjected. Chip looked slightly green and was staring at a puddle of cocktail sauce on his plate.

"Mom, I think poverty is a really important dinnertime conversation," Georgiana countered. "I think that's a big mistake we've been making as a family, only talking about things that make us comfortable. We need to talk about what life is actually like for most people."

"But we don't need to talk about menstruation!" Tilda objected.

"Fine," Georgiana agreed calmly. "But I don't want to hear about white asparagus or trunk shows. Let's talk about something real."

"Okay." Tilda wrinkled her brow in concentration. "Sasha, would you like to tell us what it was like growing up poor?"

The entire table swiveled their heads to look at her. Cord, Darley, and Malcolm wore looks of horror. Georgiana bit her lip. Hatcher gnawed on a buttered dinner roll.

"Sure." Sasha laughed. "But I should clarify that I didn't actually grow up poor. My family was middle class."

"Oh, of course, dear," Chip interjected. "You know, seventy percent of Americans define themselves as middle class. But the reality is more like fifty percent . . ." He trailed off and Sasha smiled, amused at his insinuation.

"Okay," Sasha started. "Both my parents worked. My mom was a school guidance counselor at a middle school two towns over and my father worked for a company that made uniforms for sports teams." Sasha was trying to think of what might seem strange about her life to the Stocktons. Maybe it all did? She knew that to the vast majority of people she met, the life that she was describing was completely ordinary, but they were listening to her as though she were describing an upbringing in a yurt on the salt flats.

Some part of her must have secretly wondered if she felt shame before her in-laws over her relatively modest origins. Chip and Tilda had never seen her childhood home, had barely spent time with her parents, but as Sasha spoke, she was surprised by the ease with which she told her story. She pressed on. "I had jobs on the weekends and then summer jobs when I got older. When I was fourteen my dad was laid off and things were stressful for about six months. We had to cut back. Then my dad got an even better job, this one at a company that put custom logos on branded clothing, and everything went back to normal. We got a new car and a few years after that he bought his boat."

"What did you do for vacations?" Darley asked. She had been listening closely as Sasha spoke.

"Oh, we did lots of fun stuff. Normal stuff. We drove to Niagara

Falls. We went to Orlando when I was nine. We drove to Quebec and I practiced my high school French, and we took a funicular up the hill in the old city."

"Oh, I've been on that funicular," Georgiana said.

"I mean, I had a good education and I graduated from college without debt, which is kind of shocking these days. And now I have my own business, and before Cord and I got together I was making plenty to pay for a nice apartment and a car and an upgrade every time I cracked my iPhone on the sidewalk. I've been lucky. I hope I can one day pass that on the way Georgiana did today." Sasha smiled meaningfully at Georgiana.

"But Georgiana is still so young," Darley interjected. "She doesn't know yet what she might need her money for. You have a husband and a house, Sasha. Even if everything went sideways, you'd still be okay."

"Even if everything went sideways, I would still be okay too," Georgiana spoke up. "I have thirty-seven million dollars. And that's not even counting the money tied up in property or what I'll inherit from Mom and Dad. There is no possible event on earth that would cause me to need that kind of money."

"But you don't know that yet, George," Cord said. "You're still really young. A lot could change."

"I'm actually not that young. I've been pampered. And I *want* a lot to change, Cord," Georgiana said. "I am so grateful for the money. I am so appreciative of you, Mom and Dad. And of all our grandparents. The money is a gift. It's a chance for me to create meaning in my life and for me to actually *save* people."

"What would you do?" Sasha asked, looking at her sister-in-law. Georgiana suddenly seemed different. Where she had been filled with such furious energy for the past several months, she looked calm and emanated a force Sasha usually associated with people who did lots of yoga or rubbed CBD lotion on their bodies.

"Well, Bill Wallis and I have a plan," Georgiana explained. "My trust currently throws off more than a million a year in dividends. Up until now I've just been leaving it alone and letting it compound. But we're thinking I can start off slow and set up a foundation that offers one million dollars a year in grants. I'll keep the principal invested for now as I get my bearings. But the goal will be that over time I will transfer all my stocks out to other not-for-profits."

"What kind of not-for-profits?" Darley asked.

"I'm still figuring it out, I need to research more, but I want to focus on women's health in Pakistan. That is what Brady was working on when he died. It's a place where my money can have a huge impact. And it's a place where there has been a lot of stigma and misinformation surrounding women's health and sexuality. Nobody should feel ashamed to get their period. Women need access to contraceptives. They need sex education."

"Isn't that what you do at work, though?" asked Cord.

"From a distance. But I want to do more. I was thinking that instead of doing communications I could be a donor and I could tag along on some projects. There's a trip to Benin, in West Africa, coming up, and I want to ask the founder if I can donate to the project and then go and observe their reproductive health program. Maybe someday I could join them on a trip to Pakistan. But I also want to work with other not-for-profits. I need to learn about more places. My friend Curtis has a whole group of people he hired to help him learn about good organizations. I'm sure it'll take me a couple of years to really understand the best way to do it."

"You don't sound like someone who is having a psychotic break," Cord acknowledged.

"Thanks," Georgiana said drily.

"But you know foundations shouldn't have to be the answer. The real problems are tax laws, antilabor policies, and the slow expansion of the welfare state," Chip said. Everyone turned and looked at him as though the dog had begun speaking Dutch.

"True." Georgiana cocked her head to the side. "But I can't control that right now. I can only control what I do with my life."

"So, while we're on the topic of big life changes, Sasha and I have something to share as well." Cord glanced at Sasha and she nodded. "We would like to offer to move out of Pineapple Street and have Darley and Malcolm move in."

Darley put her glass down in surprise. They all turned to face her, watching as her hands flew to her cheeks. "Really?" She looked around like maybe it was a joke.

"Yes," Sasha said with a smile. "I mean, it's up to you, Chip and Tilda, but there are four of you and only three of us."

"Oh my gosh, thank you! Seriously? Malcolm, if we moved in, we could ask your parents to live with us, if they wanted," said Darley.

"I'd love that," he said, nodding.

"Of course, that's absolutely fine with us," agreed Tilda. "The house is yours. You can do just anything you want with it. But as I mentioned to Sasha, you really do want to leave the drapes in the parlor. Those windows are enormous," she said seriously.

"Where are you going to go?" Georgiana asked Cord and Sasha.

"We don't know yet," Sasha said. "We're going to look around."

"There are those old tunnels under the former Jehovah's Witnesses' buildings," Cord mused. "We could live in those tunnels, right, Sasha? Like mole people? We'd bring the baby up to see the sun on special occasions, like his birthday?"

"Shut up," Sasha snickered, and poked him under the table.

———

After dinner they moved to the parlor, where Chip poured them sharp little glasses of cognac and they toasted his birthday. They toasted the new baby. They toasted Malcolm's new job. And they toasted Sasha's great success hosting her first Sailor's Delight theme dinner. It was only as the family made their way down the steps of the limestone and off into the evening that a candle on the dining-room table tipped and caught a bit of fishing net, the blaze climbing across the room in a web of fire.

Epilogue

Curtis McCoy opened his mailbox to find it overflowing with glossy holiday catalogs. Didn't people know millennials only bought things from Instagram ads? He carried them up to his apartment and sifted through the pile, dropping them one by one into the recycling. Buried halfway through the stack was a thick, creamy envelope, return address Orange Street. The Stocktons. He slipped his finger into the seam, gently pulling out a Christmas card. On the front was a professional photo of the Stockton family, clearly taken in the summer. The garden was in full bloom and yet they all wore coordinating shades of red and green tartan. Chip and Tilda were seated in the center, Chip in a wool blazer, Tilda in pearls, her hands folded demurely on her knee. Their children crowded around them, sweating in velvet and tweed, the grandchildren at their feet like beloved pets. Malcolm and Sasha flanked the wings, Sasha's pregnancy not yet visible beneath her blouse. Curtis let his eyes linger on Georgiana before he flipped the card open to read the letter.

Dear Friends:

Merry Christmas from our clan to yours! We hope this finds you in fine fettle. We have many blessings to

*count this holiday season: My tennis partner, Frannie
Ford, and I took home the Brooklyn Heights Casino
Over-Sixty Women's Championship for the third year in
a row! We look forward to facing many of those same
worthy competitors down at the Jupiter Island Club at
New Year's. Chip will be playing in the croquet
tournament if any challengers care to step forward!*

*Malcolm and Darley are thriving, Malcolm having
joined Emirates Airline and Darley diving back into the
workforce with a new job at a hedge fund. It will surely
be absolute bedlam managing two careers along with the
care of their children, but Chip and I have always
selflessly given of our time to our precious grandchildren.
Meanwhile, Cord and his lovely bride, Sasha, (baby
number one due this spring!) have bought an unusual
property down in Red Hook, a ten-minute drive from
Brooklyn Heights. We have yet to meet any of the
denizens of that particular neighborhood, but we hear it's
quite en vogue among artists and so we look forward to
their regaling us with stories from their bohemian
lifestyle! And lastly, Georgiana has decided to explore a
career as a philanthropist. She is preparing for a trip to
Benin, and I'm frantic arranging her goodbye dinner—an
Out of Africa–themed evening inspired by the scene
where Robert Redford goes to Meryl Streep's house and
she has those lovely pink calla lilies as a centerpiece. I
have secured pith helmets for us to wear at cocktail hour!*

*We do want to extend our thanks to all of you who
reached out in the wake of the fire last month at
Pineapple Street. The good news is that the repairs are
now complete, and Darley and her family have moved in
and made the place their own. The toile wallpaper in the
dining room was marred by the fire, but Darley has
replaced it with a beautiful botanical print, one with*

lovely small oranges. The Louis XVI dining table was a
total loss, sadly, but we found an adequate substitute at
Scully & Scully. The greater tragedy was the loss of the
Chippendale camelback sofa that had graced the
governor's mansion when I lived there as a girl.
But we soldier on!

Season's wishes from the fruit streets,
Mr. and Mrs. Charles Edward Colt Stockton

Curtis snickered to himself. Now that he and Georgiana were officially dating, he'd been spending quite a bit of time with the Stocktons, and the camelback sofa had been discussed at many a brunch on Orange Street. Curtis flipped the card over, where Georgiana had scribbled him a personal note.

Hey babe, Don't think you're getting out of the
goodbye dinner, Mom has already ordered you a helmet. Xx

ACKNOWLEDGMENTS

I wrote half this novel in my apartment on Pineapple Street at five in the morning while the neighborhood slept, or perched on the closed toilet lid as my kids played for hours in the bath, the cleanest little prunes in Brooklyn Heights. I wrote the other half at the dining room table of my in-laws' house in Connecticut as my husband conducted Zoom school and learned kindergarten math all over again. I'm grateful to my family: Carol Williams and Ken Jackson, Dan Jackson, Roger and Fa Liddell, for taking us in, feeding us salty oat cookies, hunting hermit crabs, and reading bedtime stories.

This novel was partially inspired by Zoë Beery's fantastic article in *The New York Times*, "The Rich Kids Who Want to Tear Down Capitalism." I also drew from Kate Cooper's reviews of *Melania the Younger* and *Melania* in *The Times Literary Supplement*, Emilia Petrarca's hilarious "Before We Make Out, Wanna Dismantle Capitalism?" in *The Cut*, and Abigail Disney's "I Was Taught From a Young Age to Protect My Dynastic Wealth" in *The Atlantic*. Thanks to my early readers: Todd Doughty, a true pineapple; Lexy Bloom; Lauren Fox; Sierra Smith Nimtz; and Ansell Fahrenheit. Thank you to Alli Mooney. To my Knopf family, Maris Dyer, Tiara Sharma, Jordan Pavlin, Reagan Arthur, Maya Mavjee, and Dan Novack, who would be played by Daniel Craig in the movie adaptation, I'm lucky to have you.

It has been a joy to work with Pamela Dorman, Venetia Butterfield, and Nicole Winstanley, who edited this book with care and humor and have shown me incredible friendship. Thank you to the team at Pamela Dorman Books and Viking: Marie Michels, Jeramie Orton, Lindsay Prevette, Kate Stark, Mary Stone, Kristina Fazzalaro, Rebecca Marsh, Irene Yoo, Jane Cavolina, Brian Tart, and Andrea Schulz. Thank you to Madeline McIntosh. I'm grateful to Tom Weldon, Claire Bush, Laura Brooke, Laura O'Connell, Ailah Ahmed, and the group at Hutchinson Heinemann. Thank you, Kristin Cochrane, Bonnie Maitland, Dan French, Emma Ingram, Meredith Pal, and the entire team at Penguin Canada. I'm grateful to Inés Vergara, Hedda Sanders, Alix Leveugle, Quezia Cleto, Cristina Marino, and Anna Falavena. Thank you, Jenny Meyer, Heidi Gall, Brooke Erlich, Erik Feig, and Emily Wissink. Thank you to DJ Kim, and the entire genius force at The Book Group. Brettne Bloom is an astonishment, and her friendship over twenty years is a gift that only grows.

Finally, thank you to Wavy and Sawyer, and to Torrey Liddell, for keeping a shoebox full of fresh batteries, for magically getting the printer to connect, for making life so much fun, and for letting me steal all his jokes.